Romancing the Darkness

Book I

Romancing the Darkness

Book I

Tyler R. Snyder

Romancing the Darkness Book 1

2021 © COPYRIGHT Tyler R. Snyder
2021 © COVER COPYRIGHT Crystal Publishing, LLC

Edited by Malory Wood, Patricia Phillips, Stacy Long, and Claire Shepherd

Cover illustration by Ryan Durney
Cover and interior design by Deanna Estes, LotusDesign.biz

Published by Crystal Publishing, LLC Fort Collins, Colorado

ISBN 978-1-942624-62-2

Dedication

To my mom, Rose Snyder, my first and biggest fan. Remember when I brought you page after page when I finished writing for the day? I'd bring you my progress and eagerly wait for your opinion the next day. It feels like forever ago when that happened. However much this book has changed, I have changed. But you have always been there from the good to the bad, picking me up time after time through this entire thing. I don't think I could have gone this far without you. No amount of thanks would justify how much I appreciate all you have done for me and our family. Thanks for being there for me. Hey, Mom—we did it!

Chapter 1

The Lasting of Innocence

Rayna gazed toward the horizon. She focused on the flickers of light coming from the rocky caves in the distance. Her eyes twinkled, and she bit down on her bottom lip. Tristan saw mischief forming across Rayna's face even before she opened her mouth.

"Hey, Tristan, take me to the dragon stables."

Tristan shook his head. "You know we're not supposed to go. Not without a supervisor."

"Aw, c'mon, Tristan. It'll be fun." She headed to the doors, turned around, and gave Tristan that playful grin he could never say no to.

"I really don't think we should." He headed toward the castle. "It's dangerous, Rayna."

Rayna grabbed him by the arm and pulled him back to her. "Tristan, I am the princess, and you are the guardian. So, you, my sweet little elf, must do what I want." Rayna wound her arms around his neck to tickle the slightly pointed ears he tried to hide.

"Half-elf." He emphasized "half."

Tristan pulled her hands from around his neck but continued to hold them at her sides. He hesitated. He didn't enjoy disappointing Rayna, but it was hard to perform his duty to protect the spirited princess. "Rayna…"

"Please, Tristan. I want to see the baby dragons. They're so cute." She backed a step away but kept her hold on his hands. She lifted her brows to widen her eyes and smiled.

"Rayna, no. You could get hurt. Just stay with me."

"Please," she whispered.

Tristan's shoulders slumped a little in defeat. Guardian or not, he always surrendered to her will. He could never deny her anything she wanted. "I've already lost this battle, haven't I?" he asked with a resigned grin.

"If you want to protect me, you're going to have to follow me." Rayna sprinted out the door toward the cave with unnatural speed. Her feet glowed slightly as she effortlessly ran through the grass.

"Wait!"

Rayna glanced over her shoulder and shouted, "Come on, slowpoke. Catch me if you can." Besides being tired from the day's training, Tristan's average height didn't help his stride any better. He wasn't as tall as the other guardians because of his elvish heritage, but what he didn't have in height, he made up for with his elvish dexterity and determination. However, Tristan knew he could never outrun Rayna. She was a trickster when it came to using magic against him, but he chased after her, anyway. Rayna's magical wind ruffled his unkempt platinum hair. He usually liked to keep it short out of sheer laziness, but lately, he found getting it cut a hassle. The wind carried Rayna's youthful laughter back to him, and he couldn't help but smile.

Panting, he sputtered, "I-I already r-ran four m-miles today during training, cheater."

Rayna tilted her head and made a funny face as she made her way through a patch of flowers. "I'm gonna win, Tristan!"

Tristan gasped for air but managed to yell, "Not fair!"

She reached the cave first, but Tristan was right behind her. She pointed at him with a triumphant grin on her face. "Ha, I beat you! And they say you're the fastest in your class."

Rayna leaned against the mouth of the cavern to catch her breath. Her chest rose and fell delicately. Sweaty and out of breath, Rayna still maintained her royal poise. Tristan slumped forward with his hands on his knees.

"And I would've caught you if you hadn't cheated." He gulped mouthfuls of air. Tristan recovered his faculties and propriety quickly and scanned the area for the dragon keepers. He knew better than Rayna the consequences of being caught in a place they shouldn't be.

"Your majesty, we must leave. You know we shouldn't be here." Rayna stared into his royal blue eyes. "I love the way your eyes sparkle in the sun. It's like I'm looking into the ocean." She shook her head to regain focus on her quest. "Come on. Let's go in." Rayna grabbed his hand and laced her fingers through his.

"Please," she begged. "We never get to do anything we want anymore. And there are baby dragons!" Sensing his submission, she reassured him, "I promise. We'll only stay for a few minutes and then go."

Tristan shook his head and squeezed her fingers tightly. "If you say so, Rayna."

When the two entered the cavern lit by steam-powered lamps, they heard the roars of the dragons ahead and felt the heat from the nests. They reached a small opening, where man-made nests for at least a hundred dragons surrounded them.

Tristan gaped in awe when he saw the nests honeycombed all around, stacked hundreds of feet high on the walls. Dragons hovered around the giant hives, checking on the young, adjusting the nests, and bringing in extra food. The steam-powered lights flickered up the stable walls to reveal dragon-fire erupting from one of the beasts, presumably to keep its recently laid eggs warm. The heat from the flames made them sweat. Several gusts of wind hit them as a more massive dragon hovered down to sniff them. Tristan recognized the rock dragon from its thick brown scales. Massive horns on its head curled around to the back of the neck. The dragon lowered its head, gesturing them to come closer. Tristan's heart raced as fear overtook him. Although these dragons were used to soldiers riding them into battle, he still didn't see them as tamed creatures. He backed up a couple of steps.

Rayna pulled her hand away from his. Without fear, she approached the creature. She extended her hand, and the dragon allowed her to pet it. Other dragons came down from the nests on the walls to receive some attention.

Petrified, Tristan's training failed him. There was no way to protect her from so many creatures. "Rayna," he whispered.

One of the newly hatched rock dragons crawled down the wall and growled. It did not have a saddle on it like the other dragons did. It had not yet been broken. Making quick leaps at them with its underdeveloped wings fully expanded, the dragon hissed and bared its pointy yellow teeth. Not wanting to hurt one of their young, the older dragons let it be.

Rayna stood still, paralyzed by fear of the younger, untrained dragon. Tristan, recovering some of his nerve, darted forward to grab Rayna's hand. He could hear the dragon's high-pitched roars behind them while dragging the stunned princess out of the stable. They both flinched when little sparks of fire escaped the dragon's mouth and landed at their feet. Thankfully, it wasn't old enough to produce a full stream of fire.

When they reached the outside, they inhaled the cool air. A growl behind them told Tristan the fight had just begun. He yelled for help, hoping the guards would hear, but his plea was cut off—the dragon leaped high over them, using its wings to project upward. It landed ahead of Tristan and Rayna. Tristan unsheathed his dagger, holding it in front of him, and stood between the dragon and his princess. The baby dragon roared with fury, exhaling fiery sparks. Behind him, Tristan heard Rayna cry out for her mother.

When the dragon charged, Tristan stumbled backward, bumped into Rayna, and knocked her to the ground.

"Let's get out of here, Tristan!" she screamed.

Tristan struggled to his feet and pulled up Rayna. He grabbed her hand and led her toward the castle. The young dragon, not wanting to stray too far from its nest, returned home.

"Why don't we just go straight to the castle garden and meet your sister like we were supposed to." Tristan shook his head indignantly.

"Good plan." Rayna panted.

Tristan and Rayna made their way back up to the castle, laughing and joking about their brush with the dragon. They found their way through the outside corridors that were so vast they were like a maze of white marble to Tristan. Rayna signaled him to stop behind her when they reached their destination. They peeked around the corner and saw Rayna's sister, Morgan, tending to the castle's garden. Curious, Tristan stepped out a little farther while she watered the plants. Rayna yanked him back behind the wall. Tristan gazed down at her while she signaled him to be quiet.

"Okay, elf, go sneak up on her and scare her," she whispered.

Tristan nodded with an impish smile. "Half-elf."

Rayna rolled her eyes. Tristan peeked once more to make sure the coast was clear and then stealthily tiptoed out of cover to pursue his prey. Tristan couldn't keep his mischievous smile at bay. With care, he approached Morgan from behind, and by avoiding dead leaves and loose rocks, he got so close that the smell of her perfume tickled his nostrils. He closed his eyes for a moment, intoxicated. Tristan drew a deep breath, prepared to lunge any second. Instead, a big gust of air lifted him up and threw him onto the ground at Morgan's feet. He landed with a thud.

"Ugh!" he managed to say as air escaped his lungs. "Why did you do that?"

Morgan kneeled and attempted to gain eye contact with the defeated boy. "Tristan, you know, for an elf, you really aren't that stealthy."

"Half," he said as he regained his breath.

In the background, he heard Rayna howling with laughter. Morgan stood up to extend a helping hand. Just when Tristan reached to grab her hand, she abruptly pulled back, and he fell backward, askew.

Rayna roared with laughter once more and trotted up to them. "Serves you right for trying to scare my sister. I would have done the same thing, Morgan."

"What? This was your idea!" Tristan cried out.

"Whatever do you mean, Tristan? I would never plot such a thing against my sister," Rayna said with a wicked smile.

"Why, you little liar!" He playfully lunged at her to tackle her to the ground, rolling around in the dirt until he had her pinned. "Say it was your idea!"

"Never!" Rayna laughed.

Morgan lightheartedly kicked Tristan in the side to stave off his pretend assault on Rayna and pressed him to the ground with her foot. He saw her look him up and down; their eyes locked.

"Attacking two princesses in one day? That's treason, Tristan. You could go to prison for this." She smiled before adding, "Hey, Rayna. I like how brave he is. Maybe he should be my guardian."

"No!" Rayna shoved Morgan off Tristan. "He's my guardian."

As she fell, Morgan grabbed hold of Rayna's sleeve and pulled her down. Rayna's fist connected with Morgan's stomach.

"Stop!" Morgan grunted. "I didn't mean it, Rayna. Now, stop acting like an idiot. You're eighteen years old. Act like it." Morgan let go of Rayna.

Tristan chortled while he sat up.

"What's so funny, elf?" Morgan chided.

"It's unbecoming for two princesses to fight on the ground, isn't it?" But before he could continue, Tristan saw the princesses' attendant approach. There was no mistaking the scowl on her face. He knew they were in big trouble when the screeching started.

"Princess Rayna! Princess Morgan! What are you doing on the ground? Your dresses are ruined! Stop all this nonsense. Get yourselves into some clean garments and go to your lessons. Now! You girls need to take your roles as princesses more seriously!"

The girls stood up, and their moods sobered. Rayna's sleeve dangled from her hand, and Morgan's hair fell across her face. The attendant wagged her finger in Tristan's face. "And you! This is your doing! Do your job! Stop being a bad influence on these young women. You're nothing but a commoner." She spat at his feet and spun toward the princesses. "Now, get changed! Both of you!"

"Yeah, Tristan. You should really stop getting me in trouble. Good day to you, sir!" Rayna said sarcastically.

"You behave, Tristan." Morgan winked at the elf. "Good day to you."

The next morning, Tristan's bedroom door burst open with a loud thud. Startled, he found Rayna standing in the doorway with her hands extended, palms up. She raised her hands, and Tristan's body levitated.

"Oh, perfect. You're awake." She laughed.

"Put me down, Rayna. Now!" Tristan screamed as he fumbled to get down.

"You're no fun, Tristan."

Rayna flipped her hands over, palms down. Tristan crashed to the ground. Rayna's hands reached for Tristan's to help him up. "Why are you on the floor?" A mischievous grin crossed her lips.

"Why did you drop me?" He pushed himself up.

"Sorry," she said unapologetically. "I have a job for you!"

Tristan yawned. "Oh, joy. I can't wait to serve you."

The sounds of engines and propellers drowned out this last bit of sarcasm. An airship passed overhead, blowing dirt through the open window. Tristan and Rayna coughed from the dust.

Rayna bolted to the window. "He's here! Tristan, please escort me to my father at the airfield."

Tristan brushed the dust off his shirt. "You got here by yourself, didn't you?"

"Pretty please, Tristan," Rayna pleaded, batting her eyelashes. "Tristan, you're my guardian, aren't you? You need to protect me." She slid her arms around his waist and gazed up into his eyes.

"Princess Rayna!" a stern voice bellowed from Tristan's doorway.

Tristan turned his head to see his mother storm in. He grabbed Rayna's hands and pushed them down to her sides.

"I understand you are eighteen years old, but you two will act with decency while you are in my home! Rayna, if anyone sees you two like this, you know how much trouble Tristan will be in!"

Rayna stepped away from him promptly and stood with a lady-like posture. "I apologize, ma'am. I was just fooling around."

"You may call me Sana, your highness," she offered with a respectful bow, but the lecture continued. "You know the law: royal blood and common blood cannot mix."

Tristan rolled his eyes, mildly annoyed at his mother's over-protectiveness. Sana walked toward the door but paused at the threshold. "Please," she pleaded as she walked away, "just behave, you two. The consequences of this are greater than you realize."

After Rayna peeked out the doorway to make sure the coast was clear, she closed the space between them and brushed Tristan's platinum hair off his lightly tanned skin. She leaned in and kissed him sweetly. "What's the world know, anyway?" She winked. "Meet me outside."

Tristan absorbed the intoxicating feeling her lips gave him every time they kissed. He hurriedly outfitted himself in his training uniform—a dark blue, long-sleeved shirt with dark blue pants—and then exited the small stone cottage. He stopped to survey the kingdom: swarms of beggars, children, mucky dirt roads, and the rancid, sulfuric odor spilling out of the sea. Over the sounds of hawkers and crying children, he heard the pounding hammers of the blacksmith and gunsmith. Tristan's eyes darted around the highly regulated city, searching for Rayna. In every direction, he saw groups of soldiers stationed in bunkers and gun nests. When he spotted Rayna across the way, he hurried over to her.

"Ready, princess?" he asked sarcastically. He smiled and pointed at the scene in front of them.

"I am, Tristan. Thank you for asking." She countered his sarcasm with an exaggerated curtsy.

After several blocks, they heard another loud roar of engines. Tristan observed an airship overhead. The green-glowing engines showered them with dust and mana, the magical force that bestows life. Tristan fanned his hand back and forth as the smoke and scent of vanilla filled his nose. "I hate that smell."

Rayna spun around, dancing in the mana. Its misty green specks fell on her face before evaporating. "I love it, Tristan!

These airships are just the beginning of the advancement of our world. How can you hate it?"

Tristan snorted. "It just stinks, Rayna. I hate smoke and the smell of vanilla. Plus, being that high in the air still makes me a little uneasy."

Rayna tilted her head. "Vanilla and smoke? No. It smells like cherries."

Suddenly, Morgan appeared out of nowhere and rushed past them, heading for her father's airship. She turned to them and explained, "It's mana: whatever our minds perceive it to be. Plus, you're both wrong. It actually smells like ocean berries." She continued ahead.

Tristan gestured to Rayna, not understanding why she didn't go with Morgan. He shook his head as Rayna seized the moment to move in close to Tristan. The playful look on her face became dead serious.

"Since you pay little attention in class, allow me to explain this to you, Tristan. These airships are a few years old now, but we would never have had them if it weren't for the magic orbs that fuel the kingdoms. We call them sphaeras—large green spheres of crystal, constantly absorbing and expelling mana. With an orb in every kingdom, they absorb the mana in our world. The sphaeras reside in every castle for safe-keeping. We have harnessed the mana to fuel our airships, mages, and even power our lights. We have recreated smaller similar crystals for our airships to receive the mana from the sphaeras and power them. They're an everlasting magic source that continuously fuels our world." She led him past a firing range where soldiers tested their weapons that made a loud crack when they fired. The cambustpowder made Tristan sneeze. "I know you think it stinks, but not all of us are so fragile."

"Fragile? I'm not fragile. It just stinks, Rayna. Where does mana come from?" Tristan knew the Council of Mages had created cambustpowder to give the world a chance against the guardians. They extracted the highly methane-filled gel from the glands in the dragons' mouths. When the gel hardened, the mages ground it to powder and forged explosives and bullets with this newly found tool. The council shared this information with the rest of the world, except for Sorriax. What the council did not predict was that Sorriax would get ahold of this technology and forge their own weaponry.

"The gods, of course. Are you sure you're ready to be my guardian?"

Tristan shrugged. "I prefer combat training. Everything else usually puts me to sleep."

Rayna rolled her eyes. "The gods radiate with so much mana they have an ethereal glow to them. When they walk among us, their excess mana protects our world."

Rayna pointed in front of them, past the town, to the hundreds of vessels that occupied the airfield. A stone tower stood in the middle to guide the ships as they took off or landed.

"Father says we'll win the war against the world with these. The Sorriaxian army has tools that make us more powerful than any other country. You should know all of this, dummy. You're the tool we're going to win with."

The *Naughtalesk*, the flagship for the entire Sorriaxian army, landed in front of them. The heavily armored black ship was twice the size of a standard flagship. Row after row of cannons protruded from the sides of the ship. Numerous deck-mounted machineguns lined the railings. The sheer size of the ship always impressed Tristan. After the ramp lowered from the side of the *Naughtalesk*, King Eadric strode to the platform and perfunctorily saluted no one in particular. His elaborate black armor cast a shadow as he started down the ramp.

Rayna shouted excitedly, "Father!"

From the day Tristan was born, his parents and elders had told him stories about King Eadric and his remarkable accomplishments, but Tristan always had a strange feeling around him. Eadric's subjects bowed, making way for him.

Rayna ambled up to her father and hugged his arm. "How was your trip, Father?"

Tristan's attention turned toward the gates that were a few hundred yards away from the landing field. He heard the echoing march of the Sorriaxian army returning from battle. The sound rattled him. The idea of war and men he didn't know wishing him dead chilled his bones. The army paraded down a road near Tristan and into town. Amidst the thunderous footsteps of thousands of soldiers, he heard the cries of pain from multiple voices. A group of wailing soldiers and a few injured horses had separated from the melee into the landing field so nearby medics and healers could rush to their aid. Tristan's ears did not digest the screaming well; it left him unsettled.

A white horse among the group neighed in panic. The soldiers' efforts to calm the elegant creature failed. Tristan moved toward it, extended his hand to the creature, and bid the horse come to him. Its breathing was heavy but calmed with Tristan's touch. Even though he was only half-elf, it did not hinder his ability to form a connection to nature. Tristan studied the animal. "You are beautiful, aren't you? What's wrong, boy?"

Tristan reached under the steed's neck to loosen its reigns only to feel a slimy substance. The goo was clear, instantly flooding Tristan's hand with an intense cooling sensation. He looked at the other side of the mount and gasped when he saw the other half of the poor creature's charred body. Dim embers embedded in the skin crackled as if the fire were still fresh. He angled his face to escape the smell of burned flesh; instead, he saw a dozen screaming men in similar condition.

One medic shouted, "What the hell happened to these men?"

Medics swarmed the injured, covering the burns with more of the same slimy salve used on the horse.

"What the hell happened to these men?" the same medic shouted again.

"An ever-burning dragon hit this squad," a calmer medic said, reaching into a bucket of healing salve and slathering the burned soldier with it.

Tristan could no longer watch and dropped to his knees next to a soldier. The soldier's legs ran deep with char; occasionally, an ember sparked from the wound. Tristan dipped his hands into the salve and spread it across the man's burns. Morgan hurried to help.

Tristan's voice quivered. "Morgan, is this what dragon fire looks like?"

Morgan sniffled in an attempt not to shed any tears. "No, this isn't normal dragon fire. Only certain dragons can develop an ever-burning fire. The fire becomes enchanted." She spread another handful of salve thickly over the soldier's wound. "Even after the fire is extinguished, the embers still create a burning sensation that will forever be seared into whatever was scorched."

"But what does that mean? How do we heal them?"

Morgan wiped her forearm across her brow and surveyed the scene. "Tristan, the only cure is amputation or death."

When the soldier heard the options, he panicked and grabbed Morgan. Tristan reached for the soldier's hands to loosen his grip on the princess.

"Please, don't let them kill me! I have a family!" the man pleaded through his sobs.

Morgan put her hand on the suffering man's cheek. "I won't let you die."

Tristan heard an odd grinding sound behind him. A gurgling scream erupted shortly afterward. Tristan didn't want to look, but as though compelled, he turned his head to the sounds of anguish. He closed his eyes, wishing for the power to unsee this reality.

Two healers with a hacksaw were attempting to remove another man's burned arm. One healer held the injured man's arm away from his body while the other had his knee on the man's chest and held him down. With his remaining hand, the man shakily brought a bottle of yellow liquid to his mouth.

Please let that alcohol numb his suffering, Tristan prayed to the goddess Aerra.

The king, observing the many soldiers dying before him, slowly passed by with Rayna in tow. "These men have served their purpose," Eadric addressed the healers. "Kill them and feed the burned horses to the dragons in the stable." Without hesitation or any indication of remorse, Eadric turned on his heel to walk away.

Morgan pleaded, "Please, Father. These men can be saved."

The healer in charge stood up to confront the king. "Sire, we can save these soldiers; they can perform guard duty along the castle walls."

Eadric's calm transformed into disgust. He unsheathed his sword, swung it, and sheathed it so fast Tristan could barely follow the movements. The healer fell to the ground with two separate thuds.

"Never undermine me. Never question me," Eadric said to the remaining healers. "We will not waste any resources on the mortally wounded. Kill them and feed the horses to the dragons. I will not repeat myself again."

Without hesitation, the unburned soldiers detached themselves from any moral compass. They pulled out their sidearms, took aim at the pleading men, and fired their weapons. Cambustpowder hung heavy in the air.

The king glared at Tristan. "Shouldn't you be at your guardian lessons? Leave my sight, boy."

Rayna, fear-stricken, bent down to help the saddened Morgan. She looked at Tristan and whispered, "You should go. I'll see you tonight."

Tristan, still in shock, nodded in response. He left, despondent and devastated by the horrors of war and the king's lack of mercy. He ran through the rutted streets of town, his mind reeling over what had just happened before his very eyes and what he'd soon be asked to do. He'd never get used to death smelling like smoke and vanilla.

≈

That night, Tristan violated the kingdom's curfew and slipped out of the house through his bedroom window. He pushed past all the drunks who stumbled along the bumpy dirt roads and ducked into the shadows to avoid getting caught. As Tristan approached the entrance of the castle, he heard the flags gently flap in the wind. Hanging close to the outer castle wall, he listened to the guards above talking to stay awake.

"Have you seen the woman coming and going from the king's chambers? Blond hair?" one of the armed guards asked. "The one with no face?"

"The same one we saw in the gardens the other day?" another asked.

"I didn't see any woman in the gardens," the first guard responded.

"I thought I saw a strange woman coming out of the throne room when I was on patrol inside last night. No face that I could see," a third voice added before bursting into laughter. "But maybe we've had too much to drink."

A goblet of ale fell to the ground next to Tristan. "Drunken idiots," he whispered.

Tristan took off toward the hills and sat under the lone tree where he and Rayna had been meeting for almost a year. He glanced up at the clear night sky and the crescent moon that hovered above. Tristan counted the stars in the constellations as he had done every other night. Tonight, though, he sensed an eerie, magnetic pull to a cluster of pulsating stars he had never noticed before. Absorbed by their faint blinking, he tried to connect the stars to form a shape. It was a game he'd played since he was a little kid.

Startled out of his reverie, Tristan heard footsteps running through the grass behind him. He turned around and saw Rayna, her dress hiked up and tucked into her waistband. She dove on top of him, pinning him down.

"Caught you," she said with a snicker.

"I let you." He brushed his lips against her cheek.

"So, are you going to the banquet with anyone?" she asked, making herself comfortable on his lap.

"Well, I don't know." He tucked her hair behind her ears. "Are you going with anyone?"

She grinned. "I am, as a matter of fact."

"Oh?" Disappointment changed the tone of his voice. "Who are you going with?"

She scoffed. "Who else would I go with? I'm going with you, silly elf." She added sarcastically, "I'm sorry. Half."

"Don't tease me like that."

"Were you really worried?" she joked.

"Of course," he answered quietly. "I know I didn't ask you, but I didn't want you to go with anyone else, either."

He leaned against the tree with his mind at ease. She rested her head on his shoulder. His arms folded around her petite form.

"I didn't want anyone else going with you, either," she whispered. "I heard Mira wanted to ask you. I didn't want her to take you."

"Well, she asked, and I briefly considered…"

"You did?" She pushed herself away from him.

"I'm only kidding." He laughed and pulled her close to him again and stroked her hair. "Being selfish again? I could never go with her instead of you."

"Don't tease me now, Tristan. When it comes to stuff like this, I will be as selfish as I want. You're mine."

Tristan sat there, quietly observing the stars. Looking down at Rayna in his arms, he rested his head on hers.

"I'm yours?" he whispered.

"Of course."

Even through the protection offered by the night sky's mantle, thoughts of the day's events crept into Tristan's mind. He pulled his head up from Rayna to look off into the distance—toward the airfields. The pit in his stomach grew, but he knew he had to ask her.

"Why did the king kill those men?"

"What do you mean?" She lifted her head from his shoulder. "You heard my father. We didn't have the resources to waste."

Tristan pushed her away from him. "So, our wounded soldiers are a waste? Is that what you think? They only got wounded fighting for your father."

"You know that's not what I meant, Tristan," Rayna snapped back. "Don't put words in my mouth! I didn't like it any more than you did!"

"Then why didn't you speak up?" He searched her face for a measure of compassion. "Morgan did."

"He's, well, he's…he's my father, Tristan. And Morgan's not his favorite," Rayna tripped on her own bitter words. "He is the king.

You know how he rules, what our predicaments are." Rayna paused to gather her thoughts into a more coherent statement and control the contempt in her words. Tristan noticed her doing this frequently lately.

"Resources are running thin," she started again in what sounded like a rehearsed statement. "Not just on our side, but the enemy's, too. This is war, and it's a chess match. We can't win if our pawns are broken."

Tristan hated the thought of comparing the soldiers to pawns. He saw many of the king's attributes in Rayna.

"I was just asking. I don't want to be treasonous." Tristan, forever the peacekeeper when it came to Rayna, relented. "Let's not fight, Rayna. I don't want to spend the little time we have alone like this."

Rayna grabbed him by the collar of his shirt and forcefully pulled him in. Their lips were only a breath apart.

"Treason, young guardian? If you commit treason, the only person you'll answer to is me." Tristan cleared his throat and nodded. "Can we stay out just a little longer?" She buried her flushed face against his chest. "Please."

He leaned his head against the rough bark of their tree. Tristan realized the magnetism of the constellation's strength when an uncontrollable urge forced him to fix his eyes on the stars. Through the starry glint, a foreign influence held his attention. He felt as if another set of eyes looked back at him. Transfixed, he closed his eyes, and said, "Anything you want, Rayna."

Chapter 2

The Kelpie

The sun shone on their faces as Tristan and his friend Lazarus walked through town. Busy people scurried about carrying trade goods for their businesses and gathering food for their families. Two horses trotted by, pulling a carriage full of soldiers headed out of town.

"Good morning, Tristan!" said a woman bending down to pick up a pile of pelts.

Tristan rushed over to her side to help her lift the heavy fur. "Good morning, ma'am. How are you this morning? How's business?"

She smiled and grunted as they lifted the pile and set it on a table. "Just another busy day." She wiped her brow with the back of her arm.

"Well, keep up the good work." Tristan wiped the debris from his hands. "We're counting on you so we can stay warm." He smiled at her and trotted back to Lazarus so they could continue.

"That was heavy, Laz. You could have helped."

"I didn't know it was do-a-good-deed day." Lazarus shrugged.

Tristan opened his mouth to speak, but a voice shouted from his right before the words came out.

"Good morning, Tristan!"

Tristan and Lazarus looked over and saw the baker waving.

"You really know everyone, don't you?" Lazarus asked snidely.

"Good morning! The bread smells delicious!" Tristan said before returning his attention to his friend. "It's not about good deeds. If someone needs help, you help."

"Should we really risk injury to ourselves doing some minor task to ease the life of a commoner?"

"When did you advance to being more than a commoner?"

Two younger women passed in front of Tristan and Lazarus. They both sang with an orchestra that entertained the royal family during banquets and balls. Tristan recognized them from their last performance where they had introduced themselves to him afterward.

Both ladies greeted him at the same time. "Hello, Tristan."

"Good morning, ladies. Are you off to work on a new song? Lazarus and I really enjoyed the last performance." He added Lazarus' name to try to divert their attention to him.

Lazarus sneered. "Yeah, it was terrific!"

"Really? Then we will practice extra hard for a memorable show." The women giggled coquettishly and gamboled off with excitement.

Lazarus leaned in and whispered in Tristan's ear, "I don't remember them."

Tristan rolled his eyes. Ignoring the whisper, he returned to their previous conversation. "I hate to break it to you, my friend, but you are still nothing more than a commoner."

Lazarus stepped over horse droppings while Tristan plowed through them, not paying attention.

Tristan stopped to look at the bottom of his shoe and swore. "Dammit! This is disgusting." He dragged his foot on the ground to remove the excrement.

Lazarus snickered, indulging in the humor of the incident. "Risking injury isn't a small thing, Tristan. We are soldiers and guardians, and that is where our responsibility rests. We are trained to protect the royal family." Lazarus surveyed the street crowd. "Not everyone else."

"Trainees, Laz, mere trainees. As such, we are also here to serve the people, are we not? Maybe we should set the example as future guardians."

Just ahead, a man struggled to get his carriage wheel out of a hole in the road. Tristan hurried to the man's aid. Lazarus reluctantly followed.

"Good day, sir. Get in the driver's seat to steer the horses," Tristan said. "We'll push from behind."

The man nodded and climbed onto the carriage. Tristan and Lazarus positioned themselves and leaned into the carriage. Seeing the commotion, four more men came to assist the laboring guardians.

Tristan shouted, "One. Two. Three!"

The men pushed as hard as they could, rocking the wheel back and forth until it gained enough momentum to climb out of the hole. The man waved over his shoulder, shouting his thanks. The carriage made its way down the street. Tristan thanked the men who had helped.

"Awe, Lazarus," Tristan teased, "you came to my rescue. I do declare, my good sir. Your good deed will not go unnoticed!" Tristan slugged him on the shoulder playfully.

Lazarus shook his head at Tristan and said, "How about we become guardians first? Let's get Zro."

≈

Tristan heard church bells when they approached the holy place where the people worshipped Aerra, the wolf Aeon that watched over Sorriax.

Two massive pillars carved into the shape of wolves decorated the outside of the church. More carvings of the Aeon graced the walls, and giant tapestries of Aerra adorned the windows. The façade was awe-inspiring. The only other building in Sorriax as beautifully decorated was the royal castle.

Zro and his family walked down the stone steps toward them. Once they reached the base of the steps, Zro joined Tristan and Lazarus, and together, they trekked toward the castle.

Zro faced Tristan and asked, "Hey, why do I never see you at church?"

"I don't know," Tristan said, shrugging. He has never really given much thought about going to church before. "To be honest, my parents never made me. Guess I don't see the point in going now."

"What do you mean you don't see the point?" Zro looked a little befuddled. "Since the discovery of the Aeons, everyone goes to church. Even the royal families who were chosen by the gods. Even they don't believe they're above going to church."

Tristan shrugged and contorted his face as he contemplated his answer. "I'm not saying I'm above church. I just don't see the point. We know the gods are real; they can shape and reshape our world however they see fit. We don't talk badly about them because we know they can hear us. I believe in them. I just don't see the point of going to a church when I can pray or talk to them just as easily outside. What else is there to learn?"

Zro smiled with pride. "Well, the priest did teach us something today." Eager to impress his friends with his newly acquired knowledge, Zro puffed up his chest and announced, "The Council of Mages has been conducting a study along with different churches around the world. They have jointly concluded that there could be more Aeons out in the world that have yet to be discovered. We all know that Amaranth is the first Aeon and our true god. She's in charge of the rest of the Aeons who are also gods under her rule. The Aeons under Amaranth govern and watch over the world according to her will."

Zro's friends still didn't seem impressed. He raised his arms in disbelief. "Come on, guys! This is amazing! There could be Aeons out there that nobody has ever seen before! You too, Lazarus? Really? You go to church."

Lazarus bent down, picked up a blade of wheat from the side of the road, and clamped it between his teeth. "My parents make me go. Don't get me wrong. I have my respect, but I'm with Tristan on this one. Besides, the odds of seeing an Aeon are improbable—kind of like Tristan passing his guardian test."

Tristan punched Lazarus in the shoulder, but Zro, focused on Lazarus' words, stumbled over a rock.

"But the priest said…" Zro argued.

"He can never not be a know-it-all, can he?" Tristan said to Lazarus, cutting off Zro. Tristan faced the defeated Zro. "Come on, man, we probably have to run laps around the castle today. Save your breath for that."

Ichiban, a large blue Irkshdan wolf wearing heavy armor, walked up to the friends on their way to the day's lessons.

"You boys didn't forget about your teamwork test today, did you?"

"Of course not, sir," they answered in unison.

"We're on our way right now," Tristan replied.

Ichiban heard the hesitation in Tristan's voice.

"Good. Let's go then." Ichiban lead the way to the forest to meet up with the rest of the trainees.

≋

Tristan charged toward the woods. As he breached the threshold of the dark forest, he saw another young man in all black exit the forest. Tristan noticed the man's ears—elf ears like his own. Their eyes met briefly.

Chills traveled up his spine. Tristan's heart hammered with fear and excitement. He was finally ready to perform the job he had trained for his entire childhood: to be a guardian, a protector of the royal family. But first, they had to pass this test. Their futures depended on it.

Screams came from a small pond on the other side of the woods. Tristan's breath became shallow and rapid when he unsheathed two daggers from his belt. His hands shook, and beads of sweat formed on his forehead. He peered through some bushes into a clearing. He saw the guardian trainees looking helplessly at one of their rank, Ry, dangling from the mouth of a magnificent creature. Its black-and-blue scaly skin glistened like the sunlit water's surface. Its mane dripped while a continuous torrent of water spurt from its head and neck: a kelpie.

Tristan caught something moving out of the corner of his eye. He looked down at the ground to see a black and white rabbit also observing the scene. The rabbit should have run away at the first sign of trouble, yet it stayed. A unique sapphire horn protruded from its head. The rabbit thumped its foot while emitting a few tiny barks. Tristan raised an eyebrow at the curious creature. *Rabbits don't bark,* he thought, *do they?* He shook the question out of his head. "Get somewhere safe, little one," he said to the idle rabbit.

Tristan moved toward the larger, strange beast. The kelpie's tail whipped around, brushed off the excess water, and drenched the few of them still standing in front of it. Its toed-hooves squeezed the ground beneath it, prepared to charge headlong into the sopping group of guardians. It spat Ry's unconscious body onto the ground. Its black, brooding eyes dared them to approach.

Lazarus yelled, "Get that kelpie away from our injured!"

Tristan quickly assessed the scene. To the right, his friends Charity and Mira had taken cover behind some rocks. Charity lay on the ground, blood trickling from her head. Mira tended to her while keeping an eye out for any oncoming attacks. Mira put her hand over Charity's head wound. Calling upon the mana around them, she shouted, *"Curate omnia!"* White light formed under her hand, and the wound mended. Two more small groups of trainees tended to the other wounded. The kelpie had kicked one boy in the chest: broken ribs. Everyone surrounding him tried to make him comfortable. The encounter had left the young warriors defeated, meek of spirit.

Tristan rushed to Mira and Charity while giving orders. "Mira, you take Charity back to Ichiban. She needs more help than we can give her here." He scanned the other groups of trainees. "The rest of you, if you can help, pick up who you can and follow Mira! We're right behind you!"

The other trainees aided each other in their attempt to flee the battle.

Three other fledgling warriors still challenged the shapeshifting beast with their weapons ready, waiting for it to make a move. Lazarus stood in front of the kelpie, now a giant horse; Zro remained on its left flank and Bianca on its right. It darted between Tristan and the others. The beast turned to him and opened its mouth. The force from the wall of water knocked Tristan off his feet as it collapsed on him.

Lazarus quipped, "Every time I look over at you, you're on your ass!"

Tristan mumbled curses at Lazarus as he struggled to get his footing in the now muddy ground.

Zro jumped at the kelpie's neck and jabbed his dagger into it. Zro shouted, *"Lux fiat!"* A bolt of lightning from the dagger shot out into the kelpie's shoulder. The beast neighed loudly enough to shake the trees. Lazarus leaped to its side and stabbed the creature with fury. The creature bucked up and down, sending the two young guardians flying off to land on their backsides.

Tristan drew his hand across his face and pushed his pale hair out of his face. His uniform hung in saturated ruins. Taking a deep breath, he charged the kelpie by diving directly at it. The creature's body transfigured into water; Tristan passed right through it, getting inundated once more. The process of turning into a waterspout physically took a toll on the creature.

The kelpie panted while its body reformed. Immediately, the kelpie refocused its attention on Bianca. Neighing and rearing up on its hind legs, it kicked ferociously. Expecting another charge, Tristan got up and ran at the beast's hind legs; he sliced into both of them with his daggers. The kelpie fell backward, hit the ground hard, and kicked violently. One of its hooves connected with Tristan's head. The loud knock echoed throughout his skull. The force sent Tristan's body tumbling away from the beast. He collapsed in pain.

When Tristan pulled himself together, he saw the water horse get to its feet. The kelpie shrieked even louder. Suddenly, Tristan heard galloping in the distance. He lifted his dazed head and saw a wave of water in the shape of a herd of horses barreling toward them. Bianca, Zro, and Lazarus dove out of the way, but Tristan could not move. His waterlogged body held him firmly on the ground, and his head wouldn't stop spinning.

Before the wave could pummel Tristan into the trees behind him, the unfamiliar man dressed in all black appeared from the bushes on his right. He shoved Tristan out of the wave's path. The wave's spray landed on Tristan's face as he watched the wave crush the trees he had just rested against.

The kelpie took advantage of the distraction and charged at Bianca. Raising its front leg and expanding its hooved toes, it grabbed her and pushed her against a tree. The beast snarled and roared while water sprayed all over the terrified guardian.

Tristan's vision grew hazy, but he managed to see the strange man in black pull a crossbow from the sheath on his back. After shaking his long black hair out of his face and tucking it behind his elven ears, he aimed the weapon at the kelpie's head. He fired one bolt into its snout. Tristan watched in confusion as the man pumped the crossbow like a shotgun, loading one bolt after another into the chamber. Tristan had never seen a weapon like this. The repeated pumping of the crossbow rendered Tristan motionless as the hypnotic sound echoed in his mind. He let the darkness engulf him.

≈

When Tristan opened his heavy eyes, he saw his friends standing alongside his parents. They were in a white room with some of the other injured trainees resting in beds while others sat nursing their bandaged limbs. Tristan looked to the foot of his bed and caught beautiful green eyes staring back at him. Morgan smiled and reached to touch his leg. Before she could, another hand sought Tristan's. He saw Rayna, her eyes filled with worry.

"Are you okay, Tristan?" she asked, hiding a tremble in her voice.

Tristan blinked heavily a couple of times and then tried sitting up. "Yeah, I think so. My head hurts." He inspected his pillow to find it encrusted with blood. "How long have I been out?"

The door to the room opened, and Ichiban entered. The young trainees saluted him when he stomped through.

"Long enough to waste an entire day's worth of training!" Ichiban bellowed.

"Thanks for the concern, general," Tristan said with a hint of sarcasm. "How's everyone else doing?"

"Oh, I'm fine. No need to worry about good ol' Ry here. I was just in a giant kelpie's mouth, that's all," Ry spouted from the cot next to Tristan's.

A few of the surrounding trainees laughed. Charity stood next to Mira and put her hand on Mira's shoulder.

"We're fine, Tristan," Charity replied.

He scrutinized the bloody bandage encircling Mira's head.

"Don't worry about mister smart ass over here. He's fine, too," Mira added with a chuckle.

"I was almost eaten! Eaten! Why me? You two tall bastards were within biting radius," Ry complained, pointing at Lazarus and Zro.

"Stop your whining." Ichiban's disapproving glare silenced Ry.

Bianca sat down on the cot beside Tristan. "Besides, you were the one kicked in the head. I'm surprised you have any sense left."

"Surprised? I'm surprised that damned horse didn't break its leg on his hard head," Zro said sarcastically.

Bianca gently brushed her fingers through Tristan's hair. She leaned in and kissed him on the forehead. "Thanks for coming to our rescue. We all owe you one."

Morgan butted in, "Yes, you were quite brave, Tristan."

Tristan glanced at Rayna out of the corner of his eye and noticed her jealous glare aimed at Bianca. The strange thing, however, was that he also detected the same sentiment from Morgan. Tristan looked up at Morgan, wondering if this was a new occurrence or something he had missed in their interactions.

"Brave?" Ichiban chided with a loud snort. "He charged that kelpie without a plan and instantly got knocked out."

Tristan's cheeks flushed red with shame; the other trainees snickered.

"That does seem foolish," Tristan's mother said, "but we're all relieved that you're okay."

"How's my patient doing?" The doctor approached Tristan's bed.

"Still tender, sir." He reached for his head.

The doctor pulled a chair next to the cot and took a seat. He examined Tristan's head and eyes. "I'm going to ask you a few basic questions. Answer them the best you can." While still examining the young man, the doctor asked, "What country do you live in?"

"Sorriax."

"What planet are we on?"

Tristan scoffed, "We're on Ambion."

"How old are you?"

"I'm eighteen."

The doctor grasped Tristan's head and shifted it slowly to look in his ears. "What's your job?"

Tristan flinched at the doctor's cold hands before responding. "I am a guardian trainee, a protector of the Naughtrious royal family. Rayna is the princess I am assigned to protect."

The doctor put his hands back in his lap, satisfied with his examination. "Well, there seems to be no brain damage."

"There's nothing up there to damage," Lazarus blurted.

The doctor ignored the comment and addressed Tristan's parents. "Tristan will need a day to rest. He has a minor concussion and a good contusion, but no fractures we can detect. I'd like to keep him here for observation. I'll clear him to go home tomorrow as long as his symptoms subside."

"When can he resume his duties, doctor?" Ichiban asked.

"In a few days. Maybe a week. I wouldn't push him too hard right away. Let him get his coordination back." The doctor returned his attention to Tristan. "Tell me, Tristan, what is the last thing you remember before you woke up here?"

"I remember..." he started but couldn't finish his thought. Tristan closed his eyes to jog his memory. He winced and clutched his head to steady himself. "A dark elven boy pushed me out of the way of the kelpie's attack."

Tristan's father, Faranus, beckoned to the door. "Caster, could you come in here, please?"

The door opened, and the young man from the forest entered. His long black hair and black cloak seemed to steal the levity from the room. His piercing blue eyes scanned the area before locking with Tristan's.

"Hey, elf, how's the head?" he said to Tristan.

Tristan nodded in response before adding, "Thank you for rescuing me."

Faranus kneeled next to his son. "Caster has been living in our forest for the past couple of months because his people exiled him. He's a dark elf from Xul-Fen. I have invited Caster to stay with us, Tristan."

Tristan hadn't met many other elvish people outside of his family, much less anyone who had been exiled. Almost immediately a myriad of questions raced through his mind.

"That sounds fantastic." He turned to face Caster. "I'm glad you are joining us."

"Terrific," Faranus said. "You rest up, and we'll see you at home soon, son."

As all his friends and family started to file out of the room, Tristan caught Morgan's eye. She gave him a gentle smile.

Meanwhile, Rayna squeezed his hand to draw Tristan's attention back to her. "I'll see you in a few days. Heal quickly, Tristan."

≈

Tristan returned home after a few days of rest; his head felt lighter and clearer. He could finally get out of bed without wobbling. He made his way down the dirt road to the castle. Walking amidst the other buildings, Tristan noticed that some were overrun by black briar. He remembered when he first asked his father about the strange creeping vines that always seemed to capture his attention.

"My boy," his father had said, "the townsfolk named it black briar because only in Sorriax do roses turn black."

"Is it true, Father? What color do roses turn elsewhere?"

"They do not change colors elsewhere. They remain beautiful for their entire growth cycle. Some of the elders claim the roses of Sorriax were bewitched by a vengeful goddess who was jealous of their beauty. Here, roses start out vibrant red and then become black with bitter, poisonous barbs as they age. That's why we must never touch them."

Since that day, Tristan had been afraid to touch the poisonous barbs. He was lost in his memories when Ichiban approached him.

"How are you doing, boy?"

"Much better. Thank you, sir."

They proceeded to the castle, weaving through the townsfolk going about their business. An unusually large carriage pulled by four horses passed by—a bit too close for Tristan. "I'll never get used to the smell of horses and their shit." He scrunched his nose at the odor.

"No one ever does." Ichiban grinned. "I'm immensely proud of you and the courage you showed when your fellow cadets were in danger."

Tristan had never heard Ichiban praise any of his students before. He tried to downplay the compliment by looking at the stone buildings around them. "Thank you, sir."

Ichiban's face suddenly turned somber; the scowl was unmistakable. Tristan knew he was in for a reprimand. "What you did was also foolish. You are quite lucky none of you were seriously injured. You can't barge into any situation without calculating the danger. That's how you get yourself and others killed."

The flicker of pride within Tristan vanished. "I know, sir," he said meekly, "but the events unfolded so fast."

"Battles do happen fast, Tristan. The only thing that splits life and death is a second. You can't ask your enemies to wait until you're ready. To be a great guardian, you must know your enemy. In the second or two that you have before the fighting begins, you need to absorb as much information as possible to help you survive. A kelpie is no exception."

Tristan's shoulders sagged, and his head dropped with disappointment. In a puddle, Tristan saw the reflection of one of the two giant white marble statues of a wolf guarding the castle entrance. Ichiban cleared his throat.

"But what you did was very brave. There is no doubt that some of your fellow trainees may have lost their lives in that skirmish. Just don't let it go to your head. Humility is a lesson we must all learn."

Farther up the lane, Tristan and Ichiban saw a rather large wolf walking on all fours. Gray and white fur. Green eyes. The wolf had a slight glow—Aerra. Tristan glanced around and saw everyone in the city kneel. Ichiban and Tristan followed suit when the wolf approached. Tristan lifted his head slightly since he had never seen an Aeon before. The warmth emanating from her presence cascaded over Tristan.

Ichiban whispered, "Aerra, my Aeon, what is your will?"

Aerra made her way to the humble Irkshdan. With each step Aerra took, plants and flowers sprouted. A gentle breeze ruffled his hair, and Tristan respectfully lowered his head.

A female voice resounded from Aerra, "Ichiban, my faithful." She lowered her head and pressed it against Ichiban's. Ichiban trembled as a single tear rolled down his furry cheek. The Aeon pulled her head back and walked into the crowd of people.

Tristan watched Ichiban shut his eyes to regain his composure. When he reopened them, he glanced at the curious Tristan. "Humility," he said, "even amidst gods."

Chapter 3

Awaken Destiny

That night, while everyone slept, Tristan rolled out of bed and saw Caster sitting by the window, observing the moon.

"Why are you awake?" he whispered.

Caster pointed upwards and faced Tristan. "Watching a blood hydra."

Tristan scuttled to the window. "Really?" he asked, forgetting to whisper. "Let me see!"

"It was a joke, Tristan."

"Not a very good one." He sulked away in disappointment.

"I'll ask you the same question. Why are you awake?"

"Simple," he said, stifling a yawn. "I'm not tired."

As Tristan changed into fresh clothing, Caster rolled his eyes and laughed. "Your abilities to deceive leave something to be desired, young cadet."

"I have no idea what that means. Seriously, why are you up so late?"

"Looking at the stars. They say if you look hard enough, and you know where to look, you can see dragons flying among them."

Tristan scrambled back to the window in astonishment. "Really? Where? Let me try."

"And your ability to be deceived is even worse." Caster shook his head in disbelief.

"Will you stop making fun of me any time soon?"

"Look up at the sky." Caster ignored the question. "Do you see that cluster of stars? The shape of a diamond that has two lines of stars coming out of it?"

"I see the diamond." Tristan looked at the stars again. "What does it matter?"

Caster closed his eyes and moved away from the window. "It matters to everything, Tristan. However, very few people know about them, and even fewer know what they are for. There are twelve clusters, like that one right above our world."

"What is it?" Tristan said, looking perplexed.

"The constellation we are looking at is the Angel," Caster explained patiently. "There are twelve constellations, each with their own ruling set of gods. The constellations are on a constant rotation, so each set of gods rules Ambion for a certain period of time. When the constellation is triggered and the world ends, the next set takes over. Next to the Angel constellation, do you see that triangle of stars with a line coming out the bottom?"

"Of course. I've already noticed that one," Tristan murmured.

"That is the Divider constellation; it is the next to rule," Caster said without disrupting his focus on the constellation.

"You seem to know quite a lot of things I wouldn't suspect other people know." Tristan stared at the dark elf. His youthful face contrasted with his eyes that reflected a lifetime of turmoil. Not holding back, he blurted out. "How old are you?"

Caster raised an eyebrow at his new roommate. "I see your guardian training does not yield lessons in manners." The comment went right over Tristan's head. Caster shook his head. "I'm 221 years old."

"Well, you don't look a day over a 105."

Caster rolled his eyes. "You are too kind."

Tristan was eager to get back on topic. "Okay, sure—but what about the other constellations?"

He angled his body to face Caster, enthralled in his story.

"Well, the dimmer groupings are finished. They've had their time to rule. When the cycle starts over, they will have their chance to rule again. The two brighter ones are the next to rule.

There's the Divider, of course, and then..." Caster hesitated. "Then, there's that one." He pointed to the bright constellation beyond the Divider.

"Why is that one pulsing?"

"The Divider?" Caster inhaled audibly as if bracing himself. He shook his head. "I don't know. It's pulsated since—well, for a very long time now."

"Why is our constellation called the Angel constellation?" Tristan asked, sensing that Caster wouldn't give him any more information about the Divider tonight.

"The constellation we're in now?" Caster asked, slightly astonished that Tristan needed an explanation. "Because the gods who rule in this constellation are the Aeons."

"Yes, I know that, but what do Aeons have to do with Angels?"

"Don't you know what Aeon means?"

Tristan shook his head in reply.

"You should go to church occasionally. Even if only to learn something. Aeon means 'vital force.' Each constellation chooses a species to be their messengers, and when the time is right, they end their reign and make way for the next set of gods. It's only fitting that the messengers of the 'vital force' or 'being' would be the Angels."

"I've never met an Angel. How are they the messengers of the Aeons if the Aeons are really here and the Angels aren't?"

"There are Angels in our world right now, Tristan. The Aeons may be here with us, but so are the Angels."

"Angels?" Tristan laughed. "Tell me another one, Caster. They aren't even real."

"You believe in gods but not Angels? You laugh now, Tristan. I met a few before I came to the Land of Sorriax," Caster paused and scrutinized Tristan before continuing. "In fact, I'm talking to one right now."

"Right, because I'm definitely an Angel," Tristan laughed, but his smile disappeared when Caster slowly nodded. "What are you talking about, Cas?"

Caster smiled. "Angels are quite easy to spot. Most of the time, it's their unrelenting kindness that gives them away. You may not realize it yet, Tristan, but you will get your wings soon."

"I'm half-elf and half-human, which makes me zero percent Angel." Tristan finished dressing and stared at the ground for a moment, deep in thought. Feeling uneasy and not even half-believing what Caster said, he changed the topic. "Hey, Caster, you've been around a long time, right?"

Caster nodded.

"They explained this in class, but maybe if I hear the other side of the story, I can understand it better. Why is the rest of the world at war with us? With Sorriax?"

Caster's smile faded. Restless, he stood up and crossed the room. "I have been alive only a few years longer than this war. So long that fighting has become second nature. I'm not sure what you've been taught, so I'll just start with what I know."

"About two hundred years ago, Lucian, King of the Land of Sorriax, gathered all the royal families together in one spot. From the old stories, everyone knew he seemed a bit off, different, if you know what I mean. The Sorriaxian family and country were always deemed a little darker than the rest of the world, but this was out of character, even for them."

"Then why did they all come together?" Tristan interrupted.

"The gathering intended to discuss the unity of the world: peace. It was something they all desperately wanted. However, Lucian brought unity to the world at the cost of a young prince's life. He ran his sword through the boy, made an example of him, and took the sword. Lucian wanted Rephalas, but I don't think he knew what that sword's true purpose was. He escaped the gathering with the royal family from Corriander, and they have been Sorriax's ally ever since."

"What is Rephalas?"

"A sword that will bring about the end of the world. That's how the next constellation's gods take power."

"Where is the sword now?"

"Rephalas is the culmination of the royal families' swords merging together as one."

Tristan scratched his head in confusion and looked around the room, searching for answers to his questions as he did back in his childhood lessons. "Okay. But how is that possible? And do you mean the swords physically connect together somehow? Or do you mean it represents the strength of everyone fighting on the same side?"

"Good questions, Tristan. But I can only tell you what I know."

"If all the world is fighting us, wouldn't we have lost from attrition alone?"

"You'd think," Caster chuckled with sarcasm at Tristan's curiosity. "That's where you come in, Tristan. A handful of guardians is worth a legion of soldiers. With every battle lost, those who survive are either forced to fight for Sorriax or are executed. Most join the fight in hopes of making it home one day."

"If it's a matter of collective power, why didn't the world attack Sorriax all at once?"

"They did. Every royal family of every land except one, the Land of Phalanxia, gathered to attack the Land of Sorriax in a coordinated effort. Lucian prepared for the attack, though. The Sorriaxian and Corriandarian royal families and armies united. Lucian attacked with over three hundred guardians fighting alongside him. That's the kind of power Lucian wielded. Without the support of Phalanxia and its king, the world's forces had no choice but to retreat."

Tristan raised his eyebrows; questions sparked in his eyes. He couldn't believe the power the old king had once had. Before Tristan could open his mouth, Caster's head cocked, and his astute elven ears twitched.

"Your father is awake. You'd better go if you're meeting Rayna."

"How did you know?"

"I've seen the way you look at her. It's not that hard to guess," Caster said with a knowing smile. "Go on. I'll tell him you're asleep."

Tristan paused. "Uh, Caster? Have you ever seen a woman's face in the stars?"

"Now that's a story for a different night, my young friend." Caster ushered Tristan out the open window.

≈

During the few days Tristan had off from his guardian training, he and Caster were inseparable. Tristan had convinced Caster to join the castle guard.

As they walked through town, Tristan couldn't help but stare at Caster. "How old were you when you decided to stop your aging?"

"Why?" The question caught Caster off guard. "Do I look old?"

"No, no," Tristan snickered. "I know you're a dark elf and that your kind is immortal and can control your aging process. I'm simply curious."

"Well, how old do I look?"

Just then, a horse-drawn carriage passed by. Tristan tried to shout over the racket, but the carriage rattled by quickly, muddling his words. "Eighteen," he shouted a second time, not realizing the commotion had dissipated. The surrounding townsfolk stopped what they were doing to gawk.

Caster scowled at Tristan. "You don't have to yell, you know. I'm right here. You're killing my ears, kid. Mine work just as well as yours do."

Tristan playfully shoved Caster. "Maybe it's those ridiculous rings hanging from your ears." Tristan paused, considering what Caster had said. "Hey, kid? You really are old!"

Caster laughed. "Age is only a state of mind!"

They proceeded through town until they passed an inn. Perched on top and around its sign were rabbits of all colors; their long droopy ears touched the ground. Sapphire horns protruded from their foreheads. Some of the rabbits sat on the ledge of an open window. Wafts of stew from the small cottage engulfed the air. Tristan's stomach lurched in hunger.

"Dark elves aren't really immortal," Caster returned to Tristan's earlier line of questioning. "We can control the aging of our physical appearances, but once we grow older, we can't go back."

"Alright, old man," Tristan jibed.

"Do you consider 221 old?"

"So, you were alive before the war?"

"Briefly." Caster sighed.

Tristan darted in front of him, unable to contain his excitement. "Tell me. What was it like?"

"Okay. Okay, Tristan. The world was truly a wonder then. The kingdoms built a relationship and worked together to prosper. Now, they work together to stop the Sorriaxian king. The rest of the world is so focused on creating machines and magic for destruction, I feel they have forgotten what it is like to live. To me, it feels as if progress has stopped and regressed to a more primal state. The kingdoms in their glory, Tristan, were magical. Xul-Fen, my home, had trees that touched the clouds. Creatures of the fey enchanted our kingdom with their presence. I lived in a castle with a nest of faerie dragons that glowed at night."

Caster studied Tristan's mesmerized face and smiled. "What I regret most, and I don't know if your kingdom did this or not, but the children who became adept at magic were given a choice to go on a trek with a wizard from the Council of Mages. From there, they were taught to use their magical gifts and enhance them on their journey in real-life experiences. I didn't get a chance to do that." A tinge of regret colored his voice.

Tristan shook his head. "No, we had nothing like that here. If you had magic, you were automatically forced into the military."

Caster surveyed the bustling town, feigning interest. "Here I am rambling about myself. What is it like here? This war has been going on for so long now, and I've been in the forest for ages."

Tristan hesitated, pondering how to answer. He stared at the ground for a while before making eye contact with Caster again. "War is all most of us have ever known. Though I have never been on a battlefield in the war, only 'tests,' it's normal to hear gun shots and explosions and see dead bodies. The city is always flooded with a sea of soldiers wearing our kingdom's colors: dark blue and silver."

"Dark blue? I've always thought it was black."

"I used to think so, too, but look for yourself." They were in front of the brilliant white marble castle, where the blue and silver flags embroidered with Aerra's likeness waved from every tower. "Time to go. See you at home later?"

"Yes, I'll see you at home." Caster headed off toward the castle.

Tristan called after him. "Good luck! But you aren't done talking about your home. I want to hear more about this fey realm."

Continuing to catalog his questions mentally, Tristan strode toward the marketplace. A shopkeeper selling fruit waved and greeted him. Tristan grinned in response and examined the rosy apples filling the shopkeeper's cart.

"These look delicious, sir. I'll take one, please." He rummaged through his pockets for a copper piece to exchange for the apple. The shopkeeper deposited the coin into his bag and thanked Tristan.

Tristan held the apple to his nose and inhaled the delicious fragrance before biting into the juicy fruit. Juice dripped down his chin, and he wiped his sleeve across his face. It wasn't exactly the appropriate behavior for a royal guardian, even one in training. Occasionally, he thought, it's okay to let your guard down and act like a kid.

A whisper of a breeze ruffled Tristan's hair. He cocked his head to shift the hair from covering his ears.

"Boy!"

He glanced around to find who called out to him. No one was there.

"Boy!"

Compelled, he turned again. A familiar feeling flooded his memory. He drifted through the crowded marketplace, searching for the source of the voice.

"Boy, let me show you the end."

Tristan stopped to study the crowd. Life buzzed around him: traders and customers bartered goods while horses and carriages trotted through the muddy dirt roads. The noise faded to a faint murmur once he focused on a hooded girl across the lane. He could only see her lips, nose, and a few strands of blond hair peeking through the shadow of the hood.

She repeated, "Come. Let me show you."

Tristan didn't bother to look if any horses impeded his path; he blindly crossed the road. He couldn't stop his movement, nor was he sure he wanted to. This pull he felt was inviting, yet cold. Each horse and carriage narrowly missed him when they passed by, neither stopping nor slowing down.

He approached the girl. "Who are you?"

"Come." She grabbed his hand.

Tristan flinched at her icy cold grip. Tristan struggled to keep his senses as the air around him dissipated and all light vanished. Tristan's body jerked so hard he couldn't tell if he were still standing. The weight of his own body held him immobile. Nausea claimed his stomach when his head started to spin. He observed the girl—she seemed perfectly calm. Tristan's lungs screamed for air. Before he succumbed to the disquieting sensation, a cool mist covered his skin. Tristan inhaled a fresh wind, and his lungs gratefully expanded. The fogginess in his head cleared, and his senses returned. The cool air melted into unbearable waves of heat washing over and through him.

What Tristan saw filled him with terror: tens of thousands of men and women fought hooded figures. A shockwave drew his attention upward; winged people fought more of these hooded creatures above his head. Explosions erupted everywhere, causing the ground to quake. The black sky spewed red lightning around the warriors. A ground-shaking roar forced him to cover his ears. When he watched a massive golden dragon breathe fire upon the world and engulf the horizon, a panicked Tristan cried out, "What's going on? Where are we?"

"This is Ambion," the hooded girl replied simply. "And this is the end."

Tristan tore his eyes from the monstrous dragon to focus on a teenage boy in black armor, standing still amidst all the carnage. He had long black hair, but Tristan could not see his face. The boy started to turn, but before Tristan could make out his features, the hooded girl drew Tristan's gaze to her. Tristan felt her eyes piercing his soul, emptying him of his thoughts.

She moved in closer. "Help me find him, Tristan," she whispered and kissed him gently. When her lips touched his, a strong, almost painful, shiver shot down his spine.

His name, spoken in her voice, echoed in his mind, louder and louder. "Tristan, Tristan, Tristan…" His head spun while his senses failed again. He awoke in his bed in a cold sweat. He looked out his window—the sun was out. *How did I end up in bed?* he wondered.

≈

Over the next few months, that event unnerved Tristan, often disturbing his sleep. He couldn't determine if it was real or not, nor was he sure he could even call it a dream. "Hallucination" made him sound a little crazy, and "vision" carried too much responsibility. The blond girl from his dream haunted him; he still felt the pressure of her lips on his and recalled her whisper invading his mind. Tristan couldn't forget the boy with the long black hair he was supposed to find. How was he supposed to find a boy he couldn't recognize?

After waking in confusion once again, Tristan saw Caster waiting by the window. He smiled, and all thought of the dream vanished. It was time for their nightly ritual of sneaking out of the house for a walk after Tristan's parents went to sleep. They spent countless hours gazing at the brilliant stars, sharing stories of Caster's homeland and the latest royal gossip.

"So, tomorrow you're going to be a guardian," Caster said, catching Tristan off-guard and punctuating the last word with a playful punch.

"What of it?" Tristan asked, adding his own little shove.

Caster grabbed Tristan in a headlock. They wrestled for a few minutes before Tristan finally yielded.

"What about you?" Tristan asked.

"What do you mean, 'what about me'?"

"You made Honor Guard Captain." Tristan clapped Caster's back. "That's something to be proud of."

"I have been awarded such honors before. It hardly matters, although I do appreciate Ichiban taking me under his wing. Tomorrow is your day, Tristan, and it will be a special one." Caster patted Tristan on the shoulder.

As they continued down the lane, Tristan found himself drawn to the stars glistening in the dark sky. He gasped. "Caster, look!" A flash of purple fire with a bright light in its center blazed across the sky. Tristan gazed deep into the streak of darkness.

Caster whispered, "A black falling star."

"What's that? I've never heard of it."

Caster watched in stunned silence. "It's a rare occurrence. One I have never witnessed. But I have heard stories that black shooting stars signify a god falling from the heavens."

The falling star disappeared beyond the horizon.

"But then again, it could just be a hot rock falling from the sky. What do I know?"

Tristan chuckled at the notion of rocks in the sky, but the idea that gods fell from the heavens to be among them fascinated him. Caster had taught him a lot during their time together, but now Tristan observed the constellations with a touch of nervousness. He couldn't stop thinking about what Caster had told him. The stars shined with immense beauty, yet they were ominous. The Divider constellation loomed, pulsing over him.

Tristan nudged Caster with his elbow. "You never told me how you know so much about the constellations, about the Dividers. You mentioned a 'she' once. You said you would tell me when I was older, but I don't want to wait. Who is she?"

Caster, deep in thought, found his way to the edge of the fountain where a group of the ruby-horned rabbits perched. He took a seat and angled his head slightly away from Tristan's. "I'm not sure it's time." Caster eyed the rabbits apprehensively.

Tristan tried to shoo them away. The rabbits tilted their heads at him but refused to budge. They persisted in staring at him with their beady red eyes.

"Dumb critters."

"These aren't just critters," Caster said. "They are the eyes of Lephirus."

Tristan mocked the rabbits, wiggling his nose and tilting his head at them. "What in the world is a Lephirus?"

"Lephirus is an Aeon, an Aeon that walks the world and does as it pleases. These rabbits are his eyes. He sees what they see, and they are everywhere."

Tristan bent down and looked one of the rabbits in the eye. He started making faces at the still rabbit. "So, an Aeon is watching me right now?"

Caster shook his head. "He's watching an imbecile, yes."

Tristan stopped, wanting to reel the conversation back in. He gave a half-smile before he sat down next to Caster again.

"We've only known each other for a few months, Caster, but it feels like we've been brothers my whole life. If you don't want to tell me about her, I understand."

Caster smiled at the sentiment. "No, no, it's nothing like that. I feel our brotherly bond as well, my friend. The question just caught me off-guard."

Caster fidgeted with his hands. He stared up at the stars as though he could find the answers written in their depths. "I think about her every day, Tristan. I cared for no one else in this world, and I ended up proving that. She is the reason I'm here now. Gods, she's beautiful."

Tristan watched with concern. He had never heard Caster speak like this. "What was her name? Is she still around?" Curiosity overcame him.

"Her name is Nashira. She's here, and she isn't," Caster answered enigmatically. He finally looked at Tristan, who had cocked his head to the side in confusion.

"What does that even mean, Cas?"

"She's the Dividers' goddess. She rules the Dividers."

"So, she's—uh, where?" Tristan paused, hoping Caster would continue.

"She's up there right now, watching us. She came down one day, years and years ago, long before your birth, to proclaim her love for me."

"Really, Caster? You want me to believe a goddess came down from the Divider constellation to tell you she loved you? How could she even see you from that far away?" Tristan laughed and raised an eyebrow. "Forgive me, but that does sound more than a little far-fetched."

"Not at all. It may seem a little far-fetched, but I wouldn't be here now if it weren't for her. She visited me frequently. We were inseparable, just like you and Rayna."

"I'm sorry. What happened?"

Caster stood up and couldn't maintain eye contact with Tristan. "Seeing her came at a price I was not aware of. Watcher, a friend, warned me about this. He was a servant of Nashira. She sent him to protect me in her absence. Wherever I went, he was always perched at my side but in my ear about how manipulative Nashira could be. He was right. Her love and power did more harm than good. It changed me over time and eventually ended up costing me my best friend's life."

"She killed him?"

"No." Caster waited until Tristan looked into his eyes before he added, "I did."

"But why? He was your friend." Tristan's voice cracked.

Caster nodded before he dropped his head and started pacing. "He found out what I was doing—what she wanted me to do for her. She made me choose between him and her. I chose her." Caster paused to take a deep breath before he resumed his story. "I realized what I had succumbed to and what I had become. I took the only way she and her power could reach our world and scattered it throughout the kingdoms. So my people branded me a traitor and exiled me. I roamed the continent until I eventually came to the Land of Sorriax. I was looking for a fresh start when I found you, Tristan. The Aeons blessed me with you. I may have lost my friend and my love, but I've gained a brother and a family."

"Of course, you're my family. You never need question it. Whatever you may have done in the past, I know you're a good person now. You would never hurt us." Tristan placed his hand on Caster's shoulder. "You know that, don't you? You're a good person, Cas."

"Thank you, my friend."

They stood in silence for a few more minutes until Tristan spoke again. "I need to meet Rayna. See you when I get back?"

"Of course. I don't want to keep you. I should get to bed anyway since Ichiban wants to meet with me early. He said something about teaching me your army's battle formations."

Tristan patted Caster on the shoulder and started to make his way toward the castle when Caster grabbed Tristan's elbow. "But, Tristan," he spoke again, nearly in a whisper, but with a sense of urgency, "we need to talk more about this. I want to tell you the rest of my story so that you can learn from my mistakes."

Tristan studied Caster, ready to ask him what he meant by his "mistakes." Caster stared up at the Divider constellation; he closed his eyes and raised his hand up toward it.

"What color hair did she have?" Tristan asked.

"Blond. Why do you ask?"

Caster studied Tristan, looking for a reaction. All Tristan could do was nod.

Chapter 4

Playing the Part

Tristan sat on the hill, under the tree, in the middle of the warm night. With a clear sky, the moon illuminated the land stretched out before him. While waiting for Rayna, he watched a small fleet of ships in the distant sky. From what he could tell, the Sorriaxian army swarmed the oncoming vessels to give them proper inspections. Moments later, Rayna spoke from behind him.

"What's with the airships?"

Startled, he replied, "I'm not sure."

He stood to face her. They remained there for a moment, staring into each other's eyes. Tristan's mind felt more at ease with Rayna's presence.

Rayna pulled Tristan close to her, and he wrapped his arms around her waist. He studied her face before leaning into her lips. Rayna stood on her tiptoes to meet him halfway. Their lips met softly; Tristan pulled Rayna even tighter against his body. Her hands slid up his chest and wrapped around his neck, deepening their connection.

When Rayna pulled away from Tristan, she placed her cheek against his chest and sighed deeply. "Isn't it beautiful, Tristan?"

"My view certainly is." He gazed down at her.

Rayna lifted her head and smiled. She spun around in his arms, gesturing all around her. "I mean all of this," she replied coyly.

He surveyed the landscape before them. Aside from the airships, he only saw the same hills and trees they had always seen, but Tristan did appreciate the wide-open sky that Sorriax provided. "I guess so."

Rayna pulled herself away from Tristan's hold. He tried to grasp her hands, but she moved just beyond his reach.

"What do you mean 'you guess so'?" she asked, slightly annoyed. "This is our spot. That's why we picked it. It's always beautiful here."

"The view is only beautiful when you're here."

"Please." Rayna rolled her eyes. "That was trite."

"And 'Tristan, isn't this beautiful?' wasn't cliché?" he mocked.

"No. It was heartfelt. Unlike you, you stick in the mud."

"I can tell you meant every word of it." He elbowed her jokingly.

She gasped in mocked outrage. "Tristan, attacking a royal family member is an act of treason!"

"Yeah? Just what are you going to do about it?" he joked.

The second the last syllable fell from Tristan's lips, Rayna lunged at him and tackled him to the ground. He put his arms around her. A second passed before she crushed her lips to his. Tristan broke their kiss and looked into her eyes for a moment. He stroked her hair and caressed her soft skin.

"Fair enough." Tristan raised himself up to lean against the tree. He wrapped his arms around her waist and embraced her tightly. "You are the most beautiful woman in the world."

She smiled and got to her knees, straddling him. "I know, but words like that could get you hanged," she said with a laugh.

He kissed her cheek and nuzzled her ear. "Let them," he whispered. "It wouldn't stop me from loving you."

She wrapped her arms around him and squeezed tightly, pressing her forehead against his.

"Then, they would have to hang me, too, because I would never want to live without you, my elf."

"Rayna," Tristan murmured.

"Yes?"

"Please don't ever let go of me."

She was silent for a moment before she leaned back to contemplate his face and his request.

"How could I?" she asked, meeting his eyes.

Their eyes locked, and they leaned in slightly.

"I love you so much, Tristan," she purred against his lips.

"I love you, too." His fingers twined in her hair, and he pulled her the rest of the way to him. Their lips met, sealing their words.

When they finally broke apart, they leaned against each other, catching their breath. After a few moments, Tristan propped his head against the tree and sighed.

"What's wrong?" she asked.

Tristan hesitated before speaking. He was afraid to speak his next words out loud. "I'm scared, Rayna."

"Scared of what?" she asked and brushed his hair out of his face.

"After tomorrow, we won't be under the guardians' or your family's protection at the rear line. We'll have to fight, and you will be behind us." He paused before he added, "I'm worried about you."

"Please don't be scared," she answered without fear. "You're right. We do have to fight now. But I won't let anything happen to you."

"That's supposed to be my line." He smiled and cupped her face with his hand. He stroked her soft cheek with his thumb. "Do you really want to go through with this?"

"What are you asking me, Tristan? Of course, I want to marry you." She paused a moment before asking her own question. "Do you?"

"Yes, but..."

She cut him off before he could voice his doubts. She scooted in closer and playfully nudged him with her shoulder. "To hell with our law! Who cares if I am royalty and you are a commoner? We should be allowed to marry who we want!"

She turned her gaze to Tristan; he could see the stars gleaming in her eyes. "Then say you love me! Say you want to marry me!" Her volume grew a little too loud for their secret rendezvous.

"Shhh," he whispered, laughing. "I love you, you crazy girl." He searched her face and gave her a quick peck on her lips. "You can't deny this is going to be risky; you know the law of our world. Commoner and royal blood are forbidden to mix," he said, still holding her face. "I can't guarantee I can keep us safe."

"That's why I want to do this. It won't be a legitimate marriage, but it's the best we can do." She lowered her voice to a barely audible whisper before adding, "Besides, I can't live without you."

Feeling the weight of the decision, Tristan took her hand. "Nor can I you."

Rayna curled into his embrace, resting her head on his chest with his arms around her. "Can we stay like this a little longer?" she begged.

He lingered in the silence for a few moments, running his fingers through her long silky hair and then kissing her head. "Of course, my princess."

The night slowly elapsed with Rayna asleep in Tristan's arms.

≈

Tristan awoke under the tree to the sun rising. He shook Rayna. "Wake up! We need to get you back to your room!"

Dazed, she reluctantly sat up.

"Rayna!" he said more urgently. "We have to go!"

She blinked several more times. She saw the sun breaking the horizon and gasped. Tristan rushed to his feet and offered her his hand. Together, they ran back to the castle.

They slowed upon approach to avoid unwanted attention. A fleet of airships hovered in front of the castle, each heavily armed with artillery cannons and mounted machineguns. Soldiers watched them from above. The two pretended that Tristan was simply doing his duty by escorting Rayna to her room.

Tristan rushed headlong toward the door and directed Rayna toward her chambers.

"Wait, Tristan," Rayna called. She scanned for prying eyes before she kissed him softly. "I love you."

"I love you, too." He let go of her and left. When he reached the castle entrance, he saw a familiar form leaning against the wall in the shadows.

"Caster, what are you doing here?"

"I was with Ichiban early this morning. Remember?" he asked and then pushed himself off the wall. "Your father has been looking for you."

Together, they headed toward the path that led back to town.

"Didn't you tell him I was out running like usual?" Tristan asked nervously.

"I did," he answered. Caster seemed concerned. "But he was up pretty early looking for you. Look, Tristan, what we talked about last night—you are like my brother. I would never expose you and Rayna—but you need to end this."

"But..." Tristan tried to interject.

"No," Caster continued. "What you're doing is forbidden. Not just by the Naughtrious family, but all royal families. They will kill you if they find out. Why are you doing this? Does she really care for you enough to risk your life?" Caster's sudden change of heart wounded Tristan.

"Of course, Rayna cares about me, Caster. Why wouldn't she?"

"Tactics, Tristan. Developing relationships between the bodyguard and the protected is a tactic. It makes the bodyguard give all he has to protect the one he cares for, even his life."

Tristan's eyes narrowed. He didn't like the direction Caster was taking this conversation.

"Why do you love Rayna?"

"What? How can you even ask that?" Tristan asked defensively.

"Why can't you answer?" Caster's tone grew more serious.

"I love her, Caster. Every moment we spend together makes me feel complete. I am only whole when she is with me."

"You didn't answer my question, Tristan. Why do you love her?"

Tristan became a little irritated at Caster's persistence, so he stopped walking. Caster turned to face Tristan, who began to count on his fingers Rayna's qualities. "Her smile. Her kindness. Her eyes. There isn't anything about her I don't love."

"You are describing her, Tristan. Why do you love her?"

"Damnit, Caster. I just do! She loves me unconditionally. As I do her. She would lay her life on the line for me. She would never abandon me!"

Caster closed his eyes. "I don't want you to get hurt. Most importantly, I don't want you to get caught. Watch your back."

"They won't find out. We're extra careful."

"Extra careful?" Caster raised an eyebrow. "Where were you all night?"

Tristan glared at him instead of answering.

"For your sake, Tristan, I hope they don't find out about you, but you really do have to be more careful."

Ignoring Caster's concern, Tristan asked, "Is Father still looking for me?"

"Not likely. The king summoned him to the castle. They are meeting with the admiral. Something about the fleet," Caster explained.

"Did he say anything about why those airships are here?"

"No, but the king has ordered all civilians to remain inside and all trainees to wait in the military barracks for further instructions. We might be under attack."

Under attack, Tristan thought, *that's serious.* Perhaps he'd go into battle sooner than he realized.

"I guess the guardian ceremony won't happen today. What about you?"

"The recruits and I will serve as reserve guards in case the fight gets too intense," Caster replied. "Hurry home. Grab your armor and sword. I have to go back."

"Don't let me keep you. I'll meet up with the other guardians at the barracks."

"Are you sure, Tristan?"

Tristan nodded, and they said their goodbyes. Caster headed into the castle while Tristan hurried home to gather his equipment.

He ran through the dirt roads, avoiding the hordes of panicked people scurrying through the streets. The guards shouted warnings for all civilians to remain in their homes.

Tristan tried to dodge people riding horses through the streets but fell into a bread rack outside of a bakery instead. The smell of fresh bread filled his nose and reminded him that he hadn't eaten breakfast. He saw a few of Lephirus' rabbits take refuge in a hole on the side of the bakery, maintaining their silent vigil.

Tristan rushed through the town and passed under the hovering airships. Many people scuttled about on the decks of the ships. Such activity worried Tristan, but he pressed on, making his way to the military barracks. When he arrived, he saw everyone already dressed in armored chest plates, leggings, and weapons. The trainees' special armor provided the extra layer of protection necessary for their survival.

Lazarus approached Tristan. "Where have you been?"

"I slept in," Tristan lied sheepishly.

"Yeah, well, you picked a hell of a time to start sleeping in."

"What's going on?" Tristan asked.

"The king is keeping us all on standby in case the airships attack the castle."

"Then shouldn't we be with Rayna and Morgan?"

"That's not what we've been ordered to do," Lazarus answered. "If the situation gets thick, I say we go help them."

"I second that," Tristan said and turned to the others. "What about you guys? Are you with us if the princesses are in trouble?"

Zro looked at the others and stood up. "I think I speak for everyone when I say we're in. Besides, what have we been training for if we don't get to use it?"

"Then, it's settled." Tristan donned his armor.

Lazarus waved his hands a little to interrupt. "It's highly unlikely anything will happen. They're probably here to pledge their allegiance to the king."

The group of inexperienced trainees waited impatiently inside the barracks until nightfall. Outside the door by the entrance, they heard groups of men shouting orders in a panic.

Suddenly, unfamiliar soldiers wearing yellow armor with foreign royal symbols burst into the room.

The lead soldier looked them over and demanded, "Who are you people, and what is your purpose?"

Lazarus stepped forward. "We help care for the dragons," he lied.

The soldier nodded distractedly. "Come with us. All of you," he commanded.

"Why? Who are you?" Tristan asked.

"We are soldiers from the airships above. Everyone to the castle throne room, now!" the lead soldier added forcefully.

"Why?" Tristan demanded, stepping in front of the trainees.

"That's the detention center. Come," the soldier commanded again. "Let's try to avoid any unnecessary conflict."

Tristan slowly reached for his weapon. Out of the corner of his eye, he saw Zro do the same. They paused when Lazarus lifted his hand.

"We will accompany you. We don't want any violence," Lazarus said while signaling the other trainees to stand down.

The trainees slyly moved their hands away from their weapons.

"Excellent. Disarm yourselves and make your way to the door."

The young guardians removed their weapons and made their way out of the barracks, escorted by the soldiers from the ships. They marched to the side entrance of the castle. Hundreds of unfamiliar soldiers patrolled the castle and its perimeter. Finding themselves in the hall adjoining the royal princesses' chambers, Tristan felt a spike of concern for Rayna. Portraits of Rayna, Morgan, and the rest of the royal family covered the red walls of the throne room. In the center of the gold-trimmed corridor were four guards, gagged and bound by their hands and feet.

Another group of foreign soldiers walked toward the trainees, escorting Rayna, Morgan, their two cousins, a couple of the older guardians, and some regular castle soldiers. Tristan covertly glanced at Lazarus, who returned a slight nod.

When the two groups intersected, Lazarus tripped Zro, who then fell onto a guard. During the distraction, Lazarus punched the guard, grabbed the sidearm from his belt, and fired the gun at the other guards with uncanny accuracy. Tristan pulled a sword from the downed guard's sheath. He charged the other group, furthering the confusion. The other trainees followed suit. Caught off guard, the soldiers put up little fight. The older guardians, including Tristan's father, grabbed Morgan, Rayna, and their cousins and shoved them into Morgan's chambers.

Faranus came out into the corridor. "Come here, trainees."

Tristan and his friends hurried into the room.

"Stay here. Don't let anyone enter this room. You have permission to kill all who mean the princesses harm. For your safety, do not leave this room until the battle is over, and stay away from the windows. Is that understood?" Faranus ordered.

With fear and excitement, they shakily nodded their heads. Faranus observed each of them and stared intensely into their eyes.

Suddenly, in a serious voice, he spoke the same words Tristan had heard his entire life: "Protect the royal family members with your very being. And protect each other."

The head guardian turned to Lazarus to issue instructions. "Lazarus, keep your fellow guardians safe. I put you in charge."

The group of older guardians left the room and locked the huge double doors behind them. When they were gone, Tristan and Rayna ran to one another and hugged each other tightly. Lazarus went to Morgan.

"Why didn't you use your powers to get rid of those soldiers? Where is Aerra?" Lazarus asked.

"My powers are still developing, but yes, I could've easily killed those guards. I could have easily hurt someone else, too," Morgan scoffed. "I was worried about the safety of my family, the castle, and all of you. I don't know where Aerra is. I don't have my sword with me, so I can't summon her."

"That was a smart move," Lazarus said, conceding that Morgan knew better. "Take Rayna and your cousins into the farthest corner of the room, away from the door and windows."

"Let me stay behind you," Morgan interrupted. "I can put up a barrier to protect you."

Tristan let go of Rayna to face Morgan. "That isn't acceptable. We're here to protect you, not the other way around."

"Don't be foolish, Tristan. I will be behind you, protecting you and my family. Don't try to order me otherwise."

"How can I help?" Rayna interjected.

Morgan turned to her sister. "I want you to remain right behind me but stay out of the fight. If anything happens to me, I want you right there to put up a second barrier."

"But I can fight, Morgan. Let me help," Rayna implored.

Morgan shot her sister a stern look. "Do what I ask, Rayna."

Rayna opened her mouth to reply when Mira stepped forward. "Why can't she fight? None of us have ever been in a battle before. The more swords we have, the better chances we'll have."

"That is out of the question!" Lazarus shouted to settle the dispute. "We cannot put both princesses in harm's way. Morgan knows what she's doing. Trust her judgment."

Mira rolled her eyes. "Whatever."

Tristan scrutinized the other young guardians before issuing his own commands. "Lazarus is in charge, so we will follow his orders. Do you understand?"

Everyone nodded. Lazarus turned to Tristan to determine their plan of attack. Lazarus, though technically in charge, sought Tristan's advice. "How should we mount our stand, Tristan?"

"I think the family should be in the back by the far wall. In front of them, I would like those who have bows and guns to surround the family. Morgan will be in the center. Those who have hand-to-hand weapons, up front. We'll be on the front line. The others can cover us while we fight. Morgan, protect all of us if there is any incoming fire," Tristan commanded.

Lazarus addressed the others, "Is that clear?"

"Yes, sir!" the other trainees replied in unison.

In the distance, Tristan heard the guns aboard the airships fire at the castle and town. The Sorriaxian soldiers returned fire from the castle. The grounds roared with the flames of destruction. The night sky exploded into an eerie orange and red glow.

The group stood ready, waiting in Morgan's room. Fear and tension saturated the air. Despite their years of training, none of them believed they were prepared for this.

Tristan heard shouting and fighting outside the room; sounds of clashing swords and firing guns permeated the air. The door opened abruptly. Enemy soldiers barged in.

The soldier in front shouted, "Drop your weapons and surrender the princesses to us. Now!"

Charity shot an arrow from behind Tristan's head, and the soldier dropped to the ground. Tristan charged the remaining soldiers. Lazarus and the other trainees followed suit. Melee ensued: weapons collided, and each person attacked another. Tristan cut down one enemy while Lazarus and another soldier grappled. Tristan charged at the enemy soldier, stabbing him in the leg. In a final gesture, Lazarus thrust his sword through the man's chest.

As the battle in the room slowed, Tristan heard the clang of swords in the distance. From the corner of his eye, he saw one of the newer recruits fighting one of the few remaining soldiers. Tristan pulled out his blade to move toward the young trainee.

The fight looked desperate; the boy was on the defensive. The soldier had knocked the weapon out of the boy's hand. He then rammed his sword through the boy. In devastation, the rest of the young trainees froze. Their faces reflected their disbelief: one of their own had actually fallen.

The soldier pulled his sword out of the boy's chest, and his body slowly dropped to the ground. Feeling an emptiness in his stomach and all gravity vanishing momentarily, Tristan couldn't tear his eyes away from the dying boy. However, Tristan's numbness soon disappeared, and together, he and Lazarus charged the soldier. Screaming in anger, Lazarus swung his blade and cut off the soldier's armed hand. Tristan pounced onto the soldier's body, thrusting his sword through the man's neck. He leaped backward when the body collapsed.

Tristan fell to his knees next to the dead boy. He picked up the fallen boy's sword. Breathing hard with tears welling in his eyes, Tristan studied the others. Tears streamed from their eyes and trickled down their faces of despair, but no one else seemed injured.

Lazarus took Tristan by the elbow and helped him to his feet. "Come on," he said softly. "We still have a job to do."

They joined the rest of the group to reform their lines. Though explosions erupted outside the window, they held their ranks in silence. Tristan and his friends dropped to the floor to take cover. Tristan noticed a field of blue light surrounding them. Stones knocked loose from the wall clattered harmlessly off Morgan's barrier. When the group got back onto their feet, a handful of soldiers entered the room and stopped inches from the barrier. A few attacked the barrier, but they failed to break it. Tristan stood in front of the soldiers, a sword in each hand, ready to attack. Along with the other trainees, Lazarus followed his example— Zro with his pistol and Charity and Mira with their bows.

A dark fury festered inside Tristan. Quietly, he said, "Let your barrier down, Morgan."

Morgan hesitated. He saw the worried look on her face, but she followed the order: her barrier dissipated. The soldiers and the guardians remained still, staring at one another and sizing each other up. Uncomfortable silence filled the room.

Without warning, the guardian marksmen fired their weapons into the group of soldiers. The trainees charged the men; more soldiers poured into the room from the outer hall. Tristan's ears rang when someone behind him picked up a gun and started to fire into the doorway—a valiant but impossible effort to slow the flood of bodies flowing into the room.

The number of the soldiers grew, magically multiplying before their very eyes. An enemy soldier stripped one trainee of her weapons, picked her up, and threw her against a wall while another pierced her chest with a spear. They left her hanging on the wall to watch the lifeblood drip from her body.

"Cadence!" Bianca screamed. She started to release her arrows rapidly into the crowd of soldiers. In a mindless rage, the trainees fought harder, desperate to get to the dying girl. While Lazarus, Tristan, and Ry held the soldiers back, the others pulled the girl down from the wall. Tristan peered back at Zro and yelled for cover. Zro lifted his pistol and shot with a high degree of precision into the hordes of soldiers. After placing her limp body next to the dead boy, the other trainees rejoined Tristan to push back the soldiers.

A soldier threw Tristan to the ground and raised his sword to strike. A scream came from behind when a bright light flared up, and a beam shot through the soldier. Tristan strained to see through the confusion behind him and saw Rayna with her hands thrown forward, breathing heavily. Tristan jumped to his feet, and they ran back to the fight. When they reentered the battle, a desperate soldier pulled the pin off a grenade and dove at them, making one last attempt on their lives.

Lazarus shouted, "Everybody, down!" Lazarus grabbed Tristan and Rayna, and they fell to the floor, covering their heads.

The explosion blasted both soldiers and trainees, sending them across the room and out into the hall. Tristan stood up alongside Lazarus. They grabbed the survivors to drag them next to Morgan so she could put up her defensive barrier.

In the process, they heard more soldiers running down the hall.

Morgan shouted, "Hurry! Get over here!"

Tristan and Lazarus ran to join them. The slight click from a fired crossbow resounded behind them; they dropped to the ground. Tristan watched as Lazarus fell beside him. He felt a moment of panic before he saw Lazarus turn his head to aim his pistol at the enemy.

"Don't move!" the soldier shouted and proceeded closer, pointing the crossbow at Tristan. "Disarm yourselves, or the boy dies!"

Everyone dropped their weapons, punctuating the silence with a clatter of rifles, bows, and swords hitting the ground. Two more soldiers entered the room, guarding the door.

"Princesses," the newest soldier said, "if you care about the lives of these people protecting you, come with us, or we will be forced to kill them."

Tristan looked around for a solution. Giving up was the furthest thing from his mind. He saw one of the dead soldier's weapons lying near him. The princesses hesitated and looked at each other. Morgan gave a small nod and walked toward the other soldiers. Tristan saw his chance; he grabbed the shotgun. He made eye contact with Lazarus, gesturing at the gun in his hand.

He tossed it to Lazarus, who pointed it at the soldiers and pumped it, expelling an empty shell and loading a live round into the barrel. The soldier looked fearful. He quickly raised his crossbow. Lazarus fired the gun, propelling the man's dead body into the group of soldiers securing the door.

The two remaining soldiers watched with blank stares. Without warning, they fell to the floor. Caster, wearing his black armor and shrouded by a black hood, stood behind them holding two short, bloody swords.

He strode inside and asked, "Are the princesses still alive?"

Tristan stared at Caster for a second and then hugged him. "Are you injured, Cas?"

"No," he answered, shaking his head. "How is everyone here?"

"The rest are alive and accounted for, but we have sustained many losses," Zro said, approaching them.

Caster took a deep breath and hung his head. "The same is true on all fronts," he responded. "The airships are attacking the entire city. The high guardians and Ichiban are assembling an attack force to board the *Nightingale*, the flagship of their small fleet."

"Why are you here, Caster?" Lazarus stepped forward.

"Ichiban sent me here to aid you until reinforcements arrive. We must rearm quickly. The enemy is not far behind."

"Then I want you right next to us on the frontline," Lazarus directed.

Caster narrowed his gaze. His eyes flicked from Lazarus to Tristan. "Are you in charge, Lazarus?"

"Yes, I'm the squad leader," Lazarus said.

"Then I'll be right behind you."

The group stood in formation. They heard footsteps drumming down the hall. When the first soldier entered the room, two arrows struck him. He fell. When the next soldier stepped into the doorway, a marksman fired a bullet into his head. Other marksmen shot through a dozen soldiers, holding them at bay.

One of the soldiers finally reached Tristan. Their swords clashed. Caster broke the line immediately to step in to protect his friend. He leaped onto the back of a soldier and shoved his sword through the man's neck. Caster then hopped off the soldier and watched him die like it was second nature.

Tristan and Caster charged at the other soldiers pouring into the room. Rayna cried out in protest while Tristan and Caster fought off the foreign troops. A soldier knocked Caster off his feet. When the enemy approached him, three arrows from the other side of the room struck the man's chest with resounding thuds.

Enemy soldiers quickly overran Tristan. Lazarus and the others ran to Tristan's aid until Caster could get to his feet. Their swords collided. Caster rejoined the fight, holding off the dozens of soldiers entering the room. The team killed soldier after soldier.

After a few minutes, the fighting died down. One by one, the trainees slowly calmed when they had a chance to catch their breath. Rayna ran to Tristan. He felt her gaze examine his body, making sure no harm came to him. Tears formed in her eyes. He grabbed her in an embrace, but the passion abruptly ended.

Behind them, the wall exploded from an artillery shell. Everyone dropped when a second shell fired and exploded inside the room. The blast knocked Rayna off her feet, sending her flying out the window. Panic and fear overtook Tristan. Without thinking, he grabbed his swords and followed her. Several more artillery shells exploded over Tristan's head.

He dove into some bushes next to Rayna. The small branches scraped his already bruised and broken skin. Tristan sat up. He spied an enemy soldier coming from behind. He rose and charged the soldier with a sword in each hand. The enemy pulled out a pistol and aimed, but Tristan swung his sword and knocked the pistol from his hand before he could fire. The second sword pierced the soldier's chest.

From behind him, Rayna screamed, "Tristan!"

He turned and saw another soldier with a sword charging at Rayna. She threw out her hands to attack the soldier. Tristan rolled to his left to grab the dead soldier's pistol. He fired every round into the writhing man. Tristan dropped his weapon and ran to Rayna. They held each other tightly. Tristan inspected her for injuries and found his own fear reflected.

"Are you alright, Rayna?"

She kissed his cheek and then buried her face in his chest. "Yes, I am now, my elf."

"We need to get you back inside. It isn't safe out here."

Shadows covered them, drawing their attention upward. "Tristan!" Rayna cried out and pointed.

Above them floated a giant metallic boat-shaped airship. A large gust of wind pressed down upon them from the three propellers on the three main masts. The propeller on the back of the ship turned off so it could hover in one spot. The wings, not needed for extra propulsion or maneuvering, retracted. Etched on the mighty ship's side was the name *Nightingale*. Anchors shot from the ship into the ground and the castle.

Tristan realized the enemy's plan. "It looks like they're going to demolish the castle.

"We need to do something!" Rayna panicked.

"Hold on." He faced her once again. "We aren't doing anything. You need to get to safety. The guardians will take care of it."

"They may not make it in time," she said frantically. "Tristan, save my family!"

Tristan hesitated and searched for a way to save themselves and the castle. "I can't leave you, Rayna."

"I will be fine." She gazed up at the ship; her mouth opened to yell. Tristan followed her eyes in time to see the cannons aimed at them. "Tristan!"

Rayna lunged at Tristan. She instinctively wrapped her arms around him and formed a barrier just large enough to cover them. The barrier filled the area with blue light, illuminating the castle wall. Cannons roared above and blanketed the ground with explosions. Continuous fire rocked them. Tristan never had a chance to catch his breath.

Tristan looked up again to see the cannons' attention diverted into the sky when the firing ceased. Dragon Riders flooded the flagship. Rayna let down her barrier, and Tristan let go of her. He kneeled and picked up both his swords.

He looked at Rayna, not only scared to leave her but also worried about the others trying to bring down the flagship. He didn't want to disappoint Rayna. "Stay out of sight. Keep your barrier up for however long you can. I'll do everything I can to help stop the ship."

"Come back to me. That's an order." Rayna moved in closer to kiss Tristan. He returned the kiss briefly, turned around, and ran toward the anchor's chain.

"I'm not saying goodbye, Rayna. Not yet."

Chapter 5

What Is Asked of Us

Using his elven dexterity, Tristan ran up the chain of the airship, nervously gripping his weapons. He ignored a trace of impending fear: what if he couldn't accomplish such an improbable task? When he reached the handrail of the ship, he leaped from the chain onto the deck. Every soldier on the ship, except the captain, operated a deck-mounted machinegun or cannon. No one noticed Tristan climb aboard. His heart pounded fiercely, his hands shook with anxiety, and sweat dripped from his head. He ducked behind a barrel to survey the scene.

One of the soldiers pointed and shouted, "Captain, one of our ships off the starboard is being attacked!"

The captain shouted, "Fire! We cannot let those guardians destroy any more ships."

The deck guns all fired at once. Tristan swung into action and brandished one of his swords at the captain. When the blade entered the captain's chest, he dropped to the floor. No one heard the calamity. Tristan approached the other soldiers, sword in hand. They were focused on the guardians' attacking the other ship, so Tristan seized the opportunity.

Three main artillery cannons fired from the center of the deck, each manned by two people. Tristan ran up to the cannon on the right side of the ship and took out both soldiers. The skirmish didn't go unnoticed this time. Soldiers from the artillery cannons and mounted machineguns stopped firing at the castle and turned their attention to Tristan. Each readied a gun and opened fire. Tristan grabbed the dead soldier's rifle and dove behind the cannon to take cover. His heart pounded, and tears rolled down his cheeks—he knew he was about to die.

Tristan felt the ship begin to rise. *The guardians won't get here in time,* he thought. Tristan composed himself and cocked the rifle. He charged into the onslaught of bullets. He saw the bullets zoom past him, almost like slow motion. The soldiers' movements seemed as if time had come to a halt. Tristan opened fire.

A massive explosion erupted, killing the guards who shot at Tristan. He stood up and stared down at the castle. He let out a whoop of victory upon seeing Morgan and Rayna. The two girls breathed heavily with their hands extended; smoke rose from their fingertips and palms. Morgan quickly raised a barrier, filling the gap in the wall with blue light. More incoming artillery fire came at them.

Tristan turned his attention to his own predicament. When the *Nightingale* accelerated, he sheathed his sword and prepared his rifle. He made his way to a door that led to the lower decks. Two men barged through the door. Without hesitation, Tristan fired the rifle twice, slaying both men. He hurdled over their bodies and descended the spiral staircase into a long corridor.

After the deafening chaos of battle, the interior of the ship grew silent. Tristan held his rifle tightly and advanced through the endless hall of rooms—all empty. *They all must have left the vessel to invade the castle, but why is the ship still rising?* he asked himself. He found a door leading to another staircase that went down even farther. He continued down the steps with caution. At the end of the stairs, he reached an iron door.

Tristan shouldered the door open and found an enormous engine at the center of the room. Three men monitored a large control panel with a gigantic glowing orb hovering above it on the far wall. Two fur-covered Irkshdan warriors from the Fox Tribe, both wielding bows, patrolled the room. The people of the Fox Tribe walked upright and had humanoid characteristics despite their snouts and large, pointed ears. Tristan had never seen one in person before. He did recognize another from the Wolf Tribe, like Ichiban, who carried a large broadsword in his hands.

Tristan pushed the door out of the way, firing two bullets into one of the foxes: the creature dropped. He pointed the gun at the other fox and pulled the trigger. The sounds of a disappointing click filled his ears. Tristan dropped the weapon, unsheathed his sword, and charged the second fox while the giant wolf swung his blade. Tristan nose-dived under the broadsword and rose. He swung his own blade and knocked the fox's bow and arrow from his hands. The fox pulled out a short sword to attack Tristan. Tristan fell to one knee, raised his sword, and blocked the fox's attack. The broadsword came at him again from his right. He dropped to the ground, ducking once more.

The fox pounced after him. It landed on top of the large blade and started to climb up it. Tristan crawled under the blade toward the wolf. He slid between the wolf's legs, raising his sword to stab it in the lower back. The fox leaped over the wolf, thrust its blade at Tristan's, and blocked his attack. Tristan twisted back onto his feet. Realizing he couldn't fend off both attackers at once, he shot out of the way and positioned himself next to the engine. He charged at the men operating the ship. He plunged his sword through the man on the left of the control panel. He rotated back just in time to see the fox draw back an arrow with his bow. Tristan jumped out of the way. When he hit the ground, he felt an intense stinging sensation in his left arm—the fox's arrow protruded from it.

When Tristan looked up, the wolf stood over him, holding the broadsword above his head. "Drop your weapon, boy. Surrender," the wolf growled.

He could only think about Rayna and her order: "Come back to me." With renewed vigor, Tristan thrust his sword into the wolf's leg. The wolf howled and snarled with agony. Tristan felt another arrow pierce his upper right thigh; he screamed in agony. He looked up to see the broadsword bearing down on him.

Desperate to get out of the way, Tristan grabbed the wolf's calf and slid between his legs. Once, on the other side, Tristan stole the wolf's pistol and aimed it at the fox, who prepared another arrow. Tristan fired two bullets into the other fox's head—he dropped to the ground. Tristan scuttled away from the wolf; the Irkshdan followed.

One of the remaining men left the control panel and pulled out his sidearm to fire at Tristan, who crawled behind the engine to take cover. The wolf's footsteps shook the floor as it made its way to Tristan. The gunfire stopped for a second. Tristan listened to the magazine drop from the man's gun. He lunged from behind the engine, slid on his right shoulder and back, and barely dodged the wolf's weapon when he swung it. Tristan brought up the stolen pistol and fired three rounds into the man's chest. He turned and quickly aimed the gun at the wolf's right knee and pulled the trigger. The wolf fell to the ground in agony. Tristan turned to the last man at the panel. Before he pulled out his pistol, Tristan fired one round into the man's head, dropping him instantly. "Come back to me," echoed in his mind.

Only the wolf remained. The wolf fumbled along after Tristan, dragging its injured leg. Tristan aimed the pistol at the enraged Irkshdan. Tristan pulled the trigger but only heard a click: the magazine was empty. The wolf formed a sick smile on his face.

"I'm going to enjoy killing you, boy!"

Tristan retreated, trying to get away from the wolf. He hit a furry obstacle: a dead fox. Its hands still gripped a bow and arrow. Tristan grabbed the bow, locked the arrow, and pulled back on the string. With shaking hands and blurry vision, Tristan summoned his remaining strength to discharge the arrow. Rayna's voice again echoed in his head.

He let go, and the wolf cried in agony. The arrow entered its right shoulder, forcing it to drop the broadsword. Tristan fired a second arrow into the wolf's throat—the beast fell. Tristan grabbed the fox's short blade and slowly stood above the wolf.

"Bested by a human child," the wolf gurgled through the blood trickling out of its mouth.

"Half-human," Tristan insisted.

The ship suddenly jerked to the side from distant artillery fire that ripped the engine room apart, forcing Tristan through the open doorway. The engine room erupted in explosions. Tristan pulled himself up the spiral staircase to outrun the fire that had engulfed the ship. His stomach lurched when the vessel started to lose altitude. Ignoring the pain in his arm and leg, he climbed out onto the deck toward the back of the ship—the part farthest from the ground. The ship was rapidly losing altitude and falling diagonally. Tristan wasn't sure what to do, so he crouched in a low position, attempting to maintain his balance. The ground drew near, and he froze in terror.

A grizzled, fur-covered form hurtled toward him. Tristan crashed into Ichiban's arms as the wolf jumped off seconds before the ship hit the ground and exploded on impact. Tristan's body jolted when they landed. He was close to losing consciousness.

He heard a voice. "Are you alright, boy?"

Tristan, overcome with fatigue, could only pant and mumble.

Ichiban shook him. "Come on, Tristan. Open your eyes. Stay awake!" Ichiban's gruff voice commanded.

After a few tries, Tristan managed to mumble, "Is she safe?"

"Is who safe?"

"Rayna?" he called with a forceful exhale.

Tristan gave up trying to focus and gave in to the eddy of unconsciousness. His eyes fluttered open, and he couldn't help but be reminded of the blond girl. Her words filled his head: "Help me find him." His eyes slammed shut again. He heard skirmishing, and then the darkness of oblivion overtook him.

≈

Tristan awoke to see Ichiban place a rough paw on his forehead. "How are you feeling?" he asked.

"Been better," Tristan struggled to say. "Is the fight still going on?"

"The enemy stragglers are being chased out."

"Everyone safe?" he asked.

"Yes, they are safe."

Tristan breathed a sigh and closed his eyes again. He didn't care that he would most likely be punished for his actions. Everyone was safe, and that was what mattered.

"Indeed," Ichiban continued. "Tristan, you did a very foolish thing earlier. You put yourself at risk, and furthermore, you risked Rayna's life by leaving her! What were you thinking?"

"I apologize, sir," Tristan said after a few seconds. Through the haze of medication, he continued. "I was only doing what Rayna ordered me to do."

Confused, Ichiban asked, "She ordered you to board that ship to destroy it?"

Tristan turned to the wolf and tried to nod. "Yes, sir."

Ichiban closed his eyes and shook his head. "That was a courageous thing you did for her."

Rayna's resounding command crowded his head again.

"I would do anything she asked of me," Tristan said, his voice stronger, more adamant.

Ichiban gazed out the window, deep in thought. "Tristan," he warned, "becoming a high guardian requires you to act with rationality, use logic in your decision making, and not follow orders blindly."

Tristan closed his eyes in confusion. "But they came from…"

"I know who those orders came from, boy. Royals always come first, but sometimes what they say or do isn't always accurate. So, if they do ask something of you that does not seem right, trust your instincts. If you are correct and the family is wrong, you will be forgiven."

"Yes, sir." Tristan cleared his throat and managed a salute.

Ichiban returned the salute. "The doctors will keep you overnight. I shall return to take you home tomorrow."

"Thank you, sir."

Ichiban walked to the door when he stopped and turned around. "Tristan," he said, demanding attention. "You will make a fine guardian. Well done."

"Sir," he responded.

The guardian ceremony was delayed so the palace could recover from the attack. After being transported home the next day, Tristan learned he was under severe restrictions until he fully recovered. Tristan chafed at the restriction, mainly because it meant he couldn't see Rayna.

He lay in bed, daydreaming about one of their visits under the tree, when he felt a sudden jostle. He startled awake.

"Come on, bro," Caster said, throwing Tristan's clothes on his bed.

"Cas, what's going on?"

"I'm getting you out of here. Rayna wants to see you."

The mention of Rayna brought Tristan fully to his senses. "I want to see her, too, but you heard Mother. House arrest."

"That hasn't stopped you before," Caster said with a laugh. "Do you or don't you want to see her?"

"I always want to see her."

"Then, get out of bed."

"Will the others be there?"

"I imagine so." Caster smiled at his young friend. "They all want to make sure you're still alive."

Tristan rose from the bed and carefully dressed. The arrow wounds in his arm and leg were well-bandaged but still fresh and tender.

With a little dexterity, they managed to leave the house unnoticed. Tristan appreciated Caster's support while they walked through the town. Maybe the doctors and his mother were right to prescribe bed rest.

Once they reached the wrecked castle garden, Tristan felt immense grief when he saw what was left of the young guardians surrounding the princesses. Quite a few lives had been lost that night. Tristan beamed at the sight of his best friends: Lazarus and Zro, along with Ry, Charity, Mira, and Bianca. Both princesses had also survived. Tristan knew they all owed thanks to Morgan, whose extensive powers had helped carry the fight. She stood next to her sister in the center of the group. Rayna wore a black cloak with the hood up, even though the day felt quite warm to Tristan. The sight of her made Tristan smile briefly until an image of the blond girl in black appeared in his head. He shook his head slightly to eliminate the thought.

While he and Caster made their way up a small hill, Lazarus glanced over and laughed. "Hey, gimpy has arrived!" he shouted.

Everyone turned their focus to Tristan. He knew he must look pathetic, held up by a crutch and Caster.

When Rayna saw him, she rushed toward them. The wind blew back her hood, and Tristan could see tears in her eyes. When she reached him, she buried her head in his chest and held him tight. Tristan dropped his crutch and let go of Caster. He held onto Rayna while she supported his weight.

Weeping, she said, "I'm so sorry."

He rested his head on hers and whispered into her hair, "You don't need to be sorry."

"I will never do that to you again. I got you hurt, and you could have died, and it would've been my fault." She surrendered to her sobs.

"I'm here with you now, we're all okay, and that's all that matters."

She shuddered. "I'm still so sorry," she mumbled into his chest.

"It's okay. I would do anything for you."

"I know you would."

He felt her tears saturate his shirt. Tristan couldn't stand to see her cry. He gently lifted her head and stared into her eyes. He brushed her tears away with his thumb and smiled sweetly at her. Not caring about the others or even if the guards would notice, Tristan pressed his lips against Rayna's. For a moment, she didn't react, but then she returned the kiss. Rayna clasped her hands behind Tristan's neck and gently pulled him closer.

"Rayna, what are you doing?" Morgan shouted. Morgan's eyes flicked between her sister and Tristan. She couldn't believe they would have the audacity to go against the royal decree. In public, no less. "You do remember that there is only one rule in this social order that you must obey, right? Royal blood and common blood cannot mix!"

Ignoring her, Tristan melted into the kiss. When they finally pulled away from each other, Rayna had stopped crying, and Tristan smiled.

"I can't stand to see you cry," he whispered. It took all his might to raise his left arm and cup her cheek.

Morgan stormed over to them and slapped Tristan. "Do you have any idea what you're doing?" She shrieked as she grabbed her younger sister's hand and pulled her away from Tristan.

Without Rayna to support him, he dropped to his knees. His right leg sent volts of excruciating pain through his body. He cried out.

Rayna struggled against her sister and shouted, "Morgan!"

Caster helped Tristan rise. He had no choice but to stand by and watch Morgan berate her sister.

"There is no excuse for this kind of stupidity, Rayna. You could get caught out here! You're putting all of us in danger!"

Lazarus picked up Tristan's crutch and held it out to him. "What are you doing?" Lazarus asked, as astonished by their behavior as Morgan.

Tristan watched his friend and the others; each looked at him like they didn't know him. They all began to speak at once. Tristan turned away at the disappointment.

Lazarus shouted the loudest, "What the hell are you thinking? When the king finds out, you'll be executed!"

"How stupid are you?" Zro yelled.

A roar of complaints from everyone in the group berated him. Tristan was grateful to see Caster stand in front of him, warding off the words of the others.

"Back off, all of you!" Caster shouted.

Ry reached past Caster and grabbed Tristan by the shirt collar. "Do you want to die? Is that it?"

Caster grabbed Ry's arm and threatened, "Touch him again, and you will pull back a stub."

Though their threats and taunts continued, Rayna pushed her way through the crowd and grabbed Tristan's hand to face the storm with him.

The shouting and rebuking stopped only when Morgan shoved her way to the center. Everyone focused on her. "I need to know how many of you knew about this," she said sternly.

Caster, alone, raised his hand. He glanced around and confessed, "I've known since Tristan and his family took me in."

Morgan's austere face addressed everyone as she delivered her proclamation. "Obviously, these two are fools, but they've made their choices, even after my pleas to let it go." Morgan glared at her sister. "I would like the rest of you to promise that none of you will ever mention anything about Rayna and Tristan to anyone. As far as the rest of the world is concerned, their relationship extends no further than guardian and princess. Is that understood?"

The rest of the trainees stared at Morgan, silent. One by one, they nodded their compliance.

Relieved, Tristan smiled at Rayna. His joy reflected in her eyes.

Chapter 6

Crossing the Boundary

The day Tristan had waited for all his life finally came. The castle and its occupants had recovered well enough to hold the long-anticipated guardian graduation ceremony. The ceremony was always conducted outside so that Aerra might witness it. In front of the castle, hundreds of people gathered for the trainees' graduation to full-fledged guardians.

Tristan stood with Ichiban and the rest of the prospective guardians at the back of the crowd. Ahead of them stretched a long silver carpet. It wound through the gathered spectators like a shimmering river and snaked up the castle steps. Guardians and high guardians lined both sides. At the very top, the king stood at a podium, prepared to make his speech.

His voice boomed. "Welcome, my people, to this glorious day, a day on which we now recognize the efforts and achievements of a group of extraordinary people. The hardships these young people have endured have been long and painful. Even though they were not prepared for such battles, they still prevailed. Each of these brave young men and women survived trials and tribulations. All have witnessed their comrades and superiors fall in battle, yet they pressed on, always mindful of their duty to protect our royal family."

The king paused to glance at the surrounding area. Extending a hand toward Tristan and the other trainees, King Eadric continued. "Ichiban, my loyal friend and protector, please escort these brave young warriors to the front of the stairs."

Ichiban slowly nodded his head and moved forward. Tristan followed—hands shaking and beaded sweat drenching his forehead. When they reached the stairs, Ichiban turned and barked. "Cadets, attention!"

Tristan immediately straightened his spine and held his arms at his sides. The others did the same.

"At ease," King Eadric said. The new guardians relaxed their stance and clutched their hands behind their backs. "Tradition dictates that the royal family members create and forge their guardians' weapons and armor to suit each guardian's abilities and enhance their strengths. The weapons also represent the bond between guardian and royal. My young guardians, please step forward to receive the special equipment fashioned by the family member you will now protect."

The new guardians climbed the stairs and advanced toward their assigned members. Tristan approached Rayna. The beaded sweat now dripped from his head when he approached with her bracer in hand.

The king turned to his family members and spoke with pride. "My children, my family, present the armor you designed for your guardians."

Guardians traditionally dressed in blue dragon-scale, diamond-coated, or adamant armor; however, some of the high guardians' armor was often more elaborate and colorful. Each family member revealed matching black and blue dragon-scale and adamant chest plates, greaves, shoulder coverings, and gauntlets at the king's announcement,

While the other family members dressed the guardians in their new armor, Tristan and Rayna continued to stare at each other. Breaking eye contact, Rayna opened the chest in front of her. Tristan gasped. He heard whispers rustle through the crowd behind him. Without getting permission, Rayna had changed the design of her guardian's armor. Instead of black and blue, pure white dragon scales adorned Tristan's new armor. She had refashioned the traditional plate armor into a tight and flexible bodysuit that covered him from the neck down—though it was sleeveless.

Seemingly unaware of the disapproving eyes focused on them, Rayna helped Tristan dress. When she finished, she pulled out a white hood attached to the back of the suit with a silver chain. Tristan quickly glanced over to see the king raise his eyebrow in displeasure at the sight of the atypical armor, but the ceremony proceeded.

"Now, my family, present your guardians with the weapons you created to match their skills and abilities."

This time, each family member pulled out a different weapon. Tristan watched Lazarus receive a massive sword of Irkshdan make. Zro received a gray and black sniper rifle with a broad scope and a five-round magazine. Bianca, Charity, and Mira each received uniquely designed bows. The crowd cheered when they demonstrated how each could transform into a bladed melee weapon. Ry's long elven sword looked a little heavier than usual but capable of slicing through any substance except adamant.

Finally, Rayna pulled out two swords for Tristan. "There's a switch on each sword at the top of the handle," she whispered. "If you push it, the blades will shoot out, spring-loaded of course, attached by a chain that lies within the hilt. The chain is small but can extend some distance. To retract the blades, just push the switch again."

Tristan accepted the weapons eagerly and examined their curved elven blades and exquisitely crafted Sorriaxian hilts.

"Now, my guardians," the king spoke again, "sheathe your weapons and face the person you now protect."

The guardians did as they were told.

"Each of you, present the bracers that will bond you to each other."

Each guardian and family member held out their bracers.

Rayna leaned close to Tristan and whispered, "Do you, Tristan, take me to be your wife? With the Aeons as our witness? Under the light of Aerra, will you love and honor me until death do us part?"

Though Tristan still felt hesitant about the whole idea of the forbidden marriage, he proceeded and whispered, "I do."

"Now, my family members, place the band on your guardian."

Tristan felt the king's eyes upon them. Unnerved and frazzled, he knew he would be killed on sight if the king ever discovered what they had been doing.

The sight of Rayna bolstered him, and he continued with their vows. "Do you, Rayna, take me to be your husband? With the Aeons as our witness? Under the light of Aerra, will you love and honor me until death do us part?"

Rayna smiled and whispered, "I do."

"Guardians, place the band on your family member."

Bracers in place, each royal family member now recited in unison the vow that would prepare each partnership for the magic binding ritual. Tristan knew what the other family members would be saying: "By the name Naughtrious, you are now given the title guardian. You, above all others, have the sole responsibility of protecting my family and me. If I die in battle or from any other cause, your life will end, and you will follow me to the afterlife, but in return for your allegiance and loyalty, you will be granted my power. Will you bond your life to my own?"

However, at the same time, Rayna spoke quietly, professing a different vow, "By the name Naughtrious, you are now given the title guardian. You and I, above all others, have the sole responsibility of protecting each other and my family. If you or I should die in battle or of any other cause, your and my life will end, and we will follow each other to the afterlife. But in return for your love and loyalty, you will be granted my power. Will you bond your life to my own?"

Whereas the others had responded, "I will," Tristan replied differently. "I will. Now, will you bind your life to my own?" He spoke quickly to avoid the attention of the other family members and guardians.

"I will," Rayna said.

Truly feeling the weight of his forbidden decision, Tristan looked around at the royal family and the crowd. He looked up to the sky. Even though no one else had heard his vows to

Rayna, the gods did. The consequences of his actions were in their hands.

After the exchange of oaths, the king said, "It is done, and now I shall seal your vows with this ancient binding magic passed down through generations of Sorriaxian kings."

The king chanted to himself, not loudly enough for anyone else to hear the incantation. The area around them darkened. When the king summoned the magic, a green star and the family's moon-crescent symbol appeared beneath him. A green mist of energy emanated from the emblem and covered the pairs of guardians and family members. The symbol soon sat under each pair, and the armbands glowed a dark green.

Tristan raised his arm to examine his bracer. Without warning, the armband turned a bright red and seared its symbols into his arm. The screams and cries of agony around him told Tristan that the others were experiencing the same fiery pain. Tristan immediately grabbed Rayna and pulled her in; she cried into his chest. Tristan closed his eyes and bit his lip, trying to divert his attention from the burning pain. He bit so hard that his lip started bleeding. After several minutes, the light from the armbands faded, and the burning ceased. Everyone recovered enough to finish the ceremony, but Tristan still felt occasional flares of pain shoot up his arm.

"I now proclaim you, royals and guardians, bonded," the king spoke with enthusiasm. "Congratulations."

The entire crowd roared in celebration: a new generation of guardians they would call heroes was born.

As they basked side-by-side in the applause, Rayna whispered, "After the ceremony, my parents are leaving for a few days."

He witnessed a blaze of passion spark in her eyes. "Meet me in my room tonight," she whispered.

≈

At nightfall, Tristan surreptitiously made his way to Rayna's chambers. Surprisingly, he met no obstacles or people questioning why he was out so late. When he approached her room, he knocked softly. The door opened slightly; Tristan glanced around to ensure no one was watching before he squeezed through the small gap. He closed the door with a gentle click.

In her chambers for the first time, Tristan took in the scene before him. Candles cast a heavenly glow throughout the room. Rayna stood before him in a simple, white silk dressing gown.

"Rayna," his voice cracked. He rubbed his palms across his pants, wiping off the nervous sweat.

"Tristan," Rayna whispered, though there was no reason to. "I knew you'd come."

"You told me to. But we both know I shouldn't be here."

"Then leave," she dared him.

She gazed at him and bit her bottom lip the way she always did when she meant mischief. He grinned shyly at her while coyly she approached a few steps.

"You know we can't do this," he explained.

"It's not wrong, Tristan," she claimed. "We're married, after all."

"But, Rayna, it wasn't a real marriage."

"Close enough for me," she said, untying her dressing gown.

"I'm a commoner," he replied, trying to hold her gown closed. "You're the princess."

"Tonight, we're just Tristan and Rayna. No titles. No rules. No worries about blood."

Rayna closed the distance between their bodies. Their breath mingled. She ran her hands up his arms and molded herself around his body. Tristan knew the consequences if they were caught breaking the royal decree: royal blood and common blood must not mix. He didn't care, pressing his lips to Rayna's, anyway. He knew experiencing heaven in Rayna's arms would be worth the harshest punishment the kingdom could promise.

≈

A few days later, Tristan made his way through the castle grounds, slipped into the castle at night, and stole out of Rayna's room the next morning. Since he was her official guardian now, he had developed a habit of sneaking into her chambers while the rest of the castle was fast asleep. He had found certain less-used routes that provided an amount of security and anonymity.

He heard a familiar voice shout, "Boy!"

Tristan's secret shortcut led him directly to King Eadric and his entourage. He hastily marched to him and bowed in greeting. "My king."

"You are Rayna's new guardian, are you not?" the king asked haughtily.

"Yes, sire. Just finishing my rounds of the castle," he lied, loathing the way the falsehood rolled off his tongue so easily.

"Very good. Before you leave, I have a command for you."

"Anything you ask, my king."

"My daughter Morgan is headed to Gelfhiend for the day. I would like you to escort her. It's only a few miles away. It shouldn't take long."

"What about Lazarus, sir? He is Morgan's guardian."

The king raised his eyebrow. "Are you questioning my directive, boy? Lazarus has another task today. Morgan is boarding the queen's ship as we speak. Gather your weapons and armor and board that ship immediately."

"Forgive me, my king," he said, bowing once more. "I shall leave at once."

At the castle armory, Tristan equipped himself with his newly acquired weapons and armor. Once prepared, he shielded his eyes from the sun with his new hood and quickly made his way to the airship docked next to the castle.

He boarded the queen's ship and saw Morgan standing next to the helmsmen giving instructions. Saluting, Tristan said, "I'm here to escort you to Gelfhiend, Princess Morgan."

Morgan grinned as she faced him. "What took you so long?"

"I apologize, princess," he answered sheepishly. "I wasn't exactly expecting an assignment today."

"That's what you get for sleeping at the castle," Morgan said with a wink. "You were the only guardian around early this morning."

Tristan blushed and glanced around in panic; no one else was close enough to overhear. The ship's propellers started and elevated the vessel into the air. Morgan grasped the handrail and stepped down the stairs toward the front of the ship. Tristan followed.

"So, what are we doing in Gelfhiend?"

"We're delivering supplies to the town and soldiers there. I'm visiting them to help with morale."

"Morale? Is something wrong with the soldiers?" Tristan gazed out into the horizon, not paying any attention to where he was going. He bumped into one of the soldiers.

"Watch where you're going, boy!" the rough-looking man grunted.

"I-I apologize, sir." Tristan stumbled over his words.

"Tristan, you're a guardian," Morgan scoffed. "You outrank everyone here, except me. Try to act like it. The men will look to you for courage and strength when the battle comes." She walked on toward the ship's bow.

The sailor Tristan had collided with flinched at the princess' words. "Guardian? I apologize," he said. "Please forgive my ignorance."

Tristan waved his hands at the man, trying to reassure him that it wasn't his fault. He jogged to catch up with Morgan, now standing at the front of the ship. Her eyes closed while she smiled at the morning sun, letting the cool breeze enfold her.

She glanced at Tristan and asked, "How are you, Tristan?"

"I'm doing well, your highness. How about you?" he answered with a smile.

"I'm fine. Thank you. You know you can call me Morgan, Tristan. We've known each other long enough."

"But it's informal. I could be reprimanded. Besides, didn't you just tell me to act like a guardian?"

She looked at him and smirked.

"Between you and me, it will be okay. My sister was right. You do prefer to follow the rules, except with her, of course. You don't need to be so uptight with me."

Tristan turned away and mumbled, "I'm not uptight."

Morgan gazed out to the horizon. Tristan leaned against the handrail to seem more relaxed.

"Thank you for coming with me."

"You're welcome, but I didn't exactly have a choice." He paused before asking, "Do you know why I am here instead of Lazarus?"

"I requested you," Morgan retorted. "Next to Lazarus, you are the second strongest in your group of guardians."

Tristan felt his ego shatter a little. "Great. Second best to Laz," he said, dropping his head. "Please don't say that in front of him."

Morgan laughed and glanced back at him. "That isn't the reason I picked you when I realized Lazarus wouldn't be able to come, though."

"What are your intentions, princess?" he asked.

"Curiosity, I suppose," she said, ignoring his playful banter. "Rayna talks about you incessantly, but I don't know you that well. We've never spent any real time together, so now we can."

Tristan gave a sharp laugh. "I bet you designed this whole trip knowing that Lazarus would be busy just so I would have no choice but to go along with your plan and spend the day with you," he joked.

She calmly looked deep into his eyes. "Maybe I did."

Tristan, taken aback by the response, simply stood next to her in awkward silence until the ship reached Gelfhiend.

When they arrived at their destination, Morgan and Tristan exited the ship. The people of the city had gathered to see their princess and shower her with praise. With guards beside her, Morgan walked along a path created by her subjects. She went back and forth, greeting as many people as she could. Tristan walked behind her, reveling in how kind she was to everyone. This was a side of her Tristan had never seen before—her behavior was unlike that of the rest of her family. Tristan couldn't help but smile while she emptied her coin bag, distributing as much gold as she could, providing kindness and a sympathetic ear when the money was gone. As though she could feel his approving stare, Morgan glanced around to catch Tristan's gaze and smiled back. Tristan blushed and immediately looked away. After a few moments, he turned his eyes back to her, but her attention on him had not dwindled. Tristan, growing uncomfortable with the crowd, signaled her to move on away from the people. Though the guards made motions to disperse the crowd, Morgan was not ready to board the ship again.

Tristan escorted Morgan through the town. She led him through the areas with the most devastation. Tristan's sympathy grew when he gawked at the damaged buildings, the overgrown pathways, and the beggars in the lanes. This town had known many burdens his home had not. Abandoned buildings ruined by overgrown thistles appeared ready to topple any moment. Among the holes in the buildings, Tristan saw more of the horned rabbits that watched the world for Lephirus.

"There isn't much here, is there? A little rough around the edges," he said quietly. "A little unsettling, actually."

"Then, I guess you'll have to protect me from these fearsome and adorable rabbits, won't you?" Nonchalantly, Morgan weaved her arm around Tristan's elbow. He flinched slightly at her touch before examining their linked arms. He cocked his head and gave her a puzzled look. Morgan hadn't touched him except in battle. "Does this bother you? I can let go."

"I-it-it's fine. Um, how are you?" His voice cracked.

Morgan laughed and waved at a passing couple as they bowed to her. Again, Tristan was amazed at Morgan's ease in dealing with the many poor citizens they had seen during the day. She had great compassion for their plight.

"I'm pleased to be here with you, Tristan. You are superb company, despite what Lazarus says about you," she joked without losing her decorum.

"Thanks, I enjoy…Hey, what does Lazarus say about me?" Tristan asked in slight indignation.

Morgan laughed again and nudged his side with her elbow. "I was kidding. He doesn't say anything."

Tristan's raised eyebrows and smirk said he didn't believe her. She smiled and laughed at the guardian.

Tristan scanned the desolate town and how ravaged it was by war. The people looked grim to Tristan. Though when Morgan crossed their path, they greeted her with what cheer they could muster.

"So, what else do we have to do?" he asked.

"There's one more thing I would like to do before we leave. It's somewhat out of the way. The ship can wait."

"Where are we going?"

"Just outside of town. You'll see," she said with an enigmatic smile.

Morgan picked up the pace. They walked down a dirt road leading out of town and into a forest. Once they were out of sight of the airship and the townsfolk, Morgan stopped. She touched Tristan's bare arm for a moment.

"I'd like to give you something, Tristan." She took off her golden armband and placed it around his bicep.

Tristan considered it for a second and then asked, "What's this for?"

Morgan blushed. "It's a token of my appreciation for taking me out here. Remember me and our friendship when you look at it."

"I don't need anything to remember you, Morgan." He held her hand in his. Her skin was soft like Rayna's. They stood in the road and gazed at each other for a minute.

Morgan knocked him on the head, instantly changing the mood. "Yes, you do, you dummy!" She laughed.

They veered from the road onto a man-made path. Tristan heard water and music that resembled flutes. Farther down the trail, they found a herd of terpsichore. These serpent-like horses had round dragon-like faces with big gentle eyes and golden horns on their foreheads. Their two sets of wings had long tubes of bone supporting the webbing. No terpsichore tube structure was ever the same. When they flapped their wings or in any kind of wind, their tubes played a "song." Each had its unique song. When the creatures opened their mouths, a sound like a whale came out, but it was softer and more majestic. The males had green scales and silver manes, while the females had blue scales and black manes. They called out to each other with their wings fully extended.

Morgan gasped at the sight and whispered, "Tristan, they're singing to each other! It's so beautiful!"

"Then dance with me." Tristan decided to listen to her words about how uptight he could be and let loose a little. He grabbed her hand and twirled her around while she laughed in delight.

Morgan came in closer to put her arms around Tristan's shoulders. "I didn't know you could dance."

"I thought you were leading me into a trap."

They swayed back and forth to the creature's rhythmic sounds.

She pulled him closer so his cheek touched hers and leaned her head against his. "What if you already sprang my trap and don't even know it?"

He shuddered as his heart rate increased dramatically.

"Tristan," she whispered.

The wind died down, slowing the strange terpsichore music until it stopped. Tristan twirled her one last time and gave her a gracious bow. He winked at her. "Thank you for the dance, my lady."

She curtsied. "You're most welcome, my good sir." Morgan slung her arm around his, and they continued down the path.

Together, they approached a narrow creek running in front of a small tree with red and green leaves. Hanging from its branches was a strange-looking fruit. Morgan dropped Tristan's arm and walked toward the tree.

"This is what we came here for," she explained.

"What is it?" Tristan asked, eyeing the tree suspiciously.

"You've never seen one of these before? That's surprising."

Tristan shook his head.

"Then you simply have not had the greatest berry in all of Ambion. This is an Almboch tree. Its fruit are ocean berries," she said and reached for his hand. "Help me cross?"

"Ocean berries," he said, remembering Morgan had claimed they were what mana smelled like.

Tristan walked down to the creek. Stepping into the icy water, he extended his hand to Morgan. Smiling, she took his hand. He lifted her across the water onto the other side of the creek.

The far bank wasn't as sturdy. Taking a couple of steps toward the tree, Morgan lost her footing and slipped backward. She reached out and grabbed Tristan, dragging him down into the water with her. They laughed as they fell.

Tristan landed on top of her. Placing his hands on either side of Morgan's shoulders to catch most of his weight, he pushed his upper body off her small frame. When he saw her eyes, his smile slowly faded. He used one hand to brush her damp hair off her face. Tristan's heart thudded fiercely against his chest as his body sat heavily on top of hers. Morgan's breath quickened beneath him.

A bird noisily squawked in the tree, breaking the spell they were under. Tristan pushed himself the rest of the way up and offered Morgan a hand. She stood and began straightening her sodden clothes.

"I'm sorry, princess. You're all wet," he said. "Let's get your berries and go."

Morgan closed her eyes and hid her flushed cheeks. Catching her breath, she said, "Of course."

Chapter 7

Into Levvandia

A month had gone by since Tristan's promotion to guardian. The group's first official mission had finally arrived: all guardians and royal family members were summoned to the king's airship, the *Naughtalesk*. Painted black and heavily armed, this was the flagship of the Sorriaxian Empire and almost as large as any carrier. The ship sailed to the frontlines, employing twelve propellers and masts to keep it airborne. It made its way to Ambion's capital and largest city, the great elven city of Levvandia. Levvandia was home to the most advanced and powerful elf warriors. They wielded the most advanced technology, which gave them an advantage in the war against Sorriax. No one had ever defeated them because they had never given so much as an inch to any Sorriaxian soldier.

The royal family, guardians, and generals commanded the legions on the ground and surrounding ships from inside the war room of the *Naughtalesk*. King Eadric commanded the attention of everyone who sat or stood at the round table.

"For far too long, we have been at the borders of this elven city. It is time we took this fight into our own hands," the king explained. "Admirals Gardner and Evens, take the armada and surround the city. You may fire when your ships are ready. General Ander, take your artillery cannons and surround the city by land. Do not stop bombarding until we break through their front lines.

Keep your infantry close. Snipers may be inside the buildings of the outer rim of the city. Captain Hayden, have your dragon squads stay with the ships and provide cover. Now, my guardians, I give you command of both armies. I trust your judgment, and so do your men. Hold nothing back. Slaughter all who do not swear their allegiance to me."

Tristan shouted, "Yes, sir!" along with the rest of the guardians.

"Remember, the goal is to obtain the royal family's swords, first and foremost. Now give your king this city!" King Eadric shouted and slammed his fist on the table.

The guardians and soldiers exited the war room to the deck of the ship as the clouds dissipated. When their view cleared, Tristan saw the magnificent city of Levvandia for the first time. His stomach churned, making him feel nauseated. He couldn't tell if it was the uneasy swaying of the ship or the battle in front of him. His palms sweat when the smell of gunpowder invaded his nose. His ears rang at the sounds of artillery encircling the ship. He retained his calm by focusing on Ichiban's training. With a great roar of the ship's cannons, the battle for the sky began.

The king shouted into his earpiece, "Enemy carriers are releasing their smaller assault ships. Dragon warriors! Defend our airships."

Soldiers mounted their dragons and scattered into the sky. Tristan saw that all the scout ships and mounted machineguns were manned.

"So, we have complete control of our forces?" Tristan asked the guardian standing next to him.

High Guardian Torrance, dressed in elaborate red armor, stared at Tristan and shook his head in frustration before answering, "You heard the king."

Tristan nodded and stepped up to assume control. He shouted into his earpiece at the soldiers on the deck. "Forward deck guns, lay down cover fire! You!" He pointed at one of the men on a scout ship. "I need a ride!"

"Tristan, what are you doing?" Ichiban growled.

Tristan hopped onto the scout ship and peered over his shoulder at Ichiban.

"I'm getting my king his city. Keep the smaller ships off me. Okay, scout, go!"

"Aye, aye!"

The ship launched into the sky. Not long afterward, a small squad of enemy planes rapidly closed in on Tristan. The nearest ships fired a barrage of bullets and rockets. The planes not shot down broke formation and flew past Tristan without firing a shot. The Dragon warriors joined the fight. Explosions erupted all around Tristan and the scout; the driver weaved through the fire.

"Scout, you see that ship straight ahead of us?" Tristan yelled.

"Yes, sir." The scout turned his head toward Tristan.

"Make one pass over it so I can get off. Then, make your way back to the *Naughtalesk*."

"Are you sure, sir?"

"Take me there NOW!"

"Yes, sir!" the scout replied, doing as Tristan directed.

Tristan hopped off the scout ship and landed on the deck of the enemy's vessel. A burning enemy plane hurtled toward him. The collision demolished the deck of the ship, tossing people aside and overboard. The damage soon became too heavy for the vessel to handle; it began to lose altitude.

Tristan stumbled against the remnants of the deck. After he righted himself, he rushed to the edge of the ship and hurdled over the railing. He shot his blade into the side of the vessel, slowing his descent into the outskirts of the city. When he hit the ground, he sprinted over battle-torn roads to escape the ship's impending crash. He dashed past old, useless, discarded weapons, shell casings from bullets, and bodies of the recently deceased. The unfamiliar sight of tall, square buildings towered over him.

"Sir, get down!" a voice yelled.

Tristan instantly reacted to the warning and dropped to the ground. A barrage of bullets flew over his head. Startled, he saw a small platoon of his own soldiers out of cover, attempting to return fire. A soldier ran out from a small opening. Men surrounded the entrance and stood prepared to provide cover with standard rifles.

The soldier reached Tristan and saluted.

"Sir, I'm Sergeant Culvac of the 112th Infantry Unit. I have about 160 soldiers with me. We had to evacuate our ship. Too damaged to sustain flight. When we transferred to another ship, an artillery shell hit our airship, and we crashed into that building over there." Culvac gestured to a ship that was still partially on fire. Half of it stuck out of a large hole in the tall, unstable cement building.

"Any injured?" Tristan hastily asked.

"No, but…" his report was cutoff.

"Elven shard missile! Get down!" another soldier covering one of the buildings shouted.

"Get down!" Culvac screamed.

He covered Tristan. The missile exploded, sending hundreds of bullets in every direction. Men from both sides of the conflict shielded themselves, waiting for the shower of bullets to subside. After a few moments, Culvac got up and offered Tristan a hand. Cautiously, they both looked up at the building—Culvac's ship still protruded from it. The blast had shifted it a little, but it had not collapsed. Yet.

"I want that building evacuated now!" Sergeant Culvac yelled. He turned to Tristan. "I was about to say that I lost three of my men to snipers nested up the road. What's our next move now?"

Tristan scrutinized the scene before them and took a deep breath. "Do you have anything more powerful than rifles?"

"Yes, we have two thirty-caliber machineguns and a fifty-caliber machinegun."

"That isn't much." Tristan studied the situation. "I hate to do this, but in order to advance, we will need to split your platoon into three groups. I want a group with the fifty-caliber to stay here and keep the enemy's attention. Two small groups with the thirty-caliber guns will flank to the left and right. As soon as both thirties are in place, we will create a constant crossfire, not giving the elven any room to breathe. Is all that understood, Sergeant?"

"Yes, sir!"

Culvac rallied his men and belted out the orders. Tristan bent over one of his fallen allies and stripped him of his rifle, sidearm, and ammunition. He needed more weapons and didn't think the man would begrudge him. Tristan rejoined the group once Sergeant Culvac finished briefing the men on their new objectives.

"Our long-range radios don't work, but we do have short-range communication. I'll issue orders from here. Guardian, where will you be?" Culvac asked.

"I'll lead Squad One to the right." Tristan pointed down the road. "My short-range communication works, so give your instructions to me, and I'll relay the orders."

"Very well. You two squads need to watch out for one another. I will not tolerate any more casualties. No more soldiers will die in this skirmish. Is that understood?" Culvac said.

"Yes, sir!" the soldiers shouted.

Tristan and his squad started running. He heard Culvac's squad behind him, setting up the fifty-caliber machinegun.

Culvac shouted, "All troops, fire!"

Each soldier in Culvac's group fired into the buildings at the other end of the block, allowing the left and right squads to advance slowly to the nearby buildings.

Tristan's squad entered a building farther down the road. Soft voices and footsteps resonated above them. Tristan raised his hand to signal them to stop. After a short pause, he gestured them to proceed cautiously. They crept toward the staircase and climbed slowly, allowing the sounds to guide them. When they reached the fifth floor, Tristan detected movement. He signaled for two of his soldiers to take out the two talking elves. The soldiers sneaked behind the unsuspecting elves. Just before they reached the enemy, Tristan's earpiece shrieked so loudly that everyone could hear, including the elves.

"Tristan, this is the squad two leader. We are in position and opening fire!" the radio crackled.

The enemy elves quickly rotated, raising their weapons. The two soldiers raised their guns faster than the elves and fired. Above, on the top floor, a door opened, and another elf peered down the staircase. He opened fire when he saw his comrades fall to the floor. He pulled away to radio for backup.

Glass exploded from the windows on either side of Tristan's squad, and bullets showered the room. Enemy fire somehow came at them from every direction. Tristan took cover with his soldiers and returned fire.

Tristan shouted directions at one soldier. "I need half of you on the next floor. The other half of you stay at this window with the thirty-caliber. I'll be on the roof to make sure we aren't ambushed from the top, alright?"

The soldiers shouted in agreement, and those with assignments moved into position. Tristan reached the top of the stairs and opened the door leading to the roof. Abandoned, it offered minimal cover. Ships covered the gray, smoke-filled sky, bombarding each other with artillery fire. Dragons and small fighter ships were dogfighting around the feuding vessels.

Tristan ran to the edge of the building and fired at the enemy; his magazine emptied quickly. He ducked to reload. When he turned around, two elf-mounted dragons flew from behind the building, hovering above him. He looked at his hands for a moment. Uncertainty weighed heavily on his mind. Feeling time slow down around him, he remembered what Rayna had taught him.

≋

"You're never gonna get it by blindly swinging your swords around, silly." Rayna ran up to Tristan. He looked past her at their usual spot by the tree on the hill. The sun was about to set. Tristan dropped his sword in frustration after being there all day, attempting to master his new gifts. "Hey! That sword wasn't easy or cheap to make. Be careful. Here, let's take it back to the beginning." She picked up the sword. "You know of magic, correct?"

"Yes, I know this. We already we..."

Rayna interrupted. "Back! To! Basics! Pay attention! You know a little magic, correct?"

Tristan nodded with fleeting patience. "I know a little magic."

Rayna pointed her hand at a pile of wood and rocks. "Start a fire. We're going to be here for a while." Tristan stared at the pile blankly for a moment. Rayna tapped her toe with little patience. "You do know the keyword, right?"

Tristan raised his hand toward the pile of wood. "Of course I do. It's…uh."

Rayna snapped. "*Ignite.*"

Tristan spoke firmly. "*Ignite!*" A small ball of flame projected from his hand and ignited the wood.

Rayna nodded. "Good! You must say the keyword firmly for it to work. How do you feel?"

A small wave of fatigue overcame him. "I feel like I did ten pushups."

Rayna smiled. "That's normal. Magic takes its toll on the mind and body. Rest does recover it."

"Why *Ignite*? Why can't I just shout fire?"

Rayna raised an eyebrow. "Try it."

Tristan raised his hand again. "Fire!" A few measly sparks shot from his fingertips.

Rayna laughed. "Anyone can randomly strum a mandolin and make noise. But if you know the correct notes in the correct order, you create harmony. The keywords provide that. You, Tristan, are a novice. You are only able to use one keyword, maybe a few times a day. It takes years and years of practice to build up the stamina to cast multiple spells, especially at more advanced levels."

Tristan got snooty. "Oh yeah? Well, if I'm such a novice, then what are you?"

Rayna flicked her hair out of her face. "All royals can use two keywords or more. Three keywords are maximum unless you want to kill yourself. It's rumored that the Grand Magus in the Council of Mages can use four. Just a rumor."

Tristan smirked. "Prove it."

Rayna raised an eyebrow and lifted her hand to the sky. "*Explodite undam!*" A wave of explosions blanketed the sky above them. Rayna lowered her hand, exhaling a deep breath. "The keywords were 'Explode' and 'Wave.' I can do that two more times before passing out."

Tristan was impressed. "Wow! That was pretty amazing." Rayna nodded with a smile. "So, tell me, why are they called keywords?"

Rayna bent down to pick up an acorn. "I'm not sure. The keywords have existed for countless generations. Don't you have your spell book from your training classes?"

Tristan shrugged. "It's not really a spell book—more of a survival guide with basic spells in it to help us if we are in trouble or stranded."

Rayna rolled her eyes. "The largest collection of keywords belongs to the Council of Mages. They share the keywords with the kingdoms. Well, most of them. Some are deemed too dangerous for the people to wield."

Tristan spoke with a sarcastic tone. "A wave of explosions isn't too dangerous for the masses?"

Rayna spoke with a straight face. "We are at war, Tristan." He nodded and dropped the topic. "New keywords are discovered now and then that were lost through time. The Aeons shared some keywords to improve the lives of the people. Finally, as you know, not all keywords work together. Like so." She cupped her hands around the acorn. *"Crescite Cito!"* She opened her hands. "Fast plant doesn't work." She cupped her hands again. *"Crescite herbam!"* She opened her hands. Roots grew from the acorn; a stem and leaves sprouted. Tristan looked on with wonder. She set the acorn down.

"You weren't trained to be a spellcaster, Tristan. Raise your hand and point it out into the distance." The wind started to pick up. She moved in front of him and placed her hand over his. Her body pressed against his. "This is what you were meant for. This is our royal power—the energy passed down from the gods into us. This is greater than any magic. You were trained to wield this." Black energy erupted around them. Rayna looked over her shoulder into Tristan's eyes. "Do you feel the energy?" Tristan nodded. "Don't fight it. Allow it to course through your body. Allow it to fill every part of you. The energy will increase your strength, speed, whatever you need." Tristan's hand began to glow. It felt warm while his fingers and palm tingled. Rayna drew in closer to where their lips almost touched. "The color of the energy signifies whether the energy is used for offense or defense. Normal barriers are usually blue; energy attacks are green. On some occasions, the color of barrier or attack can differ if an outside source influences it, like an Aeon. Can you feel it, Tristan?"

Taken aback by the moment and the incredible power surging through his body, he replied, "Yes."

"Now, release it." A beam of green energy erupted from their hands. The shockwave pushed the clouds in the sky away. The castle behind them shook while some of the windows shattered. Tristan looked on at the incredible power they had unleashed. He gazed back into her eyes. "Remember this feeling, Tristan. Remember it, and you can call upon this strength to aid you in your tasks." Their lips crushed against each other passionately amidst the bright light of energy they had created.

≈

Remembering Rayna's words, Tristan dropped his rifle and unsheathed both swords. He filled them with energy until they glowed fiery red. The dragons filled their lungs, ready to exhale fire. Tristan raised his swords and shot the blades into the chests of the dragons. On impact, the energy exploded and ripped the dragons' bodies apart.

From above, an enemy airship passed by; soldiers parachuted onto the rooftop. Behind them appeared three more elves riding dragons. Tristan's radio went off.

"Tristan, it's Culvac. The enemy is reinforcing by two regiments. We don't have the firepower to hold them. Focus on the enemy across the street!"

Tristan lifted his sword to block the first enemy soldier rushing him. He stabbed the elf and dove for cover when his companions opened fire. Tristan grabbed his rifle, loaded another magazine, and returned fire.

"I'm a little busy up here. My squad—we were ambushed from the top." Tristan dropped behind cover once again. He heard the shots from the fifty-caliber gun down the street.

Culvac's voice shouted in his ear, "We need help here! We're surrounded, and the other squad reports two more regiments on their way with heavy artillery that'll be here by sundown! We won't be able to hold them."

Tristan dropped his rifle and grabbed his sword again, charging it with blue energy. He considered what to tell the troubled commander. Tristan was just as afraid as the soldiers fighting for him were, but he worked hard to maintain confidence.

"Radio for support, Culvac. I know the long-range communications don't work, but somebody out there is bound to hear it and relay it," Tristan responded.

Tristan stood up and used the blue energy of the swords to form a barrier around him.

"We'll hold them off as long as we can. Culvac out."

Tristan heard the defeat in the soldier's voice. Tristan returned from defending the rooftop, exhausted. His powers weakened, he dropped behind a wall to catch his breath.

One of the soldiers shouted over the gunfire, "Any news about reinforcements, sir?"

Tristan closed his eyes for a moment, wanting to ignore the question. He opened his eyes. "Hold on a bit longer. They won't abandon us!" Summoning his will, Tristan raised his rifle and resumed the assault across the way.

Chapter 8

Caster's Prophecy

Dark had taken hold of the elven city. The dying sunlight flashed a final moment of brilliance against the gold and emerald buildings. The sky radiated with explosions and gunfire.

Morgan watched until nightfall. She had fruitlessly spent the battle aboard the *Naughtalesk*, observing their forces breach the outer defenses. The captain of the *Naughtalesk* approached her father.

"Your highness." The captain bowed. "We have reports that a squad has crash-landed behind the enemy's frontlines. They have apparently held off four regiments for the entire battle. Shall I make arrangements to send them reinforcements?"

The king laughed in surprise, but the captain did not look amused.

"I wonder how they managed to survive so long?" the king muttered.

"There are also reports of a guardian with them. I believe it was the reckless boy who took off at the beginning of the battle," the captain explained.

"What was that boy's name again?" the king asked nonchalantly.

Trust her father not to remember a guardian's name. Morgan hid her spike of fear. Rayna stepped forward.

"His name is Tristan, Father. He is my guardian. Please send him some help," Rayna begged.

Morgan silently added a plea of her own.

The king stood there, observing the battle for the sky. "Yes, Tristan," he confirmed. "Which ship is closest to his position?"

The captain conferred with the admiral for a moment. "The queen's ship, the *Shangri La*."

The king considered the situation briefly before directing the remaining guardians on the ship.

"Lazarus, Zro, take a regiment to the *Shangri La* and barge your way through the front lines to reinforce Tristan and his platoon."

Morgan was surprised to see her father turn to her next. "Morgan, I would like you to support them."

Glad for the chance to help Tristan, she said, "Of course, Father."

"Sir, it would be better if the princess remained here so we would not have to worry about her safety!" Lazarus protested.

The king scrutinized the young guardian, unimpressed with his outburst. "She will be your support," King Eadric explained, "providing a barrier around the ship so you may reach Tristan unscathed."

"Then, I would like to go as well, Father," Rayna interrupted.

The king clenched his fists and hit the mast. "That is completely out of the question!"

Morgan was appalled at the violence of her father's answer. He had always been protective of Rayna, but his reaction seemed excessive.

"Tristan is my guardian, and I'm as capable as Morgan!" Rayna snapped.

"I said no. The subject will not be broached again," the king ordered. "Guardians, you have your orders. Now go!"

Lazarus and Zro bowed their heads and left. Morgan glanced at her sister and gave her a reassuring smile.

When they reached the *Shangri La*, Morgan took control. "I want all available hands on deck manning a weapon. Helmsmen, our new heading is north by northwest. Full throttle."

The captain interrupted, "But princess, that is straight into the enemy. We will never make it."

Morgan glared at him. "My orders come from the king. Trust in my powers. We will not be harmed. We will reinforce a platoon within the city. Is that understood?"

"Yes, ma'am!" the captain said.

"Yes, ma'am. North by northwest. Full throttle!" the helmsman shouted.

The ship headed straight for the enemy at ramming speed. Morgan raised her arms and formed a barrier around the ship. The blue light emanating from the vast barrier lit up the nearby clouds. Morgan had always been more adept at magic than her sister. She knew her father was right to send her instead of Rayna.

Enemy ships struggled to get out of the way, but they could not move fast enough.

The captain of the *Shangri La* shouted, "Grab something! Brace for impact!"

Morgan stood her ground, trusting in her power to keep herself upright and the ship safe. The *Shangri La* plowed through two enemy ships, clearing the enemy's blockade. The collision knocked everyone on the ship off their feet, but Morgan didn't flinch. She ignored the looks of awe from her fellow crew members.

When they approached Tristan's reported location, Lazarus surveyed the battlefield and swore. Morgan followed his gaze and found the ground completely lit up by gunfire from all directions, aiming at one particular area. Small Kaiser tanks parked along the roads. She recognized the weapons from her lessons.

Lazarus touched his earpiece. "Tristan," he paused, waiting for a response. "Tristan, come in. This is Lazarus. We're right above you. We're here to reinforce you."

No response. He looked at Morgan, who nodded.

Lazarus spoke directly to the ship's captain. "We're going in. Take us right above the battle and blanket the enemy with cannon fire!"

The captain followed orders and steered the ship straight into the battle while firing into the enemy battalions. Morgan maintained the ship's barrier. She provided an opening for Lazarus,

Zro, and three platoons to exit the ship and head for Tristan's squad. Morgan followed their progress as they entered the building through the roof and disappeared from view. She counted a few tense moments until she heard Lazarus' voice through her earpiece.

"We've got him!" Lazarus yelled.

She let out a sigh of relief and then touched her earpiece. "We will demolish the enemy buildings and make them take this fight to the ground. Evacuate all buildings at once."

Lazarus must have left the line open because she heard Tristan laugh at her words.

"What's so funny?" Lazarus asked.

Still laughing, Tristan replied, "That was the one thing we tried not to do."

Morgan grinned.

A few seconds later, the group of soldiers and guardians ran out of the building. From Morgan's standpoint, they looked like miniature toy figures on the ground. Two other groups of soldiers ran to join them. At Morgan's command, large beams of energy shot from the *Shangri La*, completely leveling the enemy buildings. Shockwaves from the explosions prompted a couple of the surrounding buildings to collapse, kicking up clouds of dust and debris that forced everyone to drop and cover their heads.

After the dust settled, Tristan's group sprang into action. Witnessing the soldiers exchange blows, Morgan watched in horrified fascination as her friends and guardians charged the cowering enemy soldiers. She tried to keep track of the white figure that was Tristan, along with her own armor-clad guardian. Morgan imagined this must be how the Aeons feel when they look down on their people.

A pair of dragons swooped onto the scene. Morgan screamed a useless warning when one of the dragons roared and plummeted toward Tristan. Her power drained from her as Lazarus appeared out of nowhere and thrust his glowing sword into the dragon's neck, decapitating it just feet away from Tristan. Relief coursed through Morgan.

Her guardian didn't stop there. Lazarus jumped stone by stone up a collapsed building, sending waves of concern through Morgan. He leaped off the building toward the second dragon. Morgan's stomach dropped when she realized he was going to fall short. Summoning her power, she formed a whirlwind around him and raised him to the sky. Before he reached the dragon, Lazarus met Morgan's stare with relief and gratitude.

Once again, Morgan's frame shuddered as her power released red and gold energy into Lazarus' sword. Sparks filled the sky with every swing of Lazarus' sword. It connected several times, cutting the dragon in multiple areas. Screeching in agony, the dragon threw off its rider. Lazarus swung his blade in a mighty arc, sending the dragon to the ground. Following it, Lazarus raised his sword into the sky, creating a golden beam of light. He landed and swung the golden light with a forceful chop, cleaving the dragon. The ground beneath Lazarus' feet quaked.

Upon seeing her own guardian safe, Morgan scanned the scene again for Tristan. She found him standing next to Zro, also summoning his powers. A golden orb of light rose around Zro, spiraling into the sky. Morgan heard him fire once and then watched in amazement when all five of the Kaiser tanks exploded at once. He shot multiple times and destroyed several ships with his power-enhanced bullets. That was enough of an opening for the *Shangri La*; Morgan bellowed orders to descend.

The ship landed in the center of the battlefield, and all soldiers who weren't manning deck guns hurdled over the edge to join the battle. Morgan commandeered one of the deck-mounted machineguns.

"Bring all of the wounded aboard the ship!" she shouted over the gunfire.

She fired her weapon into the hordes of approaching enemy elves. Tristan vaulted onto the side railing next to Morgan. He immediately raised his barrier. Only then did Morgan see the torrents of bullets aimed in her direction. The realization of how close she had just come to death immobilized her hands.

"Morgan, what are you doing here?" Tristan asked.

With a prickle of annoyance at his lack of gratitude, she returned her attention to her weapon. She aimed at the enemies targeting her. "Saving your ass, so don't give me that whole speech about how I shouldn't be fighting!" she yelled.

"As you wish," he replied with a playful bow. "I don't regret your help."

Glancing at him, she said, "Help me buy the men some time to get the wounded aboard. I'm going to clear a path through the elves. From there, take the fight to them. I'll cover you from here."

Tristan hesitated. "I'll go under one condition."

Morgan felt her irritation grow. "We don't have time for stupid games, Tristan!"

"One condition, Morgan." Tristan ignored her anger. "Keep your barrier up, at least around yourself. Laz and I won't be near enough to protect you!"

His concern erased her exasperation. She looked deep into his brown eyes. "Thank you," she murmured. Pausing to regain her composure, she added, "Now go. That's an order!"

Tristan observed her silently for a fraction of a moment. He left the ship, and Morgan implemented her part of the plan.

Through the barrage of bullets and the smoky haze, she lost sight of him. All she could see was the ambient green light of his powered sword expelling a blast of energy as he took out a swath of soldiers. The light dimmed as Tristan moved farther away. Trusting the guardians to complete their task, she continued to fire at the enemy and clear the path for her troops. Startled, she heard the unmistakable shrieks from the battlefield.

Tristan's frantic voice crackled in her ear. "There's an ancient dragon in front of us. I need help!"

Without thinking, Morgan hurdled over the side of the ship and ran toward the danger. She dodged skirmishing soldiers and found herself inches from Tristan.

The ancient dragon stepped forward. The ground quaked under the weight of the beast. The dragon lifted its head, exposing dull yellow scales on its chest. It expanded the large tusks wrapped around its open mouth. Its chest tightened, and the beast exhaled a fiery orange beam. Morgan watched Tristan raise a weak barrier. She couldn't tell if fear or exhaustion hindered his magical abilities, but she knew the dragon's beam would rip right through the feeble shield and consume Tristan and everyone behind him. She threw her arms around him to raise a barrier to protect him.

Strained from the attack, the ancient dragon closed its mouth; the beam dissipated. Tristan stood still, basking in the blue light of Morgan's barrier. Morgan's arms held him close to shield them both.

Resting her head on his back, she shakily asked, "Are you okay?"

"Y-y-you saved me again," Tristan stuttered.

She enjoyed the closeness for a moment. "I couldn't let anything happen to you, Tristan, or any of the guardians. Rayna would never forgive me."

"I owe you one." He glanced over his shoulder, closed his eyes, and leaned into her body while she held him. Morgan breathed in his scent. She felt him tremble when she pulled away.

"I know," she whispered. "Now, let me handle this dragon."

Tristan shook his head and answered, "I can help, Morgan."

"You don't have the energy left." She smiled and squeezed his hands. "Trust me. I can take care of myself."

Tristan took a deep breath and closed his eyes. "I know you can. That's the problem."

"Make sure no one sneaks up behind me."

Tristan squeezed her hands. "I will."

He stared at her for a moment before letting go. She couldn't read the look in his eyes. He made his way past her but stopped as if he had something to say. Instead, he shook his head and joined the battle in progress behind them.

Morgan returned her attention to the ancient dragon watching her with the utmost intensity. She unsheathed her sword, a white blade veined with silver. The sword pulsated with energy. The ground shook when she summoned her power. Black clouds spiraled above her; bolts of blue energy erupted from where she stood. Small rocks and debris slowly rose into the air while the wind blew around them.

Morgan twisted her wrist slightly; her sword rotated. Energy expelled from the blade and cracked the ground below. Morgan swung her sword twice and quickly unleashed two green lashes of energy toward the dragon. In midair, a blue light absorbed Morgan's energy. *The dragon must have a barrier of its own,* she thought. Stillness filled the air when she locked eyes with the beast once more.

Without notice, the dragon whipped its tail at Morgan. She rolled out of the way. Morgan charged, swinging her sword at the barrier. The magical blade connected and pierced it slightly. Electricity coursed over the dragon's barrier. Since its protection was jeopardized, the dragon took to the sky. Both sets of wings flapped violently. The dragon's wings glowed with black energy. The first set of wings flapped again and projected black sickles of energy that made a loud crack when they fired. Morgan ran a circle underneath the dragon, avoiding each shot.

With her hand extended in front of her, a whirlwind appeared. She leaped into it and let it carry her into the sky, straight toward the dragon. She swung her blade, and this time it sliced through the ancient dragon's barrier. She flew forward, readying her next attack. The dragon flapped its wings again, sending two more bolts of black energy at Morgan. She didn't move fast enough, and the sickles sliced through her barrier and penetrated her armor. Sharp pains surged through her waist and shoulder. The impact sent her reeling backward. She screamed in anger as much as agony.

Plummeting, she summoned the strength to raise her hand and fire a white beam into the vulnerable underside of the dragon, sending it to the ground. Plumes of dust rose in every direction. Morgan landed with a thud. The ground beneath her fractured from the force. Blood oozed from her wounds; the sight gave her a cold sweat and sent a shudder down her spine. Battling the impending shock, she struggled to her feet.

When the dragon stood up, its eyes turned a dark red, glowing with rage. It growled and hissed while summoning more of its ancient power. The fire within the dragon radiated a heat Morgan felt from several feet away. Not sure of what the creature would do next, Morgan searched her surroundings for weapons and solutions to defeat the beast. Stones emerged from the ground, surrounding her. Summoning all her strength, Morgan filled her sword with white energy. A reptilian golem charged her. She quickly spun around, swung her sword downward, sliced through the rock, and shattered the golem. Another advanced on her right. She swung her sword again, splitting the golem in half. She raised her hand and fired a white beam at a third.

Mindful of her injuries, Morgan sprinted as quickly as she could toward the dragon as more golems surfaced from the ground. The dragon inhaled quickly and exhaled its fiery orange beam at her. Morgan summoned her whirlwind again, and the swirling winds sent her flying far above the dragon. The dragon's beam melted a few of the golems behind her, and then its head tilted toward the sky to track Morgan.

She spread her arms out wide and let go of her sword that remained floating in front of her. Calling upon the powers of Aerra, she created a white barrier to shield her. Bolts of energy erupted from it. The dragon's fiery beam collided with the barrier, but Morgan held firm as her new shield absorbed the attack. Morgan's blade flashed a white light and reflected the dragon's beam back at itself. The beam struck the dragon's barrier and shattered it. With the dragon now defenseless, Morgan knew this was her only chance. Her barrier glowed even brighter when she raised her right hand to the sky to summon enough power to end this fight. Through the black clouds, three small beams of white light rained upon the dragon. The beams shredded away at the dragon's scaly body, causing it to roar and writhe in pain. Finally, Morgan's beams combined into one immense, powerful stream of light, blanketed the entire dragon, and seared a crater into the ground.

Silence fell as the light began to fade. The dragon sprawled motionless on the ground. Morgan let her whirlwind dissipate, dropped down onto the dragon's head, and plunged her sword into its skull. It let out one final shriek. Morgan crawled down from the dragon's head and ran through the remnants of the battle.

When she arrived at the ship and Tristan, Lazarus, and Zro surrounded her, she breathed a heavy sigh of relief. Above her, the barricade of ships had collapsed, and the *Naughtalesk* sailed toward the elaborate castle in the center of the city.

Lazarus evaluated the situation before he issued orders. "Morgan, you and the ship's captain and the rest of the men get back on the ship and provide air cover for the *Naughtalesk*!" "Tristan, Zro, and I will head there on foot and try to stall any ground reinforcements heading to the castle."

"You heard him. Now get going!" Morgan ordered the captain.

"I meant you, too." Lazarus glowered at her.

Morgan returned his glare before she spoke. "I know, but I'm going with you. It's not up for discussion. Now, captain, that is a direct order from me. Get your men up in the air!"

The captain said, "Your father won't like this, princess."

She snapped into a regal posture and pointed a demanding finger at the airship. "Go! He sent me to do a job, and I'm going to finish it. Now get into the air!"

"As you wish, your highness." The captain saluted as he boarded the ship and took off.

Morgan's companions did not look pleased with her decision to stay.

Lazarus spoke up. "You should have stayed with the ship. I've exhausted a lot of my power. I won't be able to protect you."

Growing tired of hearing that she couldn't protect herself, Morgan interrupted him. "We've all exhausted our powers, Lazarus! The men on that ship are tired as well; they have fought all day! You three are the ones who can protect me best, regardless of your power limitations."

She walked up to Lazarus and placed a reassuring hand on his shoulder. "I trust you, Lazarus. I feel safest with you. Besides, I can still provide some protection for you in case we get into trouble." She was relieved to see him smile back at her.

"Just stay close to me." He turned to the others. "Take point, Tristan. Zro, you follow him. Morgan and I will stay at the rear."

Morgan walked a few more steps and collapsed onto her knees.

"Princess!" Tristan shouted. He knelt by her side. "Where are you hurt?"

The other two guardians rushed beside them. Morgan shook her head to answer their concerns.

"I'm not hurt, just got a little dizzy. That's all."

Tristan put her arm around his shoulder and his other around her waist to lift her. His calm strength bolstered her. "Thanks for coming to get me," he said quietly enough so the others wouldn't hear.

Morgan looked into his eyes and studied his face. "You don't have to thank me, Tristan. We all play our parts in battle."

Tristan swallowed a little pride. "I don't think I'd be here now if you hadn't shown up."

She watched Tristan caress her hand with his thumb. "I'll always be here for you," she said sweetly.

Tristan examined their linked hands. He realized his hand was still stroking hers and stopped. "Let's say you show me how to make a pie out of those ocean berries when we get back." He released her hand.

Morgan blushed and looked down. "I already ate them."

"Well, then, we'll have to get some more." Tristan smiled.

Zro nudged Tristan with his foot. "Hey, stop kissing ass. We've got a job to do."

Lazarus reached for his radio. "She has used too much of her power. She's too exhausted to fight. I'm calling someone to…"

"I'm fine," Morgan interrupted. "We need to keep going. I said move!"

Tristan and Lazarus exchanged glances, clearly in disagreement with her. She stared them down, so they inched forward. Zro positioned himself in front of Morgan to keep her completely covered. In the distance, they could hear explosions signaling that another vicious battle had already started. Around the corner, a fierce battle raged between a row of buildings and the royal castle.

A bright beam of ethereal light shot out of the sky, shattering the building next to them. Through the wreckage, they could see a high guardian. The beams of light pounded into the man. After only a few seconds, the beams shattered his barrier and blasted through his body, killing him instantly.

Tristan tasted fear. His hands shook when he watched the seasoned warrior die so easily. He peered through the demolished building and saw a golden-clad, white-haired elf wielding a claymore with a silver blade.

He felt a tug on his arm—it was Morgan signaling him. Her face had blanched, her eyes were wide, and her breaths quickened.

"We need to go," she whispered. "That's Prince Averror, first son to the royal family. This fight is beyond us. Walk away, Tristan."

Averror strode confidently toward them. Tristan couldn't move. Zro raised his rifle and shot two rounds at him. Zro's bullets bounced off Averror's golden barrier. Averror swung his claymore with one hand. The force from his blade opened a crack in the earth between Morgan and Tristan; a small wave of rock and debris hit them. Tristan recovered his senses, grabbed Morgan, and dove out of the way.

Zro ran to the side of a building to distract the prince. "Hey, pretty boy. Over here!" Zro shouted.

Zro fired the rest of his magazine at the elven prince and slapped in a new one as fast as he could. Averror swung his blade at Zro but hit the building behind him. The sheer force of the blow sliced the building in two. Zro dove away from the falling brick. Lazarus charged, swinging his sword down at the prince. His blade connected with the barrier in a bright flash of light.

"Tristan, get Morgan out of here!" Lazarus shouted.

That was not what Tristan wanted to hear. He couldn't leave his best friends here to die; he looked at Morgan, searching for an answer. She wasn't looking back at Tristan, though. Her attention focused on the battle between her guardian and the prince. She raised her left hand and fired a white beam at Averror. The attack pierced his barrier and knocked him to the ground.

"We are not leaving without you, Laz!" Morgan shouted.

Tristan felt a surge of pride in his team's unity. The beam dissolved, and she lowered her hand and grunted as if someone had put a thousand-pound weight on her arm. Tristan knew Morgan had nothing left to give. Lazarus quickly backed away while the elven prince stood firm. Tristan readied his swords and adopted a defensive stance.

Averror emitted a glowing golden light; he focused all his powers upon Tristan and his companions. Within the burning light, a great dragon's head formed. Averror swung his blade and unleashed a golden wave of energy. The dragon's head at the front of the beam engulfed everything in its path. Lazarus sidestepped when the beam passed a bit too closely. Paralyzed with fear for his friend, Tristan didn't see the prince's energy beam approaching. Morgan grabbed his hand and jerked him out of the way seconds before the energy almost swallowed them both. They toppled to the ground. Tristan's hands shook, and his breathing became shallow.

Averror approached the guardians and their princess. Tristan, frozen in fear, covered Morgan on the ground, protecting her from the unmatched enemy. Lazarus reemerged, ferociously swinging his sword, and lunged at the prince. The prince gathered the energy surrounding him and tossed Lazarus aside. After pulling himself from the wreckage of the collapsed building, Zro fired round after round to divert Averror's attention. Averror nonchalantly flicked his wrist at Zro and expelled a small orb of energy in the guardian's direction. It exploded on impact and threw Zro to the ground.

"Tristan, get up! Get up! Tristan!" Morgan yelled and squirmed to release herself from his hold.

Blood coursed through his ears, drowning out Morgan's cries. She clutched the guardian's shoulders and shook him. The dread covering Morgan's face bolstered Tristan into action. He shot to his feet, taking direct aim at the prince.

The clangs of their exchanged blows resonated off the rubble and ravaged everyone's ears. Tristan knew his skills and speed were no match to the prince's abilities, so he immediately went on the defensive. Tristan dodged the sword, lunged at Averror, and head-butted him twice. The prince only smiled deviously at the attempt. Heat blazed around Tristan's stomach. A hand formed from the prince's energy shoved Tristan back to Morgan. Pain rendered him immobile.

Two arrows glowing with energy left a stream of sparks as they fell from the sky. They exploded next to Averror. From the bow of the ship that had just entered the fight above them, Bianca, Charity, Mira, Ry, and Rayna stared down at the outmatched guardians and Morgan. Rayna's fierce gaze reinforced Tristan's strength. He got to his feet to help Morgan.

The explosions did not affect Averror. The elf prince swung his illuminated blade upward, casting beams of golden light. The beams rose in a straight line in front of him and concentrated on the ship. The beams tore through the vessel, disintegrating it from the bottom up.

"Jump!" Ry shouted.

He grabbed Rayna and vaulted from the ship; the other guardians followed suit. Each landed safely. After Ry set Rayna down, she instantly ran to Tristan. Already on their feet and ready for the fight, Bianca, Charity, and Mira each fired another arrow at Averror. All three stuck in his barrier and exploded. Ry filled his sword with green energy and charged Averror, swinging his sword at the barrier.

"I've been waiting for this all day!" Ry yelled.

With each strike, huge sparks erupted from the prince's barrier, but the blade made no visible marks. Averror swung at Ry. The guardian lifted his blade to block the attack and erected his own barrier. The prince's powerful weapon sliced through Ry's defenses and clashed with his sword. The sheer force sent Ry off his feet, careening into a building.

More arrows fired at Averror, preventing him from pursuing Ry. Averror glared at the arrows, and they stopped in midair. He raised his open hand and waved the arrows back to their source. The arrows raced back to the guardians too fast for them to put up a proper defense.

Rayna darted out in front of the guardians and erected a black barrier. The arrows disintegrated before they reached the barrier. Power emanated from her body, spiraled into the sky, and spun the black clouds above them. Her energy shredded the ground beneath her feet. Anguish crossed Rayna's beautiful face as fury escaped her lips. The dark power enveloped her, and without preamble, wings sprouted from her back. Her body hovered above the ground as an eerie black light pulsed from within her.

Tristan stared at Rayna in awe until he saw the same black power forming around him. His fingers flexed involuntarily, and the power latched onto his fingers and crawled up his arms, inundating his body. Power blazed through his insides, and Tristan fell to his knees and screamed in agony.

The energy sent loud snaps and cracks throughout the night sky, simultaneously echoing sounds of pain and domination. Unaware whether this power came from Rayna or from another attack from Averror, Morgan signaled the other guardians to retreat from the dark energy.

Averror swung his blade, sending a pulse of energy at Rayna. When the wave hit, her barrier absorbed the attack instantaneously.

She glowered at Averror and screamed, "Executioner!" A large pentagram with eight moon symbols appeared beneath Averror's feet.

Tristan raised himself from the ground, feeling his strength and rage return. He flexed his wrists and found his swords now blazed with black light. Overwhelmed by this foreign power, a strange sensation gripped Tristan: two feathery white wings had emerged from his back. Not quite sure how he did it, he flexed his muscles; the wings responded and flapped through the air. Rayna's dark energy filled Tristan, sending him into a frenzy. Trusting his instincts, he readied his swords and flew at Averror. Behind him, he heard the other guardians' shouts of protest.

Tristan reached Averror and destroyed his barrier, swinging both swords at the elf prince. Averror raised his claymore to block each attack but found he was no longer fast enough to keep up with Tristan's newfound power. After each attack, Tristan flew to the prince's other side and swung his sword again. Averror struggled to put up a defense.

The moon symbols on the ground shot out eight beams of black light, tearing away at the sky. The black light closed in on Averror's position. Tristan, compelled as though by another force, flew in front of Averror with his hand pointing at the elf's face. Tristan fired a wave of black energy that hit Averror and caused him to fall back toward the encroaching beams. Tristan soared away just as the light's attack consumed the prince. The rays covered Averror, tearing away at his defenses and his body before merging into one large beam and elevating him into the sky.

The rays of black light gradually dissipated. Compelled once again, Tristan flew to the elven prince, rammed his sword through Averror, and drained the life from him. Tristan removed his sword and watched Averror fall to the ground. Tristan held his sword in front of him and watched it fill with black light. He aimed at Averror and fired a large black energy wave that consumed the elven prince and destroyed everything around him.

Tristan crashed to the ground with a thud; the dark power disappeared. He fell to his knees once more, unable to continue fighting. His lungs ached, and his muscles throbbed as he fought to catch his breath and composure. His head whirled with the confusion of what he'd just done.

Lazarus rushed over to the fallen guardian. He hoisted Tristan up from the ground and led him to Rayna and the rest of their friends. Lazarus supported Tristan's limp frame as everyone surrounded them. They waited in silence for an explanation of what had just happened.

"Where did you get that extra power? Since when do you have wings?" Lazarus asked.

Out of breath, Tristan just shrugged; he didn't know how to answer his own questions, much less those of his friends. "I'm not sure."

"What do you mean you're not sure? You mean to tell me you pulled that out of your ass?" Zro asked.

"I think I can answer," Morgan interrupted. "When Rayna's power grew, so did Tristan's. The same thing could happen to you and me, Lazarus. It isn't all that surprising if you think about it. She is still discovering what she is capable of, and so is Tristan. I can't explain the wings, though. But to have the ability to defeat, let alone stand against a royal family member singlehandedly, I don't know what that means, either."

Morgan bent down and picked up the claymore that had fallen from the dead elf prince's hand. She glanced between the lifeless prince and his sword. "So, this is what all this bloodshed is for?" she asked no one in particular.

She walked back over to the others and assumed her role as commander. "Charity, radio the *Shangri La* and tell them we are ready for pick up."

"Yes, your highness." She reached for her radio. "Come in, *Shangri La*, this is Charity. I have two princesses and some wounded guardians here that require immediate evacuation. Over."

Charity held her earpiece, listening for a response. "They are on their way, princess."

"Good. Thank you, Charity."

Lazarus left Tristan on the ground again while he helped sort out everyone else.

Rayna hovered over him, comforting him and checking for injuries. "Tristan, are you alright?"

Somewhat dazed, Tristan examined the destruction their battle had caused and noticed more rabbits peeking through the rubble. *These things are everywhere*, he thought.

"What?" He refocused on Rayna. "Yeah, I'm just tired and a little spooked about what happened."

Tristan thought about what Caster had told him. He nervously touched his back where his wings had been. *Am I an Angel? Is Rayna's power good?*

Rayna continued to run her hands over his face and body to check for wounds. "What do you mean, you're spooked?"

"Well, it was like I wasn't in control of what I was doing. I saw it all happen, but I couldn't stop myself. It just…" Tristan heard the quiver in his voice.

She kissed his forehead and whispered against his skin, "I would never let anything bad happen to you."

"I know," he said. "Please help me up."

Careful of his injuries, she helped Tristan stand. She wrapped her arms around him and rested her head against his chest. He tilted her head and kissed her softly as the *Shangri La* appeared above them. They pulled apart quickly, hoping no one had witnessed the intimate moment.

The group boarded the ship that had landed next to them. The soldiers from the vessel picked up the body of the high guardian, and the ship took off. Watching over the side, Tristan observed the ruins of the once beautiful city. Minimal enemy resistance remained while most of the surviving enemy forces surrendered and kneeled before the king. Tristan looked toward the ravaged castle and beheld King Eadric carrying four other swords.

"He must have defeated the other family members," Tristan said.

Rayna looked puzzled and asked, "Who?"

"Look at your father." Tristan pointed at the front of the castle.

Rayna followed Tristan's gaze. "Wow! I guess he did. So, does this mean the fight is over?"

"In this city," Morgan said, stepping next to them. "We have a long way to go."

Queen Christina joined her daughters. "Yes, we do, my child, but with the progress we made tonight, who knows what possibilities may come to us."

The queen glared at Tristan and Rayna, looking concerned and disappointed. A spike of worry seized his thoughts. Had he and Rayna been discovered? The concern faded when the queen walked away—saying nothing.

When the *Shangri La* reunited with the *Naughtalesk* in the sky, the queen stepped onto the larger vessel, followed by the guardians. She walked to her husband and, with a bow, presented him the claymore.

With much gratitude and relief in his voice, he asked, "Whom do I have to thank for this?"

"Your daughters and their guardians." The queen smiled as she presented the princesses and their friends.

Incredulity washed across his face as he scanned the group. "Are you certain?"

"Yes, my husband. Rayna and Tristan got the kill, but the others did their part in the fight."

"Well, then, you are all to be commended," the king said, not trying to hide his astonishment. "I thank you for protecting my daughters and obtaining the sword of a royal family member. No guardian has ever stood against royalty and survived."

All the guardians bowed their heads to the king and awaited any further instructions.

"Tomorrow night, we have a banquet to celebrate Rayna's birthday. The royal family of Corriander has graciously accepted the invitation. Normally, we do not invite guardians to such events, but I believe each of you has earned it. Will you accept my invitation?"

Lazarus bowed and answered for all of them, "Of course, your majesty."

"Splendid! I shall arrange an appointment for you with our royal tailor at the castle to have you fitted for your dress clothes."

"Thank you, your majesty," Lazarus answered again.

"That will be all. You may rest on the *Shangri La* if you wish. The soldiers and the high guardians will clean up the rest of the elven resistance." The king nodded his head in dismissal.

The guardians bowed once again and left the *Naughtalesk*. Drained from the exertion of battle, they were quiet as they returned to the ship. Most of all, Tristan was happy to return to his bunk to collapse into the welcoming arms of deep sleep. Reexamining the events of the night—the epic fight with Averror, his new powers, and his memory of Caster's cryptic words—would have to wait.

Chapter 9

Unrequited Love

Tristan couldn't sleep from the rocking of the *Naughtalesk*, still hovering over Levvandia. Caster's prophecy about him and the events of the fight with Averror clouded his mind. He tossed and turned but could not find comfort. Around him, he could hear the snoring of his comrades.

Tristan climbed out of his bunk and left the quarters. He walked down a hall to an open door where fresh air filled his lungs. The sounds of distant explosions, cannon fire, and propellers rang in his ears. He continued down the deck, gazing out into the distance at the brilliant light exploding out of the city's darkness. He found Morgan leaning against the deck rail, also examining what was left of the battle.

He approached her. "Couldn't sleep, either?"

Startled, she gasped, "Tristan, you scared the hell out of me."

"Sorry."

She shook her head, ignoring his apology, but she returned his smile. She sighed and leaned back against the railing. Tristan leaned next to her.

"I couldn't rest. Not here anyway," she said. "I'm still trying to take in everything that happened."

"Yeah, it was quite a day." Tristan sighed. "Thank you for rescuing us."

She glanced at him out of the corner of her eye and then back into the distance.

"I think we rescued each other, Tristan."

"We make a good team."

"I enjoyed being out there with you." She leaned in to bump his shoulder with hers.

"You enjoyed slaughtering elves with me? That's a little sick," Tristan said, chuckling.

"No, you ass. I didn't mean it like that." She glared at him until her expression softened. "I saw you out there. You jumped in front of a bullet for me. I saw the real you."

Tristan stared at the battle in the distance as he thought about that for a moment. "Well, what is the real me?"

"Although Lazarus is my guardian," Morgan said, blushing, "you—you are my hero, Tristan. I see why she cares so much for you. You aren't like the rest of the people in Sorriax. Your eyes are gentle, and so are you. You are as strong as you are brave. And you treat your soldiers like comrades instead of slaves or underlings."

Tristan was flattered and humbled. He smiled and peered at his feet shyly.

"Thank you. But I have to say, you're the same. You are kind. None of your family goes to the neighboring towns to wish the people and soldiers well. Not even Rayna. Your attitude, the way you treat your people with kindness and generosity, and your beautiful heart are qualities everyone should aspire to. No, Morgan, I'm grateful for your words, but if there is a hero here, it's you. And I hope to become just like you."

Tristan took her hand and gave it a gentle squeeze before placing it in the crook of his arm. "Come on, let's get you to bed, princess."

Morgan squeezed his arm and held onto it until he escorted her to her room. They walked through the doors that led to a hallway filled with cabins. When they arrived at her door, she peered into his eyes and, with a bright smile, said, "Thank you. No one has ever said anything that nice to me."

"Think nothing of it, Morgan. It's something you should hear more often."

"Then you better make it a point to tell me."

Tristan blushed and turned away. "Rest well, Morgan." He turned and headed to the guardians' quarters.

"You, too, Tristan," she called after him.

Tristan was halfway down the hall when he heard a door open behind him. He glanced over his shoulder to see Rayna standing in the doorway.

"What were you two doing?"

Tristan read the misgivings on Rayna's beautiful face as he approached her. "I couldn't sleep, so I went out on the deck. Morgan just happened to be there."

Morgan heard Rayna berating Tristan. She opened her door and flew to Tristan's defense. "I couldn't sleep either, so I went out to the deck to look at the city and, you know, just take in everything that happened. It was nothing more than a coincidence, Rayna. It was nothing!"

Rayna scowled and shook her head in disbelief. "I don't believe you. Tristan, what were you doing with her on the deck?"

"Nothing, Rayna!" Tristan instantly retorted with anger. "We both just explained what happened."

"Then, why were the two of you holding hands? Don't deny it. I saw you! You don't need to hold hands to talk." Rayna fired off her words like a gun.

"My hand was around his arm. He was expressing his gratitude, Rayna. We had some very intense moments during the battle. This was our very first, and we all made it out alive. We fought another royal family member and survived. He was just grateful. Nothing more! Tristan is yours." Morgan hesitated. "I would never try and take him from you. He's my friend, and you are my sister."

"Why the hell is he wearing your armband, Morgan? Don't act like I didn't notice him wearing it or that I don't know where it came from! You have worn that since we were kids, Morgan, and now suddenly it's on Tristan's arm? Why the hell is he wearing it! I've noticed you two spend a lot of time together lately. Do you think I wouldn't notice? Do you think people wouldn't tell me? Do you really think I wouldn't find out? Answer me!" Rayna shouted and slammed her fist on the wall, leaving a massive dent in the metal.

Tristan slammed his fist into the wall, demonstrating a similar power, and the metal caved to the force of the blow. "Dammit, Rayna! Nothing's going on!"

Rayna wiped the back of her hand across her eyes. "Take it off, Tristan! You are mine. You are my guardian. I order you to take it off."

From the corner of his eye, Tristan saw the unease on Morgan's face. She opened her mouth to speak, but he held his hand up to halt her words. His own anger morphed into submission. He didn't like fighting with Rayna; he couldn't reason with her when she acted irrationally.

"I am yours, Rayna—but I'm not taking it off. Go to bed. We'll talk more in the morning." Tristan took a step in the opposite direction.

"Don't hurt me, Tristan," Rayna pleaded.

He stopped to glance over his shoulder at her.

"You're doing that to yourself!" Morgan hissed at Rayna. "He hasn't done anything."

Tristan walked back to his quarters. Morgan returned to her room and slammed the door behind her. Only Rayna remained in the hall with tears streaming down her cheeks.

Chapter 10

Rayna's Birthday

Tristan's mom burst through his bedroom door. Sana surprised Tristan and Caster when she told them they were running late for their appointments at the castle. Since both young men were expected at the ball to celebrate the princess' birthday, they had to get fitted by the king's tailor for appropriate suits.

The tailors measured and poked them. The experience was foreign to both of them. Tristan glanced at Caster with worry in his eyes. "Caster?"

Caster blew his long black hair out of his eyes since his arms were out to his side so the tailor could try on different sleeves. Through the reflections in the mirror, he made eye contact with Tristan.

"What's up?" he asked, giving Tristan a cordial head nod.

Tristan wanted to bring around the subject of Angels, but he wasn't sure how to do it without coming right out and asking. And he couldn't bring himself to do that. The implications of Caster's possible answers seemed daunting. Instead, Tristan asked another question that had been bothering him lately.

"You're my family, right? Even if you are two hundred years older than me?"

Caster laughed a little under his breath. "Of course I am, Tristan. What's with the silly questions?"

Tristan gazed out the window at the fading sun.

He returned his attention to Caster. "You're immortal, Cas. You can live forever."

"Yes, I know what immortal means. But I'm only immortal when it comes to time. I control my aging, Tristan. A simple bullet could end all that."

"Then, why would you choose to age with me?"

Caster's smile dissipated when he switched his focus from Tristan to the world outside the window. "Tristan, you are my brother. Blood does not matter between you and me." From the moment we met, I knew the Aeons had arranged for us to meet. That is another reason I believe I ended up in that part of the forest when I did. We are meant for something special, Tristan. I can feel it. Land, sea, stars, time, or even death will not keep us separated for long. When the time comes, I choose to die with you. I think a ripe old age of three hundred sounds nice. I love you, Tristan."

This sudden outpouring of emotion touched and surprised Tristan. Caster usually gave him a tough time about being sentimental and sappy. He was unsure how to respond to Caster's unexpected sensitivity. He reverted his attention to the outside.

"You sound like a girl." Tristan raised an eyebrow. He glanced back at Caster and uncomfortably muttered, "But I love you, too." Tristan felt a bit of tension in his back that instantly reminded him of Caster's prophecy. "Cas?"

Caster looked at Tristan and seeing the concern on his face. "What is it, Tristan?"

Tristan looked down at his hands, and then he turned to address the tailors. "Can you give us a moment?"

One of the tailors replied, "Of course. Let us know when you are ready for us to return." They left the room.

Tristan continued to look at his hands as they started to tremble. "You were right about me."

Caster took a deep breath and exhaled. "You got your wings, eh?" Tristan nodded. "Are you frightened?"

Tristan looked at Caster. "What am I? A freak who has wings sporadically appear on his back?"

Caster stepped off his stool and walked over to Tristan, who did the same. He put his hand on Tristan's shoulder. "Not being able to control your wings is a problem. We're just going have to fix that."

Tristan brushed Caster's hand off in frustration. "But what the hell am I? What does it mean?"

"You are an Angel. For some reason, the Aeons chose you... but I can't tell you why they chose you."

"Is it because of Rayna? She got her wings, too! Since we are royal and guardian, does that connection matter?"

Caster looked surprised. "Rayna got wings, too? That's very interesting. No, it doesn't matter. The Aeons apparently chose both of you. There really isn't a rhyme or reason for why people are chosen to be Angels. Maybe you and Rayna are destined to do something great? Maybe you will be like most others who are chosen and lead very normal lives. It's hard to tell."

Tristan stared at Caster. "Is this going to change me?"

Caster shrugged. "As a person? Most likely not. Physically? Most Angels, once they get their wings, their physical attributes increase. Some even become more adept at magic. But the most important thing is you have the capacity to fly."

Tristan was frustrated. "Capacity? What's that supposed to mean?"

"Well, you do lack the ability to learn quickly." Tristan rolled his eyes. Caster gave him a reassuring hug. "There is one more thing. Whatever you do, do not lose control."

Tristan pulled back from their hug. "What do you mean?"

Caster repeated, "Do not lose control. It's something that Angels can do. I have seen it once; it is horrifying the amount of power they generate. The feathers from their wings wilt away, leaving nothing but bone, their eyes turn red, and they cannot distinguish friend from foe. It is called 'dark' or 'going dark.' But do not worry, you are better than that. I will work with you to teach you to fly and control your new abilities." Tristan smiled and nodded, comforted by Caster's guidance.

≋

Throughout the day, ships came from far and wide to deliver attendees to the king's ball. Night had fallen. Tristan wore a black suit. His newly acquired medal hung over his chest, and his rank was displayed on his shoulder. Caster dressed similarly. Tristan, Caster, and Lazarus met in front of the castle, entering together. Tristan looked forward to the ball, but he couldn't stop thinking about the surprise they had planned for Rayna's birthday later that evening. Hopefully, he could apologize for everything that happened aboard the ship.

A guard met them at the front of the castle to escort them to the ballroom. When the door to the ballroom opened, a doorman announced their presence. "Now arriving, Guardians Lazarus and Tristan and Honor Guard Captain Caster."

Upon entering, the crowd applauded. Tristan and the other two boys made their way to the group of other guardians. He half-expected Rayna to show up and smother him with affection, but he didn't see her anywhere.

While Lazarus was talking to the other guardians, Tristan leaned into Caster. "Hey, do you see Rayna anywhere?"

Caster searched the room before he answered, "No, but I do see someone else."

Tristan followed the direction of Caster's stare and felt his heart make a small but resonant thud in his chest. Morgan. She wore a glittery black dress with a slit up to her thigh, her hair was teased into an elaborate design, and her bangs framed the right side of her face.

She saw Caster and Tristan staring. She smiled and excused herself to the gentleman with whom she had been talking. Morgan sauntered over to the boys, smiling wickedly at them. "Hello, boys. How's it going?"

Tristan was a little dumbstruck. "Uh…we're fine, and you look…just wow!" After stumbling over his words, he composed himself. "You look amazing, Morgan."

"Why, thank you," Morgan said beguilingly. "You two are very handsome tonight as well."

Morgan smiled at Tristan again. Tristan shook his head slightly. "Hey, have you seen Rayna?"

Morgan's smile faltered a little. "No, I haven't. I'm sorry, Tristan."

"It's alright," he said, shrugging. "I just hoped we could dance."

Morgan's face grew more serious. She placed her hand on Tristan's arm. "Listen, Tristan. You aren't going to like what I'm about to say, but you need to hear it. There's another reason for this ball, other than our conquering the elven city and Rayna's birthday." She paused to make sure she had Tristan's full attention. "Father is announcing my and Rayna's engagements."

Tristan's heart dropped into his stomach. "What? But what about…"

Morgan cut him off. "I'm sorry, Tristan. I'm against it as well, but you knew this day would come just as she did."

Tristan shook his head, avoiding eye contact with Morgan. She had to be wrong. After all he and Rayna had been through to be together, surely she couldn't go through with an arranged engagement. He knew he could talk her out of it if she'd give him a chance. "Is she here? I need to talk to her, Morgan."

"She is here, but I haven't seen her."

Morgan grabbed his hand. "Come dance with me." She renewed her smile and dragged him toward the dance floor. Tristan tried to ignore her, but instead, Morgan ignored him. "Dance with me."

"Go find Lazarus!" Tristan sputtered.

"Don't be so stubborn." Morgan's whisper had an edge to it now. "You know how jealous Rayna gets. If she sees us dancing, she will show her face and get in between us so you will have your chance to see her."

Morgan pulled Tristan close, grabbed his hands, put one low on her waist, and lifted the other to their side. She slowly moved her hips and began to lead him in their dance. Tristan couldn't relax into the dance; he kept glancing around the room, searching for Rayna. Detecting his tension, Morgan rested her forehead on his shoulder.

"For what it's worth, I'm sorry, Tristan," she whispered just loud enough so only he could hear. "I don't want this, either. I have plans that don't include complying with an arranged marriage."

"Like what?" Tristan scoffed. "You don't love anyone."

Morgan stopped dancing and scowled at him. "You don't know that. I could have feelings for someone, just like my sister does."

Feeling guilty for snapping at her, Tristan took the lead and danced with Morgan in earnest.

"I'm sorry for that outburst," Tristan said softly. "It's not my place to judge you."

"You're upset. I understand." She rested her head on his shoulder again. "Please don't do anything foolish when you see them together."

Tristan smirked and shook his head slightly. He knew he couldn't guarantee that.

Rayna walked toward them with a huge smile on her face. Relief coursed through Tristan's body. He immediately released Morgan and stepped forward to hug Rayna. She walked right past him as if she hadn't seen him. Tristan stopped and watched her embrace a young man with short black hair and glasses. He was a little thicker than Tristan, but he was also a full head taller. Tristan resented the man's height and stretched himself to appear as tall as he could.

Morgan stepped next to Tristan. "That's Prince Ethan, the first prince of Corriander."

Tristan's anger rose. He could taste the bile in the back of his mouth, his muscles tensed, and his jaw clenched. He started toward them, but Morgan grabbed his arm and pulled him back.

"I know you don't like it, but you can't do anything about it, especially now with so many people watching." Morgan tightened her grip on his arm. "Please, Tristan, if you need to talk to her about this, do it when we take her out on my ship for her birthday party. Please? Can we dance now?"

Tristan knew Morgan was right. He'd get them all in trouble if the king found out about his and Rayna's relationship now. He let Morgan pull him into another dance, but he only had longing eyes for Rayna and eyes full of hate for the new prince. Rayna and Ethan danced, not taking their eyes off each other.

King Eadric approached Morgan with a few nobles in tow. Tristan didn't recognize any of them. He stood to Morgan's side with his arms at rest to show respect to his king. Morgan weaved her arm through Tristan's.

"Morgan, if I could borrow you for a moment," he said with a tone that meant Morgan's acquiescence was not optional. "I would like to introduce you to your fiancé, Prince Andrew."

Tristan took Morgan's hand and removed it from his elbow. He gave her hand a slight squeeze as he held her hand out to Prince Andrew. The prince pulled Morgan away from Tristan, and a strange look of melancholy washed over her face. She stared over her shoulder at Tristan as long as she could. He watched Rayna's and Morgan's fiancés lead them onto the stage where the orchestra played.

"Ladies and gentlemen," King Eadric spoke. "I have some wonderful news for you all that will bring the families from Sorriax and Corriander even closer. My two daughters, Morgan and Rayna, are to wed the Princes Andrew and Ethan."

The two couples bowed, and the crowd applauded. Morgan did not smile; she had a stoic look upon her face. In contrast, Rayna's smile was dazzling and animated. She seemed different. Strange. A tinge of jealousy and anger cast a dark shadow over his thoughts.

Caster approached Tristan and put his hand on his shoulder. "I'm sorry. If there is anything I can do…"

Crestfallen, Tristan's gaze fell to the floor to hide the tears forming in his eyes. He pinched the bridge of his nose to stop them before replying to Caster. "There's nothing anybody can do."

Caster pulled his hand away after he squeezed Tristan's shoulder. "Well, we're going to get ready for Rayna's party. Are you coming?"

"Whatever."

While his friends left to prepare the ship, Tristan remained in the ballroom. Rejection clouded his mind as he watched Rayna, the woman he desperately loved, dance with a man he hated. Rayna had abandoned him, his friends had deserted him, and even Morgan was stripped from him. Tristan wanted to scream, but he couldn't figure out why he felt so alone. He had known this day would come, just like Morgan had said, but he hadn't expected Rayna to accept it with such enthusiasm.

≈

Tristan gazed into Rayna's eyes while they sat under their tree. Something had been bothering him for a while. He picked up a twig and twirled it in his fingers. "Can I ask you something? It's been bugging me."

Rayna looked him up and down. "No." She turned her attention to the view in front of them, but she couldn't hide her smile for very long.

Tristan raised his eyebrow. "Rude." She laughed. Tristan continued with his question in a more serious tone. "What are we going to do if your father arranges for you to be married?"

Rayna scoffed. "What? Don't be ridiculous. That'll never happen."

Tristan wasn't so easily convinced. "But what if it does?"

Rayna rolled over on all fours and slowly crawled closer to him with a devious smile on her face. "My elf, are you jealous? Now that I think about it, the idea doesn't sound so bad. Having a fat, rich, and powerful husband." She ran her fingers up his stomach and to his chest. "And on the side, I have a not so tall, dark, handsome man at my every beck and call."

Tristan grabbed her hand. "I'm not doing that. I'm serious."

Rayna rolled her eyes. She turned over and pressed her body against his. "The rest of the world is at war with us, and we kill all other royal families who oppose us. It's not like princes line up to be with us. Morgan will be single forever." She looked up at him over her shoulder. "I think I did well for myself. You know, my parents are in Corriander for the evening."

Tristan breathed a sigh of relief and then jokingly spouted out, "Yeah, who would marry you anyway? Being so fat and ugly. This is really just a pity thing we have going on."

She smiled. "Shut up and kiss me, you idiot."

≈

Thinking back, Tristan could still feel how hard she pressed her lips against his that day. He decided to leave. He couldn't handle watching Rayna smile at the other man for a second longer. He stopped in the doorway to survey the ballroom one last time. Rayna watched him turn to leave, and a glimmer of hope sprang to life. Foolishly, he thought she might run over to stop him and apologize or at least give him a reason for ignoring him the way she did. Instead, she returned her attention to Ethan. A smile illuminated her face as though he'd said something funny. The glimmer vanished, and Tristan exited the ballroom.

Slowly, he made his way to the airship docks. He kicked around some dust and stared at the ground while he walked. When he reached the *Luna Spell*, he saw Ry and Mira loading the last of the supplies onto the ship. Tristan followed them to the ship's deck. Everyone was busy preparing the decorations, food, and drinks for Rayna's party.

Tristan didn't bother to help with any of the work. No one attempted to stop him as he walked up to the higher deck and stared off into the star-filled sky. Lately, the Angel constellation had captured his focus and radiated its beauty at him.

Moments later, when everyone shouted, "Happy birthday, Rayna!" Tristan didn't care to participate. He remained on the upper part of the deck without so much as a glance to acknowledge her. The music started to play, and everyone laughed and joked around on the main deck.

Tristan heard steps behind him, but he was too incensed to turn around. He didn't want to face Rayna right now.

"Mind if I come up for a minute?" Morgan asked.

"Doesn't matter," he said, but her voice soothed his angry mind.

Morgan walked over and stood next to Tristan. "Ethan heard about Rayna's little birthday party and decided he wanted to come."

"So? It doesn't make any difference."

"You don't care that he came with her?" Morgan sounded aggravated.

"Why should I? If she can so easily dismiss her feelings for me and ignore the fact that I even exist after everything she and I have been through, then why should I care?" Tristan's tone rose. His cheeks burned red with anger.

Morgan became more serious rather than sympathetic. Her voice carried the timber of a command rather than concern. "Well, stop acting like you don't care. Maybe there's a reason she's acting this way. Maybe she's trying to protect you."

"And why are you so involved in this? What does it matter to you?" Tristan's frustration escalated.

"How could you ask something like that?" Morgan asked indignantly. "For your information, I care about you and my sister, and I don't want this engagement to hurt you more than it has to, Tristan!"

"Mission accomplished, Morgan." His voice dripped with sarcasm.

Her eyes grew watery. "You're an asshole."

"I'm sorry, Morgan," he whispered. "I shouldn't be here."

"Maybe you shouldn't." Morgan spun on her heel and nearly ran into Rayna.

Tristan quickly swiveled to avoid both of them and disembark. The ship rose into the sky, eliminating his possibility of escape. He swore under his breath and turned away from both princesses.

Rayna said cautiously, "May I speak with Tristan?"

Morgan stomped past her. "He's all yours."

Tentatively, Rayna took the last few steps and stood next to Tristan. She put her hand on his. Tristan wrenched it away.

"What's your problem?" she asked, sounding hurt.

ROMANCING THE DARKNESS

Dumbfounded, Tristan asked, "What's my problem? Isn't it a little obvious? I'm sure your highness can figure that one out!"

"You don't have to be such a jerk about it. I just asked you a question. Are you mad about the whole engagement thing?"

Tristan didn't answer. He gave a sarcastic chuckle and shook his head. He grasped the railing tighter.

"It's nothing I planned, Tristan. We knew this would happen, eventually."

Tristan, not thinking clearly, yelled, "It doesn't mean that you have to ignore me completely, Rayna! You didn't even bother to say hi to me at the ball!"

"I did say hi." Confusion was written all over her face.

"What? You walked right by me without even flinching. Your sister and I were dancing. She saw you ignore me, too!"

Rayna shook her head, lost in his words, but Tristan didn't care. He wanted an indication that she was suffering as much as he was. "So, what now? Is this how it's going to end?" Tristan's voice fractured.

"Is this how what's going to end?" Rayna's voice quivered.

"Us," he said. Tristan couldn't prevent a couple of tears from rolling down his face. "Is this how we're ending it?"

Rayna sniffled, trying to stifle her emotions. "Are you breaking up with me?"

"If you're so infatuated with your new fiancé," Tristan jibed, "then is there any reason to keep this up any longer? I don't see one."

Tears spilled from Rayna's eyes. "We vowed to be together forever. How can you turn your back on that?"

"How could you, Rayna?"

"It's not like I have a choice in the matter, Tristan."

"Then, why do you talk like you do?"

Rayna's eyes turned from sad to infuriated. "Why are you trying to make this worse? Why are you deliberately trying to make me more upset?"

"Uh, I don't know." He laughed bitterly. "Maybe because you're going to marry some spoiled idiot when you claim to love me. Did you think of that?"

131

"Shut up, Tristan!" Rayna shouted but quickly regained her composure. "I'm done talking about this tonight."

The small party froze momentarily as Rayna's shout lingered in the air. She stalked away from him before he could reply. Murmurs grew louder as people slowly began to talk and dance again. Tristan shook his head, knowing their fight was probably the topic of many conversations.

Tristan remained on the upper deck for most of the party. Everyone below seemed to have fun. Rayna escorted Ethan around and introduced him to all the guardians, except Tristan.

In the distance, Tristan saw two ships in the clouds rapidly approaching the *Luna Spell*. The vessels had flags with Corriander's symbols flying on their masts. They pulled up next to their ship and docked, not showing any form of hostility. The captains of both ships, accompanied by a small company of soldiers each, boarded. Tristan headed to the stairs leading to the lower deck to see what the commotion was. The larger, more decorated captain approached Rayna and Morgan.

"Greetings, ladies and gentlemen. I am Captain Moyyarte," he said in a thick accent.

Morgan spoke, "What can we do for you, captain?"

"Well, if I am not mistaken, you two are the princesses of the Naughtrious family, are you not?"

Morgan hesitated to answer his question. "What's it to you, sir?"

"I can see that you are unarmed, and I assure you we will make this as painless as possible," Moyyarte said with a cunning smile.

Lazarus stepped between the unknown captains and the princesses. "Make what painless? Who are you?"

A soldier hit Lazarus in the head with the butt of his rifle. Morgan cried out in alarm. The partygoers huddled behind them screamed as well.

Moyyarte resumed speaking. "If we do not have any more outbursts like that, no one else will get hurt. I do despise violence. But to answer your question, boy, we are pirates up for the highest bid, and we are here for her." He pointed at Rayna.

"So, my dear," he directed his words to Rayna, "if you wish all your friends to live, you will come with me quietly."

He extended his hand. When the other guardians started to move toward Moyyarte, his deckhands raised their rifles and forced them to stop.

"It's okay," Rayna said quietly. "I will go."

Tristan cursed himself for not bringing his weapons. His anger now focused on the pirates. He leaped down from the stairs. "Like hell, you will!"

Tristan attacked one of the deckhands, knocking the rifle out of his hand and shoving him overboard.

Moyyarte fired a round into the air and shouted, "Enough!"

Tristan froze in place.

"Throw him overboard. We don't want any more needless violence," the captain ordered.

The other guardians protested and shouted for the pirates to leave. The guards grabbed a struggling Tristan and threw him over the side of the ship. Reacting quickly, he reached out and grabbed onto a windowsill. He heard his friends' screams—the loudest was Rayna's. She screamed his name over and over, pleading for him not to die. Tristan's heart raced as he fought to maintain his grip. But now, he was more afraid for Rayna than he was for himself. He heard Rayna's struggle and the retreating footsteps of the pirates.

The ships departed into the distance. Tristan slowly climbed up the side of the ship. "Can somebody give me a hand?"

Caster and Zro's heads appeared over the edge of the railing.

Caster shouted, "Tristan! You're alright!"

Together, they grabbed his arms and pulled him back on to the deck. Caster drew Tristan into a hug. Tristan, however, couldn't contain his rage and quickly released himself from Caster's hold.

"What are we waiting for?" Tristan asked the other guardians. "We need to head back to the castle, arm ourselves, and rescue Rayna!"

"We have no way of tracking them," Morgan said.

Tristan paused. He closed his eyes and concentrated on the new powers he shared with Rayna in hopes they would allow him to locate her. After a few minutes, Tristan's shoulders slumped.

"I may be able to." Ethan finally spoke up. "Give me a moment."

Ethan glowed with gray energy, illuminating the *Luna Spell* with a dim light. A large falcon appeared out of the light. Ethan addressed it. "Follow those two ships and return to me so you can lead us to them. Now go!"

The bird flapped its wings and, with haste, headed after the pirate ships. The *Luna Spell* retreated to the castle at top speed.

Tristan grasped the rails of the ship. His anger was palpable—anger at whoever hired the pirates; anger at Rayna for going so willingly; anger at Ethan for being the one who could track her; but worst of all was the anger at himself for failing to protect Rayna at all costs. He cursed the slow-moving ship.

"Guardians, ready yourselves," Morgan directed. "I will deal with my parents!"

When the ship docked at the castle, the guardians sprinted in one direction; Morgan and Ethan went in the other. Anxious to save Rayna, Tristan was the first to reach the armory where the others met up with him. Tristan and the other guardians had almost finished preparations when a messenger arrived in the armory.

"The king and queen would like to speak with you right away," the messenger stated.

None of the guardians answered but quietly resumed dressing. Tristan nodded to the man. The messenger left the room shortly, followed by the guardians. They sprinted down the corridor into the throne room. The king stood with his arms folded; his eyes homed in on Tristan.

Morgan entered the throne room wearing her armor. She was visibly upset. Tristan thought he saw a red mark across her right cheek as if she had been slapped.

The king walked right up to Tristan and shoved him. "You call yourself a guardian! How dare you take my daughter out and not be armed. You are as foolish as this ridiculous armor that was designed for you."

He glowered at Lazarus. "I expected more out of you. You let me down." The king then turned to the rest of the guardians and his daughter and bellowed, "As did all of you. You all let me down. You let your queen down. You let the future of this kingdom down."

He aimed his glare at Tristan. He stepped close enough to Tristan to grab the chain of his armored hood and pulled Tristan a few inches off his feet. "You let down my daughter, the one whom you supposedly care for so much. Don't think I don't know what you two have been up to? Do I look stupid to you? Do I? Answer me!"

Tristan said nothing. His chest rose and fell quickly as his anger grew out of control. The king dropped Tristan to the floor.

"You're lucky I'm not without mercy, boy. Bring my daughter back at any cost. If she is alive, I will consider your punishment." The king poked Tristan's chest for emphasis.

Tristan returned his stare. "Are you done yet, sir? I have a job to do."

The king took a moment to digest Tristan's words. King Eadric then directed his stare at Morgan. "At any cost, Morgan! Take the *Shangri La* along with your ship and what men you can. I do not know when reinforcements will arrive. Ethan will stay here. I do not want any more screw-ups on your part. His bird will lead you to them."

The king turned back to Tristan and hit him across the face, knocking him to the ground so forcefully he slid across the marble floor. "Now find my daughter!" the king screamed.

Bianca and Zro ran to help Tristan to his feet. Tristan tried to demonstrate that he wasn't hurt, but he had a tough time pretending. They left the throne room. When the door shut, Tristan spat blood on to the floor and cradled his face in agony. Even through his fight with Averror, he had never felt such pain. Or humiliation.

"Come on. We need to go." Lazarus put Tristan's arm around his shoulder. "You can recover aboard the ship."

Tristan's friends helped him hustle to the docking area, where the soldiers gathered on the *Shangri La* and the *Luna Spell*.

All the guardians and Morgan boarded the *Shangri La*.

"Hoist all anchors," Morgan shouted. "I want both these ships in the air in less than sixty seconds. Is that understood?"

The deckhands shouted, "Yes, ma'am!"

The large falcon hovered in front of the ships, ready to lead the way to the pirates.

"Follow that bird!" Morgan commanded.

Tristan sat on a barrel on the deck, staring off after the falcon and willing the ships to fly faster. The other guardians carried on conversations around him.

"How do we know she isn't already dead?" Zro asked.

"Don't say that. Don't ever say that!" Morgan cried out. Tears filled her eyes.

"She isn't dead." Tristan stared down at his armband.

"Sorry," Zro said. "Of course."

Tristan took a deep breath. "I suppose I should confess our secret to you since they're going to hang me anyway."

"What secret?" Morgan asked.

"Rayna and I took a different vow than the rest of you. I know that if she dies, so do I. But if I die, then so does she."

The others stared at him in shock and disbelief. Morgan was outraged. "How could you let her do that?"

Tristan bristled. "It was her idea, and I love her. What do you expect? Arguing about it isn't going to get her back any faster."

Morgan glared at Tristan and gave him the impression that she wanted to hit him or, at the very least, yell at him some more, but she remained still and silent.

Ry interjected, "Wait. I don't understand. You guys don't have the magic or power to alter our guardian vows. So how did you do it?"

Morgan shouted, "They did it during the actual ceremony without anyone noticing!"

"If you need me to get some colored wax and parchment, I can draw it out for you," Tristan said. In the distance, the bird started circling an area for a few minutes but then vanished into the darkness.

The captain of the *Shangri La* reported, "We see two ships hovering over what looks like a small stone building."

"Kill the lights. They don't need to know we're coming," Morgan said.

Both ships went dark.

"Okay, these guys are just ordinary soldiers. Nothing special about them," Lazarus commanded. "I want Zro, Mira, Charity, Bianca, and Morgan up on the ship to provide cover fire and assist our men with taking out the two enemy ships. Tristan, Ry, Caster, and I will head down to get Rayna. This is a grab-and-go operation. Their reinforcements may already be on the way. No telling how much time we have. I want us in and out. Is that understood?"

They all nodded and stared at the oncoming threat. Tristan sensed the tension in the air. An alarm sounded, and spotlights illuminated the Sorriaxian ships. So much for their plan to go unnoticed.

Lazarus shouted, "All deckhands, give us some cover! Go, go, go!"

Tristan, Lazarus, Ry, and Caster hurdled off the ship. Explosions flared around them, and bullets whizzed by. Before they hit the ground, whirlwinds appeared around them, slowing their fall. Tristan charged the oncoming enemy first. His blades cut down one pirate and then a second. His fury grew with each person he killed. Zro's bullets eliminated pirates wielding rifles and shotguns. A beam shot from the *Shangri La* split one of the pirate ships in half. The guardians plowed through the pirates' forces on the ground.

"Tristan, go inside and get her," Lazarus shouted. "We'll hold them here."

Tristan nodded and charged into the stone building. Two pirate guards pointed machineguns at Tristan and opened fire on him. Tristan ran through the bullets with his barrier up; he cut down both soldiers before they could defend themselves. After Tristan kicked open the door they guarded, he saw Moyyarte with a handful of pirates, each pointing a rifle at Rayna.

"I thought we threw you overboard," Moyyarte said with that cunning smile.

"What can I say? I'm hard to kill." Tristan shrugged.

"Indeed, you are. Don't do anything foolish, boy. I believe you are this young lady's guardian. Your life will end with her death. We want her alive, so please do not force us to do anything that isn't necessary."

"How do you know I'm her guardian?" Tristan asked.

"Inside information, my boy," he answered. "Obviously, one of your comrades sold you out."

"Stop with the bullshit!" Tristan yelled. "Hand over Rayna, and I promise each of you a quick death."

"You are in no position to make threats, boy!" Moyyarte said, his tone changing from playful to deadly. "Now drop your weapons and surrender!"

Tristan stared across the room at Rayna. In that short second of contact, he knew she understood and trusted what he was about to do. Tristan quickly raised his sword, aimed at Moyyarte's head, and fired the blade. The blade flew by Moyyarte and stuck in the wall behind them. Tristan quickly hit the switch once more, and the blade pulled him toward Rayna. He wrapped his arms around her just as every gun in the room fired. Tristan opened his eyes to see his barrier surround him and Rayna. He looked down at her, scanning for apparent injuries. "Are you hurt?"

She shook her head. He released his hold of her but kept his barrier intact. Tristan's radio went off.

"Tristan, it's Morgan. Their reinforcements are almost here."

"Copy that, Morgan. Out." He touched his earpiece.

"You won't be able to get away," Moyyarte laughed. "None of you will survive."

"Neither will you," Tristan said, adding a cocky smile.

He fired his blade into Moyyarte's chest. Once he retracted it, Tristan grabbed Rayna's hand and led her out of the building. By the time they reached outside, the second pirate ship had fallen to the ground in flames. The other guardians climbed back up to their ship by rope.

The remaining pirates stormed out of the stone building, carrying rocket launchers and high-caliber machineguns. They resumed firing at Tristan, who kept his barrier up. He raised his sword and fired it high into the side of the *Shangri La*. Rayna understood his plan and secured her arms around his neck; he wrapped his free arm around her waist. He pushed the switch again, so the hilt hoisted them into the air. Explosions burst all around them, bouncing off Tristan's shield. Tristan and Rayna gazed into each other's eyes. Forgetting his anger, Tristan pulled her tightly to him and gently kissed her, not caring about the fact that they were dangling in the air.

When they pulled apart, Tristan said, "I love you, Rayna."

"I love you, too, Tristan."

Rayna wrapped her arms around Tristan, holding him tightly. When they reached the top of the deck, Charity and Lazarus pulled Rayna up first and then Tristan.

"We need to hurry," Morgan said. "Their reinforcements have arrived."

Tristan followed her sightline and saw a few dozen ships only a couple of miles away.

The captain's voice was full of doubt. "We can't outrun them. These are flagships, your highness. They will most certainly catch us."

Tristan looked to Lazarus for an answer, but his friend seemed just as hopeless. Tristan grabbed his bracer and took it off, revealing the horrible scar that had seared his flesh. Rayna ran her fingers over the scar.

"Tristan, what are you doing?" Rayna demanded.

"Your parents know about us somehow," Tristan explained. "I'll be sentenced when I get back, so it doesn't matter anymore if I die."

"Yes, it does." Rayna gripped his arm. "Stop acting so selfish!"

Morgan stepped forward. "Father said to get you back at any cost, Rayna. I'll stay and hold them off so you can make it home."

"No, you can't," Rayna pleaded with her sister. Her eyes scanned the group of guardians. "None of you can. I order you to come with me."

"I'll be staying as well, princess," Lazarus said.

"So will I," Zro added.

One by one, everyone volunteered to stay.

"Please, none of you have to do this," Rayna sobbed.

"I need two volunteers to escort Rayna back to Sorriax on the *Luna Spell*," Tristan said. He scrutinized the guardians before he continued. "Mira and Ry, I want the two of you…"

"That's crap, Tristan," Ry interjected. "We want to fight, too!"

Mira yelled, "Yeah, we want to help her!"

"Look, we don't know what else may be coming," Tristan said firmly. "Other ships may be on the way back to Sorriax. I don't know, but my point is that Rayna needs guardians to escort her back."

"He's right. You two go with her," Morgan said. When they hesitated, she added, "That's an order!"

"None of you have to be here," Tristan addressed the other soldiers on deck. "This is clearly a stalling mission. We aren't likely to go home."

"I speak for my men, sir," the captain said as he stood up. "We are here to protect Lady Morgan and Lady Rayna until death."

Some deckhands cheered and shouted, while others nodded solemnly.

"Thank you. All of you," Morgan said.

Rayna fought and cried all the while she was escorted off the ship. Mira and Ry didn't seem thrilled either. When they crossed onto the *Luna Spell*, Tristan grabbed Ry's arm and spun him around.

"Protect her!" Tristan placed the bracer in Ry's palm. "With my life."

Ry nodded and accepted Tristan's bracer. Tristan slowly let go and watched the ship head off in the opposite direction.

Rayna ran to the end of the ship while it pulled away. "Come with us, please!" she screamed. "Please! Morgan, I love you! Tristan! Please, Tristan!"

They all watched the *Luna Spell* disappear into the darkness.

Chapter 11

Blood Traitor

Now that Rayna was safe, Tristan looked to Lazarus for leadership.

Lazarus smiled and said, "I think you got this one."

Tristan nodded and then shouted, "I want all deck-mounted guns and below-deck guns manned. Anyone left, grab a machine-gun. No one comes aboard this ship. Do you understand me?"

"Yes, sir!" the sailors replied.

Tristan switched his focus to the guardians and Caster.

"You guardians, I want Caster and Lazarus to remain aboard the *Shangri La* to protect Morgan! The rest of us will take this fight to them. Fight with everything you have. Hold nothing back. I'm counting on each of you. This will not be our final stand. This is not the last night we will see. We will overcome our adversaries!"

Tristan's commands were brief but powerful. The guardians stood silent with rage and determination in their eyes.

The ships arrived and stopped in front of the *Shangri La*. A firm male voice came over a loudspeaker. "This is Admiral Anton. We have you surrounded. Surrender yourselves, and your lives will be spared."

"Hey," Zro said to Tristan, "if there aren't any royal family members with them, I think we can win."

"Well, let's hope there aren't," Morgan whispered.

"We'll know if a barrier is put up around the ship," Tristan said. "Now, when you attack, we should each head for separate ships."

"Thanks," Lazarus chimed in. "That still leaves a dozen or so for us to handle."

"What are you complaining about?" Tristan laughed. "You have a tank standing next to you."

He eyed Morgan. She smiled back at him.

"Drop your weapons and surrender!" the enemy bellowed over the loudspeakers again.

"Zro," Tristan said, "shut him up."

"Yes, sir." Zro smirked as he peered through his scope, aimed at the enemy admiral, and filled his rifle with energy. He fired, hitting the admiral. The bullet exploded on contact. The side of the ship blew apart and fell to the ground.

"No royal family member, then. Excellent," Tristan said.

Tristan and the other guardians ran forward and launched themselves at the opposing ships. Gunfire came from every angle, aimed at the guardians and the *Shangri La*. A barrier appeared— the *Shangri La* deflected all incoming fire.

Filling his swords with energy, Tristan shot out both blades and used them like whips. The swords caused an explosion on impact, tearing the deck apart from the outside in. Flying past him were the other guardians firing energy-filled projectiles that decimated the other ships. The vessel he attacked started to lose altitude, so Tristan retracted his blades. He fired the blades again, hitting the deck of another ship before he fell.

The blades pulled Tristan to the deck, where several enemy soldiers ran to fight him off. Tristan raised his sword to block the first attacker and knocked him to the ground with his shoulder. He swung, slaying another soldier advancing toward him. A third came from his side. Tristan dodged and countered the attack, only to have the pirate thwart it. Their swords clashed. Tristan smirked, pleased to find a worthy swordsman to fight.

A bullet hit the swordsman in the head, killing him instantly. Tristan's radio came on.

"Sorry to ruin your fun but quit playing around!" Zro said while flying by on a scout ship.

"Zro, you ass!" Tristan gave his friend a quick salute. Then, he ran to the helm, cutting down all who got in his way. Bullets ricocheted off his barrier. After cutting down the man steering the ship, Tristan turned the wheel, forced the ship into a dive, and blasted the wheel with his energy.

Tristan ran to the edge of a ship and touched his earpiece. "Hey, I need a ride!"

"I'm right behind you, babe," Charity's voice responded. "I see you."

Tristan saw Charity board a scout plane attached to the side of the ship. She detached from the ship and gained speed from the fall. The wings and propellers sprung from the side of the plane, and she took off toward Tristan. She reached out for him. He grabbed her hand and hopped onto the vessel.

"Thanks."

"Anytime," Charity said. "Where to now?"

"I don't know," Tristan said, surveying the battle scene. "This all seems a little too easy. I know the battle just started, but they aren't putting up much of a fight."

"Stop complaining and tell me where to drop you off. We're still getting shot at," she complained.

"There!" Tristan said as he pointed to an enemy carrier that had just arrived and released all its fighter planes.

"Roger!"

Charity maneuvered through bullet fire, reaching the aircraft carrier as two fighter ships came up behind them.

"I'll get off here." Tristan jumped off and filled his swords with energy. In midair, he let go of the blades. They hovered in front of him. He put his palms to the hilts and shot two green waves of energy, destroying both planes. Tristan grabbed his weapons, fired them into the aircraft carrier's runway, and hoisted himself aboard.

A bright light discharged from his right. He saw white beams of energy rise from the ground and morph into the shape of wolf heads. They emitted high-pitched screeches when they attacked, destroying the ships surrounding the *Shangri La*. Morgan's energy illuminated the entire sky but soon faded.

Tristan touched his earpiece. "What did I tell you, Laz? She's a tank."

"Get back to fighting," said Lazarus, hiding his amusement with his orders.

Tristan pointed his hand at the captain's deck and fired a green beam at it. A gray barrier surrounded it, blocking the shot. Tristan's hope for victory vanished. He touched his earpiece to give his friends the bad news. "There's a barrier on the aircraft carrier. It's time to consider getting Morgan out of here."

"Don't be stupid," replied Morgan. "We'll be there to assist you soon. Caster and Bianca are on their way to you."

"I don't think that's enough time," said Tristan.

A dark-haired elf in light black armor and a black hooded cloak stepped onto the captain's deck. He unsheathed a black-hilted broadsword.

"Someone looks a little morose today," quipped Tristan.

"Cute." The dark elf smirked.

"May I ask your name?"

"How polite. You may ask, but it will matter not in a few moments," the dark-haired elf said.

Caster and Bianca landed next to Tristan.

"Ah, I see you stalled for time. Clever, I guess, if you wish death upon your friends," the dark-haired elf jibed.

"That's Prince Talruke," Caster whispered to Tristan under his breath. "He and his family govern the country I'm from."

Talruke must have heard Caster's statement, for the prince turned his attention to him and laughed. "I see you have the blood traitor with you. Figures he would join you. No one else would have him."

"Don't you talk that way about my family!" shouted Tristan.

Talruke found Tristan's words hilarious. "Trust me, boy, he does not think of you like family." The man continued before Tristan could object. "He's an assassin, kid. He puts on an act to gain the trust of the enemy and sells the information to the highest bidder."

Tristan flinched at an explosion that rocked the carrier back and forth. He narrowed his eyes at Caster in disbelief. "Is this true?"

Guilt crawled across Caster's face. Tristan slumped, and his heart filled with disappointment.

"He has misinterpreted what I've done," answered Caster.

"Cas, is it true?" Tristan pleaded.

Caster couldn't face Tristan. He focused on the dark elf.

"I actually have a home and a family now. Tristan, I would never turn on you. Never."

Thoughts of betrayal flooded Tristan's mind; he fought the swell of angry tears in his eyes. Moyyarte's words from earlier that evening came back to him. Tristan felt like a fool for not having seen it earlier.

"You're a spy! You sold out Rayna and me! You told these bastards where to find us during Rayna's party!"

"Tristan!" Caster pleaded. "I didn't do any of those things. You have my word!"

Tristan, desperate to wake from this nightmare, yelled, "How am I supposed to believe you? There isn't anyone else who could benefit from this without getting punished. All you have to do is leave the country and spy for someone else!"

"If you would please listen, brother…" Caster's words were full of anguish.

"Don't call me brother!" Tristan screamed. Tristan didn't care about the blow Caster had received from his caustic words. Caster's shoulders slumped; his face went pale.

"Aw, it looks like you hurt the little blood traitor's feelings." Talruke laughed.

Tristan turned his rage to the dark elf and yelled with all his might, "Shut up, elf! Shut up!" As Tristan screamed, black energy erupted all around his body. His blades illuminated with a black light. The Naughtrious symbols appeared underneath their feet while the wind roared violently around them. Tristan tried to duplicate the energy he had summoned in his last battle, but once again, he was not in full control of his power. Without Rayna and the bracer nearby, the energy wasn't as strong.

Talruke emitted such incredible energy that he levitated off the ground. Tristan charged at Talruke with all his fury. He swung his blades at the dark elf's barrier and cracked it.

145

"Bianca, fire!" shouted Tristan.

Bianca fired three consecutive arrows at the crack in the barrier. The resulting explosion propelled Tristan into the air, but the barrier remained in place. He summoned energy into his blades and raised them over his head. After he reached the pinnacle of his altitude, Tristan fell with incredible velocity. He approached the barrier, swung his swords downward, and shattered it. A black spiraling beam of energy rose into the sky.

Tristan retreated slightly as the beam faded, revealing Talruke. His barrier was destroyed, but he only had a few scratches on his armor and face. Tristan's best efforts were not going to be enough to bring him down. Talruke glided toward Tristan, swinging his sword with his elvish speed. Tristan barely blocked the attack. Tristan and Talruke exchanged attacks—their swords collided ferociously. Talruke swung his sword; Tristan ducked underneath it, diving to the side. Bianca fired another arrow that hit Talruke and exploded, but it didn't appear to do much damage.

Bianca yelled into her earpiece, "We need some help over here!"

Tristan got up and blocked another assault from the dark elf. Tristan shot the blade in his left hand to the top of the staircase leading to the helmsman's deck and pulled himself backward up the stairs. Talruke glided right above him, swinging his sword. Tristan blocked the attack with his other blade. When the hilt met the blade in Tristan's right hand, he was surprised by Talruke's speed. He quickly appeared behind Tristan, thrusting his sword at Tristan's neck. Tristan released his blade, flipped over the top of Talruke, and landed behind him.

He charged, forcing Talruke to dive for the stairs. Tristan raised his hand and fired a black orb of energy that hit where the dark elf landed, knocking him down the stairs. Tristan recovered his second sword. Talruke shot into the air and swung his blade with all his might. Tristan blocked the vicious attack with both swords, but the force of the attack caused a thunderous crash that cracked the deck beneath his feet.

"Not bad, kid. Now, let's see how you act under pressure." Talruke laughed.

He raised his hand and pointed at the helm. The ship turned toward the Shangri La and picked up speed.

"You coward," Tristan murmured.

"You, better than anyone, should know how to win, even if that means resorting to underhanded tactics."

Desperate to land an attack on the prince, Tristan pushed Talruke away and swung his weapons violently. Talruke dodged all of Tristan's efforts. He raised his hand and fired a beam of gray energy that hit Tristan and forced him off his feet. The beam carried Tristan until he hit the barrier protecting the aircraft carrier. The force of the wave, combined with the power of the barrier, tortured Tristan. The energy seared through his body but hadn't burned him. As suddenly as it began, the pain stopped. Tristan heard Talruke's snide laughter. When Tristan opened his eyes, he saw Caster had the prince's arms pinned to his sides.

"Oh, did the blood traitor actually feel some form of guilt while watching the only person who cares about him be beaten to a pulp?"

With fury in his eyes, Caster shouted, "As long as there is breath in my lungs, I will never let you hurt Tristan!"

"It's a little late for that promise, blood traitor," quipped Talruke.

Using all his formidable strength, Caster turned both their bodies to face Bianca. "Bianca, now!"

"I can't! I might kill you, too!" she cried out.

"I don't care—just do it!" yelled Caster.

He continued to grapple with the struggling Talruke. Bianca took a breath and fired the energized arrow.

"Let's fix that part about breath in your lungs," Talruke said.

Talruke flipped Caster over and ducked under the arrow, which exploded a few feet away on the deck. He pummeled Caster in the stomach and tossed him into the air. Talruke flew up behind Caster, readying his sword. "So long, blood traitor."

Realizing his friend was in grave trouble, Tristan gathered his strength and cleared the last confusion from his head. He summoned a whirlwind that flew up and behind Talruke. Tristan aimed his sword at the elf prince and hit the button. The prince was impaled; Caster fell, hitting the ground unharmed. The retraction of the blade whipped the prince around to face Tristan. Talruke opened his eyes wide, and his skin grew pale as he searched Tristan for a weakness.

"Never let your guard down," Tristan mocked. "Bianca, one more time!"

Tristan ran his second sword through Talruke and kicked him backward, forcing him toward Bianca. She fired an arrow, striking the prince in the chest. Tristan raised his right hand and fired a black orb of energy so forceful that it threw Talruke into the air. The explosion lit up the sky. After the barrier around the ship disintegrated, Talruke landed on the deck.

"I may not have killed you," Talruke said, forcing out a few last words, "but the crash will."

Tristan had forgotten about that. There was no way to slow the prince's ship now, and its collision with the *Shangri La* was inevitable. Tristan grabbed his discarded sword. Bianca grabbed the prince's sword. The three of them ran to the guard railings to grab hold of something.

"Hold on!" yelled Tristan.

They all shut their eyes tightly and braced for the impact.

The aircraft carrier collided with the *Shangri La*, causing explosions to erupt on both ships. Tristan felt like he was falling. When he opened his eyes, he saw a barrier around him that was not his own. All around him, he saw dozens of barriers filled with unconscious and conscious soldiers and guardians. He looked around to find the source of the shields. From the deck of the *Shangri La*, Morgan, who did not have a single barrier around herself, concentrated with all of her might to shield everyone around her.

Tristan yelled, "Morgan, put a barrier around yourself!"

"I don't have the strength to form another one." She gave him a strained smile.

"But you won't survive!" Tristan screamed.

"No, but you will."

"I won't let you die, Morgan!"

In a panic, Tristan pulled out his sword and filled it with all the power he could. He started attacking the barrier around him, forcing it to crack little by little. He grew weaker: the harder he tried, the more energy he exerted. Tristan screamed as he thrust his blade through the barrier, ignoring Morgan's pleas for him to remain safely inside. He sliced through the barrier and shot his blade into a nearby tree. He pulled himself to Morgan and caught her while the others hit the ground unharmed. Holding onto Morgan, Tristan hit the ground and slid across the dirt and grass. They stopped moving, and Tristan cracked his eyes open. He saw Morgan kneeling above him.

"Why did you do that?" She swatted his arm. "You could have killed yourself, you idiot."

"Are we alive?" Tristan winced as Morgan gave an exaggerated nod. "Then I guess it was worth it."

"Thank you. I guess we're even now."

"Yeah, I guess we are," he said with a nod. "That's what friends do."

Morgan hugged him, and Tristan returned the embrace. Morgan stood up. "Are the others safe?"

"All of us are okay and accounted for," yelled Lazarus.

Morgan helped Tristan up. "We need to get out of here. No doubt they'll be searching for us now."

Bianca walked over and handed the sword of Talruke to Morgan. "Here, princess. I believe this belongs to your family."

"Is this the sword from the family member?" Morgan asked incredulously. "How did you get it?"

"Tristan beat him," Bianca said. "He actually went toe-to-toe with the dark elf prince and beat him."

"I didn't beat him. You, me, and Caster…" he cut himself off. Knowing that Caster might be a traitor made him feel stung on the inside.

Morgan finished Tristan's sentence. "The three of you beat the dark elven prince?"

Tristan, now distracted, quietly replied, "Yeah, it was the three of us."

"Stop being so modest," said Bianca. "Tristan did most of the fighting. I just shot a couple of arrows at him, Caster wrestled him, and…"

Bianca's tone dropped, and then she stopped talking altogether, glancing at Tristan.

"What's wrong?" Morgan asked.

"It's not my place," Bianca answered. "Tristan should be the one to… Excuse me." Bianca walked away.

Morgan eyed Tristan suspiciously. "What's the matter? Why won't one of you tell me what happened during the fight?"

"The prince called Caster a blood traitor. I think Caster may have…" Tristan's voice grew more tense when he tried to get the words out.

Morgan understood what Tristan was afraid to say aloud. She looked away from Tristan to hide the swell of sadness in her eyes. "We have to tell my parents," she said softly.

"You can't, Morgan. They'll kill him."

"We don't have a choice," Morgan argued. "If he is the one ratting us out, who knows what else he may have learned. We can't risk it."

"He's family. Don't do it, please. Besides, what if the prince was wrong?"

Morgan watched him with pity in her eyes.

"He's my friend, too, but if he's what the prince claims, then we have to let someone know. You can't just wish Caster innocent."

"I'm begging you," Tristan pleaded. "Don't tell anyone, at least until any kind of proof presents itself. You did it for your sister and me. Please help Caster. If something else happens, then you can turn him in. I don't want him executed for something he didn't do."

Morgan studied Tristan's face and hugged him once again.

"Okay, Tristan, okay," she whispered. "He gets one chance."

They stood facing each other and agreed. Tristan felt relieved and kissed Morgan on the cheek. "Thank you."

"You'd do the same for me. Now get out of here so I can explain this to Bianca."

Tristan rejoined the other guardians when Morgan called Bianca over. Zro was concentrating hard on something when Tristan approached him.

"Do you hear that?" he asked Tristan.

"What?"

Zro glanced around at the other guardians.

"Everyone, come here. Do any of you hear that?"

They listened as their confusion grew. Zro waited in silence for a few more seconds.

"Nothing. No insects. No animals. No beasts. Nothing. This forest is dead," Zro whispered. "We must tread quietly and speak softly."

Tristan hadn't noticed. He listened again to the overwhelming silence and became a little spooked.

"But there's nothing here," Lazarus responded.

"We don't know that. Whatever might be out there could have scared away the creatures and could be watching us as we speak. We should move quietly," Zro said. "And quickly."

"What if the enemy pursues us?" Lazarus asked.

Tristan said, "Then, we'll fight our way through." A sudden gust of wind buffeted Tristan.

"Above us! Enemy airships!" Morgan shouted.

The remnants of the enemy's soldiers slid down the ropes that hung from the ships. The number of enemy soldiers dropping into the forest quickly outnumbered the guardians and their followers.

Tristan and Lazarus ran back and grabbed Morgan. Lazarus ordered the guardians to run. Charity led the guardians and soldiers through the forest. Tristan heard rustling all around them, and then he heard shots. Ahead, he saw Charity dive into a ditch along with the other soldiers and guardians. Morgan and Lazarus followed. Just before Tristan dove in, he saw two men with rockets pointed at the ditch.

Tristan hurried and covered Morgan. He shouted, "Get down! Put up a barrier!"

The other soldiers covered their heads from the two explosions outside the ditch. Tristan got up. "Return fire!" he yelled.

Those who had guns formed a circle on the edge of the ditch and fired into the oncoming soldiers. Tristan had a challenging time seeing the enemy through the blue mist creeping up from the ground. Gunfire lit up the darkened forest. The gunshots stopped, and the mist grew thicker, making it impossible for the soldiers to see.

Tristan saw a shadow on the ground that grew until it loomed over them. He raised his eyes and saw a tall, black-hooded figure.

"Wraith!" Tristan shouted.

This undead creature, once alive, was cursed to roam the world after death. *Something is forcing it to be here,* Tristan thought. Tristan couldn't tell what species of humanoid it was since a hood covered its head. The stench of rotting flesh filled the air. The wraith's bony fingers gripped a scythe. Sickly pale flesh peeked through its torn robes, turning Tristan's stomach at the sight. The others quickly backed away from it. In the distance, screams of the enemy soldiers filled the forest. The wraith glided into the ditch; its presence cleared everyone out of it. All around the guardians, Tristan saw black shrouds of darkness floating through the forest.

"Tristan, watch out!" screamed Charity.

The wraith was in front of Tristan, raising its scythe. Tristan lifted his rifle to block the attack, but the sickle sliced through the gun. Two soldiers tackled the wraith from behind, forcing it to the ground. Another soldier pointed his rifle at the wraith's head and shot an entire magazine into it. Its hood fell back. The absent eyes and bullet-riddled face of the wraith caused the men to jump in fright and disgust. The wraith sat up, pulled its hood back over its head, and stood.

"It can't be killed by normal weapons! Run!" Morgan shouted.

The soldiers and guardians ran away with the wraith in pursuit. Tristan and Lazarus flanked Morgan to keep her safe. In the distance, they saw something glowing through the mist. When they got a little closer, they discovered a floating corpse. Lightly armored with a torn robe and bearing a staff, the animated corpse had pieces of flesh missing. Its eyes burned green, and it pointed its rotten finger at Morgan. A wheezy screech came from it, and the wraiths stopped in mid-pursuit to stare at Morgan as well. Tristan grabbed Morgan's hand tightly.

"You dare trespass in my forest?"

"Who's speaking? And what is that?" Tristan asked. "What the hell is going on?"

"It's a lich," Morgan answered shakily. "It must be controlling these wraiths. The only thing it seeks is power greater than its own."

"So, it's after you. Great," Lazarus said. "We need to get out of here, now! We are surrounded."

The lich wheezed. "No. Stay. Join my family." Behind him, in the distance, legions of skeletons sprinted toward them.

The lich floated past trees and rocks toward a group of enemy soldiers. Tristan could visibly see light and energy drawn into the apparition like a vortex. Liches were rogue mages who sought eternal life by using dark magic and turning undead. Their decrepit forms and rotting flesh were signs of how long they had been around. Bone had pierced through what remained of the lich's flesh, telling Tristan it had lurked around the dark corners of this world for some time. Tristan's ears twitched as he heard screams coming from the lich. He watched in horror when he saw the faces of trapped souls try to escape the creature's body. The lich ran its hand through one soldier, grabbing and ripping a transparent form out of the soldier's body. The body fell to the ground. Dozens of wraiths gathered around it and cannibalized the soldier's flesh. The lich had devoured the person's soul.

"We need to leave!" Zro yelled. "Why are you just standing there and watching?"

"We can't just leave them to die like that!" answered Morgan.

"Are you crazy? They're the enemy. Who cares?" Zro indignantly asked.

Morgan ran toward the enemy soldiers.

"Shit!" Lazarus cursed. "Zro, take the other guardians and soldiers and get out of the forest. We'll meet up with you!"

"We can't leave you!" replied Zro.

"Shut up and go!" Lazarus commanded. "Tristan, you with me?"

Tristan pulled out both swords and yelled, "Yeah!"

The two guardians chased after Morgan rushing headlong into the slaughter in front of them. Morgan reached the enemy soldiers and stood in front of them, shielding them from any further harm. The lich slowed its movements when its eyes fixated on Morgan. It smiled the most wicked smile Tristan had ever seen. Its voice sounded like footsteps on gravel.

"Your power will be mine, child." The lich then fashioned a transparent sword out of the mist.

Over her shoulder, Morgan yelled, "Run!"

The other soldiers stared at her questioningly.

"Run!" she yelled once more.

Wraiths glided toward her, but Morgan showed no signs of retreating. Lazarus ran straight at a wraith. Their weapons collided; each tried to push the other back. The lich charged Morgan. Morgan angled her sword in front of her, pointed the blade at the lich, and gathered her power. Tristan stepped between them, filling both of his blades with energy to buy Morgan what time he could. The lich swung its sword with great force. Tristan raised both blades in defense. The force of the attack brought Tristan to his knees; the lich showed no mercy. Tristan screamed, barely able to support his swords. He weakened as the creature drained his energy and life force. After only a few seconds, he was desperate to find a way out.

"Tristan, move!" Morgan cried out.

Behind Tristan, Morgan glowed with white energy. A transparent form of a wolf symbolizing Aerra stood within the light Morgan had created. Wind and debris rose up around her. The lich applied more pressure; the ground cracked beneath him.

An errant green beam came from Lazarus' sword while he fought off yet another wraith. The beam hit the lich in the face. The creature lifted its blade long enough for Tristan to drop down and dive out of the way. Morgan shouted as she unleashed all her power—a large white beam detonated from her sword.

Two smaller beams formed around the larger beam and rotated around it. The wraiths shied away from the light. The white beam shredded the ground and covered the lich, causing the creature to shriek. The attack stopped, leaving what was left of the lich's flesh to sear. The green glow in its eyes turned red. The creature slammed its staff into the ground, repeatedly muttering a chant: "*Surgite Umbras. Animate Draconem!*"

The surrounding area grew even darker. Tristan couldn't see in front of him. He yelled, "What's happening?"

Morgan shouted back, "The lich used four keywords in its spell. I only heard Draconem; I don't know what the other three mean!" A circle of eclipsed light appeared in front of the lich. The light reminded Tristan of an eclipse. It emitted a dim light while keeping the rest of the area in complete darkness. Tristan suddenly felt a pull toward the light. Soon, a powerful force from the light sucked in all the undead and everything else around it. Tristan felt himself rising into the air. He thrust his swords into the ground to avoid being taken by the light. He saw Morgan and Lazarus struggle against the force. They were shouting, but he couldn't hear anything. The force of the light was so powerful it even absorbed sound. Tristan could not believe the power of this creature. He saw Morgan repeatedly try and say a single word. The sound kept escaping her lips. The tree Lazarus hung onto began to give way. A fiery white light tried to erupt around Morgan. Each time, the lich's light absorbed it. Frustration grew on Morgan's face. She thrust her sword into the air, forming a white barrier around her. She screamed, "Aerra!"

A larger white barrier formed around all three of them. The wolf Aeon emerged from the dark, next to Morgan. The wolf stood even taller than she was. Tristan was unaware the Aeons could change their size. The bodies of the skeletons and fleshy corpses merged around the light and quickly took the form of a dragon, mostly made of bone. Its eyes glowed a deep red. The force from the light died, and moonlight returned. The creature roared. Its roar consisted of the screams from the hundreds of undead attached to it. Tristan looked at its body and saw all the skeletons and corpses merged into it. Still conscious, they tried to move and free themselves from their new form. When it opened its mouth, a cone of bone shards came out instead of fire. The shards hit Morgan's barrier. Aerra looked down at Morgan and nodded.

"Run!" Morgan shouted breathlessly. The wolf charged the dragon.

Lazarus put his arm around Morgan to support her weight, and they hobbled in the direction of the other guardians. Tristan pushed himself up and chased after them.

Behind him, he heard a hissing voice. "You cannot leave."

A low moan came from the distance. Tristan spun around to see the lich raise its arms to the sky. Its cries sent uncomfortable chills up Tristan's spine, making his hair stand on end. The ground shifted when the lich summoned corpses and skeletons of those who never managed to escape the forest alive over the years. Tristan sped up to catch Lazarus and Morgan as the corpses of the recently deceased and those who had rested in the ground for some time rose all around them and grabbed for their feet. The guardians ran past the undead climbing from the earth where they had lain. The sheer numbers of the dead chasing them shifted and moved, mimicking a busy anthill.

"Don't stop," shouted Lazarus. "Run through them!"

Upon reaching the edge of the forest, Tristan wasn't sure of the plan. When they breached the treeline, bony fingers scraped at their armor. Ahead, Tristan saw the enemy soldiers they had rescued lined up with machineguns and fifty-caliber turret guns. Behind them was their ship, where more men operated deck-mounted machineguns. Among them, the other guardians and Sorriaxian soldiers also aimed at the army of the dead.

The captain of the ship shouted, "Get down!"

Lazarus immediately shoved Morgan to the ground. Tristan fell on top of her, shielding her head. The undead rushed out of the forest as the captain ordered her followers to fire. The night lit up with gunfire. Bullets shredded the corpses of the undead and the wraiths. Tristan closed his eyes while their bodies and bones fell around them. This fight was going to create a memory he didn't want. He tightened his hold on Morgan as she tried to lift her head. "Don't look!" He covered her head again.

Bullets continued to spray while more undead poured out of the forest. They lay on the forest floor for what seemed like hours. Tristan listened to the sounds of battle, hoping for a break in the fire so he could stand and join the fight. A bright blue glow flashed through his eyelids, followed by an inhuman screech of pain.

Tristan opened his eyes in time to see Caster pull his sword from the lich's chest. The lich emitted one last screech before disintegrating into the ground. The undead and skeletons collapsed; the wraiths retreated into the mist, howling in the darkness. Tristan pushed himself up, allowing Morgan and Lazarus to stand. Caster rushed to offer Morgan a hand.

When the guardians got to their feet, they stood in front of Morgan, readying their swords. The enemy was in front of them, armed with fully automatic weapons.

Zro shouted, "Hold up, hold up! We sort of agreed on a short ceasefire."

Tristan kept his swords at the ready while the enemy's captain approached. The woman was not as elaborately dressed as the other captains they had encountered. She wore the same tattered, shabby uniform as her men, except for the insignias indicating her rank. However, her pale arms were covered by scars, and her eyes told a thousand weary tales. This woman had seen her share of battles.

"Who are you?" Tristan asked. "What do you want?"

The woman paused for a moment, closed her eyes, gave a half-hearted smile, and then opened them. The action appeared to have refreshed her.

"My name is Adalay. We are in quite a predicament here, aren't we? We are sworn enemies, yet you saved my men's lives. Should we continue our battle, or should we go our separate ways? What do you think, Kavalla?"

An Irkshdan cat sprang from the ship to the ground. Her black sleeveless armor covered her dark skin, and pointy ears stuck out of her brown hair. Her golden eyes stared Tristan down while her tail twitched. Standing taller than Tristan, Kavalla strolled over to Adalay.

"I'm not sure, Adalay," she replied in a firm but soothing voice. She scrutinized Morgan before she continued. "This one's heart does not seem as tainted as the rest of her family's."

Morgan raised her eyebrow and granted Kavalla a glower of her own.

"What makes you so sure, my dear?" Adalay asked.

"Call it women's intuition," Kavalla purred.

Adalay placed her hand on Kavalla's shoulder. "This is my first mate, Kavalla."

With pride, Kavalla added, "And I can put an arrow between your eyes at three hundred yards."

"Well, luckily, we're a little closer, huh?"

"Mind your tongue, boy," Kavalla growled. "Be grateful that we aren't going to attack you!"

Adalay held up a hand. Kavalla returned her attention to her superior but didn't stop glaring at Tristan. "I'm glad to see you two are getting along. But it is true—we shall not fire upon you. Let us go our separate ways."

Morgan smiled and approached Adalay, extending her hand in gratitude.

"Thank you so much. I am…"

Kavalla smacked her hand away. Morgan retracted and signaled Lazarus and Tristan to stand down.

"Don't you dare touch Adalay," she bellowed. "We may be sparing your lives, but that does not mean we are friends. You're all still monsters, and mark my word, the next time we meet, I will not be so merciful."

"Spare our lives?" Lazarus laughed. "Who the hell do you think you're talking to, you stupid cat?"

Kavalla lifted her sword, but Adalay quickly grabbed her arm. "That is enough!" Adalay ordered. Her glare bounced between Kavalla and Lazarus. She focused her attention on Lazarus before she continued. "But she is right. Our next encounter will not be under the same circumstances. We will be enemies once again."

"I can't wait." Tristan gave the enemy a taunting smile.

Adalay took one last look at the guardians and Morgan. Tristan kept his guard up.

"Let's get out of here. Everyone, back to the ship," she directed.

"Until next time, boys," Kavalla added darkly. She winked and turned toward her ship. After boarding, the enemy took off in the opposite direction.

The guardians and soldiers escorted Morgan back into Sorriaxian territory—on foot. They walked into the night for hours. A combination of exhaustion and grief left the team in silence for most of the journey. When they reached the borders of Gungshrid, Morgan stopped and grabbed Tristan's arm. The others turned around and surveyed the landscape.

"Keep going. We'll catch up shortly." When nobody moved, Morgan added, "That's an order!"

The guardians and soldiers trudged off.

Morgan remained quiet, closing her eyes and still gripping Tristan's arm tightly. Tristan was happy to lag behind because he wasn't particularly thrilled to be home. Morgan faced Tristan, opening her eyes to reveal her tears.

"I want you to leave," she said quietly.

"What?" Tristan searched Morgan's face for an explanation.

"I want you to run away. They're going to kill you. They won't allow you to live once you step into the castle." She was desperate for him to understand and leave.

"If I face my punishment, maybe the king will be lenient with me. Running away feels like a death sentence no matter how you look at it."

"Don't be stupid. Please go. I couldn't bear it." Morgan struggled to keep her composure. Tristan put a comforting hand on her shoulder.

"This is a price I knew I would pay, and now, I'm going to pay it," Tristan clarified. "I know this makes you angry, and I'm sorry for that. I can't let Rayna face the punishment alone."

Morgan pulled Tristan's hood over his head and wrapped her arms around him. She burst into tears, unable to constrain herself.

Tristan hugged her tightly. "I'm sorry, Morgan," he whispered into her hair.

Morgan tilted her head to gaze into Tristan's eyes and leaned in closer to him. Tristan stared back at her, trying to sort through his conflicting thoughts. His hand grazed the side of her cheek, and their lips brushed against each other. After a second, Tristan pulled his head away. "We can't. I can't."

"What's the matter?"

Tristan let go of her, but her arms stayed wrapped around his waist.

"You know I can't. Rayna and I are..."

"Rayna? You two are not married. Despite what you may think, she is marrying someone else. And as for this I-can't-let-Rayna-face-the-punishment-by-herself thing, don't you get it? She won't face any punishment. That's all on you." Morgan dropped her hands from Tristan's waist and drew back into herself for a brief introspection.

Tristan paced, trying to make sense of what had just happened. With his hands on his hips, he faced her. "Before you continue, Morgan, may I remind you that you are getting married, too?"

Morgan shook her head. Her tears cascaded in earnest now. "No, I refused to marry Prince Andrew. Father wasn't exactly thrilled about my decision. Neither was Andrew." Morgan tried to lighten the heavy conversation.

"You're not?" Tristan's eyes studied Morgan's face, searching for any answer.

Wiping away a stray tear, Morgan said, "No. Rayna, on the other hand, accepted her marriage. She didn't even put up a fight."

Tristan clutched his chest, feeling something crack inside him. Morgan's eyes filled with pity.

"I'm not trying to make you jealous," she explained. "I just wanted you to know."

He stepped away from her. Anger flushed his cheeks. "So you could take advantage of me?"

"No, Tristan." Morgan shook her head, eyes wide. "It's not like that."

"Then, how is it?"

Morgan averted her eyes, a blush rising in her cheeks. "You said on the dance floor at the ball that I didn't care for anyone." She gazed at him before she continued. "But you were wrong. I care about you, Tristan. I want to feel what my sister feels; I want to know your touch. I want to feel your lips. I want to know your heartbeat. I want you to know mine as well."

Words failed Tristan. He had never expected Morgan to confess anything like this. She looked uncomfortable. Tristan could only think of Rayna and how she would react to Morgan's revelation.

"Say something," Morgan whispered.

"We can't." Tristan shook his head. "I love your sister."

"So your mind is set?" Morgan's eyes overflowed with tears again.

Tristan just stared—stared at the road, stared at the sky, stared at his hands, stared at anything to avoid the sight of Morgan's tears. "My mind can never be set, Morgan. Not with you. But Rayna and I are married, and I still have hope in my heart that she will return to me. I'm sorry."

"Stop apologizing. I'm the foolish one." She took a few steps toward home.

Emotion stirred inside Tristan when he eyed her dejected form. He didn't mean to hurt Morgan, but the idea that she had feelings for him was bewildering.

"You're not foolish. There is nothing wrong with following your heart." He grabbed her hand and angled her to face him again. "There's nothing wrong with you—you're gorgeous, funny, smart, and one of my best friends."

Morgan shed a few more tears, but words escaped her.

Tristan rubbed his thumb over the back of her hand. "I need you to say something. I don't want this to get weird between us."

Morgan tried to hold back her tears. "What else can I say? You love my sister, you won't run away, and you plan to go back to the castle and let them kill you. You're a stubborn asshole," her voice choked on the insult. Tristan knew she didn't mean it.

"Why don't you just go?"

"What? Go with you, or go away alone?" Tristan joked to lighten the mood.

"Now is not the time to be an ass. I'm serious, and all you can do is act like a jerk. Please, be serious. I don't want you to die."

Her words sobered him. "I don't want to die, Morgan. But, if I run, I'll run for the rest of my life. It won't be much of a life if I do that."

"Maybe I can go with you."

Tristan cocked his head and gave her a grin. He shook his head slightly.

"Then, we'll have everyone looking for us. Morgan, your place is here, and so is mine. Nothing will happen to me. I promise."

"That doesn't make me feel any better."

He spoke softly, "Nothing bad will happen, not to me, not to Rayna, and not to you. I promise."

Morgan clearly wasn't satisfied with his declaration. Tristan put his arms around her again, embracing her tightly. He kissed her cheek and then leaned his head against hers. She hugged him and kissed his cheek a couple of times.

"Just don't forget that promise, okay?" she said, all choked up.

"Never."

They let go of each other and continued their return to the city. The guardians in front of them had disappeared from sight. The whole city appeared abandoned, and the emptiness left Tristan alarmed. The lights were off in every building. The street was still. Footsteps echoed around them, but Tristan saw nothing. He grabbed Morgan's hand and brought her in close, readying his sword in his other hand.

From Tristan's left, the butt of a rifle hit him in the face. In seconds, unfamiliar soldiers swarmed the street, pulling Tristan and Morgan apart. Dozens of men grabbed Tristan and threw him against a wall, binding his arms and confiscating his swords. Morgan grabbed a few of the men, tearing them away from Tristan, but more soldiers appeared.

"Detain the princess, but do not harm her!" a soldier shouted.

Soldiers seized Morgan before she could reach for her sword. Tristan squirmed against his many captors and fought with all his might. Another blow hit Tristan in the face. A rucksack covered Tristan's head, and he was dragged off to an unknown location. Morgan's screams faded into the distance.

Chapter 12

Princess Abducted

Tristan awoke on a cold stone floor, his back against a stone wall. Next to him was a cot with a thin sheet over it; bars extended across his cell door. A musty mildew stench filled the air. He was in the castle's prison. When he stood up, he grabbed the bars to keep from falling over. His head throbbed. There wasn't one inch of his body that didn't ache. He saw a guard at the end of the hall.

"Guard! Hey, guard!" Tristan shouted. When he didn't receive an answer, he called out again. "Why am I here? I'm not going to run. If I were going to run, I would have left while I was on my assignment!"

"Listen, sir," the guard finally responded to Tristan. "I'm sorry, but you need to be a little quieter."

"How long am I going to be in here?"

"Just tonight."

"Can you at least tell me what happened to Morgan and my friends? Did Rayna make it back safely?"

"There were complications, sir."

"What kind of complications?" Tristan asked nervously. The guard hesitated to answer. "Tell me!"

"The princesses never made it back to Sorriax."

Tristan shouted, "What? How? What the hell happened?"

"We don't know, but the king is on top of it," the guard said calmly. "They weren't the only ones taken. The guardians Ry, Charity, Mira, and Bianca were also abducted. The rest of the guardians are also detained at the castle now."

"What! What for?" yelled Tristan.

"Sir, they aren't exactly being punished. It's just a precaution. You're going to need your rest to be ready for whatever tomorrow brings. Get some sleep," the guard said on his way out of the holding chamber.

Tristan wasn't satisfied with what he had been told. It didn't make sense. He rested on the cot, but he couldn't sleep. For hours, he sat there, alternating between thinking about his death and the fate of the princesses and his friends. Tristan stared out his barred window and saw a quarter-moon and a field of stars shining in the dark sky. The sight of the constellations reminded him of the hooded girl—a thought that sent shivers down his spine.

The next morning couldn't have arrived any slower for Tristan. He managed to nod off a few times, but he didn't get anything that resembled restful sleep. He lay awake most of the night, haunted by his upcoming punishment.

Four guards appeared before his cell. Tristan stood when they entered to handcuff him behind his back. They led Tristan out of the dungeon and through the castle. In the throne room, he saw the entire royal family, Ichiban, his own family, and the rest of the guardians. The guards delivered Tristan before the king and encircled him to prevent him from escaping.

The king's silent glares weighed heavily on Tristan. "Death," the king said. Rage filled his voice. "Death is the consequence for the actions that you have taken in forming a more than friendly relationship with my daughter. Whether it was consummated, I do not care to know. The crime you committed is not only enforced by our country but by the rest of the world. This is a profoundly serious crime. Royal families are not to engage in any dalliance outside of royal blood. The blood of commoners cannot and will not taint our bloodline. Death is the punishment to show the world that violating these laws will not be tolerated.

And believe me, boy, after discovering your acts of betrayal, I want your head on my wall." The king shared a glance with the queen before he returned his focus to Tristan. Tristan felt a glimmer of hope at the hesitation.

"But my wife and I have had an exceedingly long and taxing conversation. Though your time in the service has been short, you have done remarkable things in this war—things no other guardian has done. Yet now, my daughters have been abducted. What I have decided will not change and cannot be negotiated. The gallows will not claim your life, Tristan. Instead, you and two hundred soldiers will be sent to the front lines. You will start on the shores of the mainland in the city Airk, move to the Elemental Islands, and eventually make your way to the undersea city of Furreshda. The islands hide a road that leads to Furreshda, but they will not make it easy for you to enter. Your mission is to reinforce our soldiers currently there and break your way through the city to rescue Rayna and Morgan."

"Two hundred is not enough to reinforce anything, let alone get the princesses back!" Tristan protested.

"I know," the king retorted. "Another part of your punishment is that if you cannot lead these men to complete your task, you will have the deaths of two hundred soldiers and my daughters on your conscience, all paying for the crime you have committed."

"How long will I be gone?" Tristan looked anywhere but at the king.

"However long it takes," the king answered coldly. "I have one more surprise for you. Guards, could you bring forth Caster and Guardians Lazarus and Zro?"

The three stood before the king. All wore handcuffs and had glowering faces similar to Tristan's.

"When I was informed of Tristan's misdeeds, your names were mentioned. You knew what was going on between Tristan and my daughter, yet you failed to tell me. As punishment, you will be sent with Tristan."

Cries of protest came from all corners of the room. Tristan couldn't believe it.

"That is unacceptable, sir," Tristan yelled over the crowd. "They had nothing to do with the situation. They should not be punished for something I have done."

"I thought I was clear when I said this matter will not be negotiated," the king, visibly upset, yelled. "Now, you complain when I am generous and sparing your lives! Well, then, I…"

"I want to go, too," Ichiban interrupted.

"Why?" the king asked incredulously. "This is a death sentence, Ichiban. You know these battles cannot be won!"

The grizzled wolf nodded. "I know. But perhaps if I join them, maybe some good will come of this instead of their dying right away. I have been on the frontlines. I could command this small army. Your majesty, do not waste the talent of these boys. Let me help make use of them."

"This is quite the bold move on your part, Ichiban. Do you really think you can make a difference?"

"Yes, sir."

The king remained silent and then nodded. "Very well. You may go. On one condition."

Sergeant Culvac raised his hand and stepped forward out of the crowd. "Your majesty, I apologize for the outburst, but I must object to Guardian Tristan's punishment. I want to volunteer my unit to assist him."

"Name and rank soldier?" the king asked, perplexed.

"Sir, Sergeant Samuel Culvac of the 112th Infantry Unit," he said with a salute.

"Please, sergeant, tell me what provokes this act of courage?"

"Your majesty, my men and I have served under Tristan once, and we would trust him with our lives. He is a superb leader, a valiant warrior, and he puts his men before himself. I speak for my men: we owe him our lives, and we wish to repay him by joining him in this campaign."

"How many men are in your unit, sergeant?"

"Eighteen hundred, sir."

Frustrated, the king looked back and forth between the sergeant and his Irkshdan general.

"You do realize this is a death sentence, do you not?" the king asked, bemused at the support for the traitor. "You will not come back from this."

"Your majesty, it doesn't have to be," the sergeant said. "My men and I can really do some good and help you win this war. We will get your daughters back."

"Do whatever you want," the king resigned. "Throw your lives away. I don't care."

"Thank you, your majesty," said Culvac, positioning himself next to Tristan.

"What are you doing, Culvac?" Tristan asked under his breath.

"Sir, I am repaying the debt for my men. We owe you."

Over his shoulder, Tristan said, "You owe me nothing."

"We feel differently, sir."

Tristan shared a glance with Ichiban, who nodded. He then turned his attention back to Culvac.

"Captain Culvac, ready our men."

"Sir?" Culvac asked.

"You heard me, captain. Now go."

"Yes, sir!" Culvac exclaimed, excited at his promotion.

"Now, if I could have your attention," the king called petulantly, his face twisted in almost sadistic delight. "Now, Tristan, for the last bit of your punishment. You shall receive ten lashes immediately in front of the castle so the entire city can witness your punishment. Afterward, you may spend your last night at home before being deployed."

"Yes, your majesty." A forced smile stretched across Tristan's face.

Everyone in the throne room exited. They followed Tristan and the guards who escorted him. When they reached the front of the castle, most of the town had already assembled. The king must have sent out a summons for a large audience.

Two poles stuck out of the ground. They were topped with shackles where Tristan's hands would be bound. A large, hooded man dressed in all black stood next to them. He carried a long black whip. The guards took Tristan down the steps, removed his chest plate and shirt, and strapped him to the poles.

With vindictive amusement, the king said, "This guardian has committed one of the most serious crimes in our nation; the beginning of his punishment will consist of ten lashes. Executioner, commence when you are ready."

The first lash came immediately and set Tristan's back on fire. He bit his lip to keep from crying out. He wouldn't give the king the satisfaction of his pain.

Chapter 13

To the Rescue

xhausted, Morgan pried open her tired eyes. She arose from an unfamiliar soft, white bed—her head cloudy. Coral walls and flooring surrounded her; she heard the faint sounds of falling water. Feeling a bit heavier than usual, she realized she still had her armor on. She climbed out of bed and put her feet on the cold floor. Fear slithered into Morgan's mind—how had she gotten to this place? She fought the urge to shout for help; she knew better than to alert her enemy. Her boots sat by the door. She put them on and stared at the door handle, hoping it wasn't locked. When she pulled, the door opened. Morgan slowly inched her head outside. The coral halls appeared vacant. She picked a direction and ran. She proceeded through room after room, her panic growing. She no longer cared about being discovered—escape was her only focus.

Morgan barged into a large, elegantly decorated room. A set of elaborate chairs stood in the middle—the throne room. Morgan's eye caught movement on the wall in the back of the throne room. The entire wall had been replaced by a wall of water held at bay by magic. In the water, a massive kraken fixed its eye on Morgan. The creature moved frantically, but its tentacles couldn't penetrate the wall of water.

"It won't come until it's released," a female voice snickered.

Startled, Morgan spun around and saw a hooded blond girl sitting on the throne behind her.

"Who are you? Where am I? How did I get here?"

"You are in Furreshda, and you can address me as goddess," the hooded woman said quietly but purposefully.

Morgan scanned the room frantically. There were no escape routes that didn't pass in front of this goddess.

"How the hell did I end up here?" Morgan asked, stalling for time.

The hooded woman shrugged and then slowly strutted, making her way to Morgan.

"Doesn't seem right, does it? It's really just due to events that are out of your control."

"Is Tristan okay?" Morgan asked. "He was with me when I was abducted."

"The half-elf? He is fine. His wellbeing, that is. But you know what's strange? Rayna and your guardians are here, too."

Morgan raised an eyebrow. "But why are we here? Where are they?" she asked, growing more infuriated at the woman's inability to give straight answers.

"I know. It's bizarre. Again, you were taken for reasons that a being such as yourself could not comprehend." The goddess rose from the throne, and Morgan reached for her missing sword. The hooded woman laughed. "It wouldn't help you in this situation anyway."

"I'm not stupid." Morgan summoned her courage. "Who are you? Why have you brought us here?"

"No, Morgan. I do not believe you are stupid. Come. Take a walk with me."

She stepped past Morgan, who followed warily. The woman directed their steps toward the wall of the throne room.

"Well, that was a short walk," Morgan said sarcastically.

Without pause, the hooded woman continued to walk. When she was about to come in contact with the wall, the castle separated brick-by-brick, clearing a path. Morgan's eyes opened wide; she struggled to comprehend how the world around her moved and bent with the hooded woman.

"Come." The goddess glanced over her shoulder to ensure Morgan followed.

Astonished, the princess watched the rooms around her separate. The furniture and paintings remained undisturbed while the rooms shifted. "What kind of machinery is this? I wouldn't think Furreshda would have such capabilities."

"They don't," said the goddess, pressing onward. "This is all me."

Morgan's gaze moved back to the mysterious young woman.

"That's right, princess, you're in deeper than you realize."

"Where is everyone?" Morgan asked, taking in all the empty rooms. "It seems like we are the only two people here, but you said my sister and the others are here, too."

They made it outside to the entrance of the castle. Morgan gazed in amazement at this city built of coral, gold, and emerald and surrounded by a wall of ocean. A towering statue of a serpent reared its head in the city's center. Morgan couldn't help but wonder how far below the surface they actually were. The goddess observed Morgan's wonder.

"They are actually two miles high," she answered as though reading Morgan's mind. "It's the perfect defense for a kingdom. If you try to swim, the creatures in the ocean will eat you. If you manage to build a vessel to dive under it, the pressure will crush you. There is a singular path from Airk that leads to the city for trade and supply purposes."

"What about the sky? There is a lot of open space above us."

"Look deeper into the water if you can. There are turret guns and an armada of airships that reside within the water. Any fleet would be ambushed and destroyed before it could reach the castle. These people are the masters of this ocean. To attack this place is suicide."

"You didn't answer my question." Morgan studied the mysterious figure. "Where is everyone?"

"They are where they need to be right now. I must tell you something, and I don't need other people to hear," the hooded woman paused. "It's something you won't believe."

Morgan's attention did not shift; she was desperate for answers.

"I am, indeed, a goddess, Morgan. I'm here for you and Rayna."

"You're right. I still don't believe you," Morgan said with a sarcastic chuckle.

The goddess snapped her fingers in the air. A wave of pure white fire passed by, leaving the ocean dry and the city in rubble. "I don't feel any need to prove anything to mortals. But it's the look on your faces that I love when you see how easily I can take away life." She snapped her fingers a second time. The wave of fiery light swept overhead and returned the land to its previous state.

"But even I have my limitations," the woman explained. She approached the stunned princess and ran her fingers through Morgan's hair. "That is why I require you and your sister. Your family is on a crusade to acquire Rephalas for me. I need Rephalas to end this miserable rule of Aeons, so I can take over."

"What do you mean you 'take over'?" Morgan jerked away. "None of this makes any sense."

The goddess waved her hand in the air. The constellations shone so brightly they could be seen during the day. She pointed to the Angel constellation. "Do you see that group of stars there? That's where we are now in the timeline. That's the Angel constellation where the Aeons reside. The one next to it is the Divider constellation. That is where my generals and I live. Rephalas is the sword that ends the rule of one set of gods and begins another's reign. There are twelve of these constellations. Think of it as a giant clock, except that the only thing that moves the hands of this timeless clock is Rephalas."

Morgan stared at the sky, trying to absorb all this information. "But that doesn't explain why you need my sister and me."

"It takes a royal family member to end the world, but the family member must also be a species of the current constellation. Therefore, it will take an Angel to end the world," the goddess explained, looking at Morgan's back. "I see you don't have wings, which is quite unfortunate. On the other hand, your sister does, and her sheer overwhelming power is more than enough evidence to convince me that she is the one to end your world and let me take over."

Morgan's face blanched; she searched the entryway for a weapon. The goddess laughed hysterically. "You do have nerve, princess. I'll give you that," said the goddess as she glanced over her shoulder. "Bring them!"

Morgan watched as guards escorted her father and sister. Rayna carried her sword, and Eadric bore Morgan's sword. The hooded woman approached the pair and stroked both weapons, bestowing upon them a black glow.

Morgan took a hesitant step forward and tried to reach out, but the pressure kept her hand away.

"Father? Rayna? Are you okay?" When neither responded, she asked the goddess, "What have you done to them?"

The goddess did not respond to her, either.

"What are you doing to our swords?" Morgan asked, her voice despondent.

"Do not fret, my little princess. I'm transferring some of your and Rayna's powers to your guardians in Sorriax. I'm giving them the power and tools they need to win this war."

"Go back to Sorriax," she directed, "and see to it that our little elf finds his way here."

Eadric gave a bow, and a black hole made of energy appeared behind him. He stepped into it and vanished.

≈

The guards woke Tristan in his empty house. They instructed him to don his armor in order to return to the castle. Tristan did as he was told, dressing slowly so as not to disturb the wounds on his back. He strapped the two swords to his armor gently and allowed the guards to escort him.

A red carpet extended from the throne room straight out of the castle. Families and friends of the soldiers lined the side of the carpet. The king and the royal family, minus Morgan and Rayna, watched the event with the remaining guardians from their thrones. The guards brought Tristan to stand between Lazarus and Zro. In front of them, Ichiban and five lines of soldiers stood. The king said nothing to send them off. He just glared at the small army with contempt. Tristan drew his hood over his head, drowning in uncertainty and fear. He raised his eyes and saw Caster in front of him. Caster nodded, reassuring him. Tristan could see his mother in the crowd, crying. His father, seemingly disappointed, stood next to the king. Ichiban glanced at the king and then at Tristan; they both nodded their heads. He then turned to the soldiers and barked, "Soldiers of the 112th Unit, march!" The soldiers marched in sequence out of the castle.

"Guardians! March!" Ichiban barked.

Tristan led Lazarus and Zro from the throne room. Tristan closed his eyes for a second, looked forward, and continued down the red carpet where the families had tossed roses on the floor. Some of the soldiers picked up a flower; others marched over them, leaving a swath of color in their wake. Tristan watched his soldiers bear his burden as they went down the long path in a seemingly endless march.

~

Hours had passed since Tristan and his small fleet had departed the Sorriaxian shores. Tristan stood by the deck rail on the flagship and stared off into the ocean. His mind raced with thoughts of Rayna, Morgan, his family, and his friends. Ichiban walked up to him and put his hand on Tristan's shoulder. Tristan glanced at Ichiban and back out to the sea. He didn't really care what Ichiban had to say.

"The first day is always the hardest," Ichiban explained. "Take some time for yourself, Tristan, but what is to come will be here sooner than you think. I have already given the other captains instructions about night watches and other issues we need to look out for. I will give everyone on the ship the same instructions, so when you are ready, come and get me. We will start the meeting."

Tristan continued to stare off into the clear blue water. Ichiban walked off.

Tristan observed his men. Some worked on the ship; others cleaned their weapons. Someone was singing. Who could sing at a time like this? Tristan walked through the crowds of his soldiers up to the helm, where Ichiban, Caster, Lazarus, Zro, and the other officers on the ship gathered. Ichiban stood in the center of the officers.

"Listen up! This is probably the first time most of you have been to the frontlines. There is no room for fear or hesitation. There will be weapons and creatures and even languages that you might never have encountered before. Always be on guard, even now. Every battle will be uphill. When we are resting…"

"Sir!" a soldier in the crow's nest shouted. "There's something strange in the waters on the starboard side!"

Tristan ran with the others to the side of the boat. A school of sharks swam next to the ship.

"Yes, the Furreshdians are watching us," Ichiban said. "They will soon know we are coming."

Tristan and Lazarus shared a glance, and then they stared back into the water.

≈

Two days had passed. Tristan stood watch on the ship with a few other soldiers. The sky was thick with the night air, the wind blew gently, and the waters were calm. Tristan sat on the deck with a small candle burning next to him. He had a quill in his hand, thinking about what to put in his letter. He had written two letters already and sent them back home with a courier riding a large falcon.

Tristan wanted to dive off the boat and swim home. But something strange happened… Rayna wasn't the first to come into his mind. In his head, he remembered the sound of rushing water and he and Morgan slipping into it. He remembered her laugh, her smile, and the feeling in his chest when she looked at him.

She flooded his thoughts to the point where he couldn't think of anything else. He wondered what could have happened. He became angry when his thoughts shifted to Rayna and Ethan. He tried focusing on the battles to come, but they seemed hopeless without Morgan's help. He did not know what else to do. Lazarus and Zro approached Tristan and sat next to him. Tristan could tell Zro had something on his mind. Tristan preemptively spoke. "Out with it, Zro."

Zro scratched his head in slight frustration. "So you're an Angel? I know it's been a few days since we have seen your wings, but we haven't really had the time to talk about it."

Tristan nodded. "That's fair. What did you want to ask?"

Lazarus interrupted as Zro was about to speak. "Why you? Is it because you and Rayna are connected? I mean, you don't even go to church."

Tristan almost heard a tinge of jealousy in his voice. "I don't know. There really isn't anything special about me. Come on. There must be tons of Angels out there."

Zro shook his head. "No, there aren't. They are truly rare. The church isn't even certain why or how certain people are chosen. Do you feel any different?"

Tristan shook his head. "Nope. Still the same old me."

Zro joked. "Now, you just have to learn how to fly properly."

Tristan smiled and ran his fingers through his hair. "Yeah, I've been kind of going off instinct. These things tend to have a mind of their own sometimes."

Lazarus spoke seriously. "Instinct will only take you so far, Tristan. Unless you have the skill to back it up."

"Courier approaching!" the shout from the crow's nest interrupted his thoughts.

Tristan stood up immediately and ran to the deck railing, excited and hopeful. The bird landed, and several soldiers rushed to him. Tristan tried his best to plow his way through the crowd but couldn't reach the front.

Over the clatter of voices, the courier said, "I'm sorry, guys. There's no mail to deliver, but if you have any letters, I will be happy to deliver them."

The soldiers quieted, and most of them walked away to grab the letters they had written. Tristan locked eyes with Zro and Lazarus while they headed toward him. They sat next to Tristan, looking just as dejected as he felt.

"Do you think our families have already forgotten about us?" one of the soldiers asked.

"How could they?" Zro said with a shake of his head. "It's only been a few days. That doesn't make any sense."

"Then, how could they be so busy they can't spare just a few seconds to let us know they miss us? Seriously, did we mean that little to them?" another soldier asked, staring at the floor. His soldiers seemed to take their situation harder than Tristan initially thought.

"They do care," argued Zro. "It's not like we have vanished from existence—it was all just bad timing. And it's only been two days."

Lazarus tried reeling them in. "Zro is correct. It has only been a few days. They are probably instructed not to communicate with us just in case the enemy gets ahold of the courier and our position, and what we are up to becomes compromised. Do not fret any longer; we have a job to do. Now return to your posts." The remaining soldiers scattered back to their positions on the ship.

Tristan stared out at the dark horizon. "Well, whatever it is, they have to deal with this just like we do. The best way to do that is to keep busy and keep our minds occupied. We'll arrive at Airk tomorrow. Send one last letter because I don't think we'll be able to write again for a while..." Tristan cut himself off before adding, "if we live through it."

The others seemed to understand what Tristan didn't say. With that sobering thought, they wrote their goodbyes.

≈

Morgan sat alone on a bench on the balcony, staring at the sky. She thought about her friends at sea and her friends running the king's errands. A magnificent flagship with the Corriander symbols on the side appeared in the distance, escorted by half a dozen other ships. *What is Corriander doing here?* Morgan thought.

Determined to investigate, she left her room and headed out of the castle. She entered the docking area and saw dozens of soldiers march past her, headed into town. Behind them walked Rayna with her arms around Ethan like he would float away if she didn't hold onto him tight enough.

"Rayna! Hello!" Morgan yelled, catching up to her sister. "Why is Ethan here? Is he here to rescue us?"

Rayna walked by without acknowledging her. Morgan stared after her sister in disbelief as the couple rounded a corner. Morgan heard the sound of pottery shattering and turned to witness her sister berating a man.

"What the hell do you think you're doing, clumsy fool?" yelled Rayna.

"Princess, I-I apologize," the man pleaded. "I don't know what has gotten into me. Please forgive…" The man's words devolved into a gasp. Morgan watched energy from Rayna's hand pin the man against the stone wall. A bit of red light glinted from her sister's eyes.

"Rayna, release him!" When there was no response except for the twisted smile on her face, Morgan shouted, "Rayna, I will not say it again. Let him go!"

The soldier looked at Morgan, barely able to speak. "Your… highness…please!" His hands scrambled uselessly around his neck.

Morgan stepped toward Rayna, and a shock sparked down her arm. It started to burn. Ignoring the pain, Morgan gathered what power she could without her weapon and formed the energy in her hands. Ethan and Rayna stared at Morgan. Rayna's lips formed a sinister smirk.

"You're not going to attack me, are you, sister?" asked Rayna in a voice that was not her own.

Morgan looked from her sister to the fading soldier. She threw her hands forward, unleashing a wave of energy that blasted Rayna into a wall. Small cracks formed behind Rayna's body.

Rayna got up and unsheathed her sword. "Ah, too bad, sister. You don't have your sword. It looks like you're going to get hurt."

Morgan retreated until she hit the stone wall. "Are you going to kill me?"

"Maybe," Rayna said with a flippant tone and shrugged. "We'll see."

A group of Furreshdian soldiers ran around the corner, aiming rifles at Rayna. "Princess Rayna! Prince Ethan! Stow your weapons and step away from Princess Morgan!"

"How dare you shout orders at me! You will pay with your lives for this treachery!" Rayna said through clenched teeth. She raised her hand toward the soldiers.

"Enough, Rayna!" the Queen of Furreshda yelled. All eyes turned to the queen and her four elaborately dressed soldiers.

"Yes, ma'am," said Rayna, suddenly docile. She dropped her hands to her sides and turned to Morgan before saying, "See you around, sister."

Rayna and Ethan joined the queen, and they departed for the castle.

One of the soldiers approached Morgan and asked, "Are you alright, princess?"

"Yes, I'm fine," she said through a long sigh of relief. "Thank you for helping."

"Anytime, princess. You are a prisoner here, but it doesn't mean we shouldn't keep you safe. If you ever need us, call, and we will come to your aid." He discreetly handed her a small radio.

Soldiers surrounded Morgan and ushered her back into the castle. When the door to her room shut behind her, Morgan leaned against it, trying to process what had just happened. She had never felt like she needed guards against her own family before. She breathed heavily, trying to suppress her tears, but it was inevitable. She covered her eyes, sank to the floor, and sobbed. She curled into a ball and cried herself to sleep.

When she awoke, the sun had already risen to the top of the sky. She sat up and rolled onto a few pieces of paper that hadn't been there last night. She grabbed the three sheets of paper. Her eyes widened upon realizing what they were. She read the two letters from Lazarus and Zro first. But when she reached for Tristan's letter, a knock sounded at her door. It opened, and a maiden walked in.

"The queen was worried when you didn't show up for breakfast and asked me to check on you."

"Oh, I'm late!" Morgan quickly stood and changed into a fresh dress. When she was ready, Morgan put the last letter into her pocket and headed to the throne room. It was empty. She ran to the dock next to the castle and saw guardians and soldiers escorting her family onto the queen's ship. Morgan hustled to join them, only slowing when she reached the Queen of Furreshda.

"You're late." The queen turned to face Morgan. "Though you are a prisoner of my kingdom, I still expect the manners of a princess from you."

"Forgive me, your majesty." Morgan bowed.

"We don't want to look bad to those in Corriander, do we?" the queen asked without waiting for a response. "Good. Now go to my dressing room. You look terrible."

Morgan didn't respond. Over the past days in captivity, she'd grown used to such treatment.

"Bianca, Charity," the queen called. "Take your princess to my dressing room and make her presentable for the ball."

Both guardians bowed and replied, "Yes, your majesty."

The guardians took Morgan's hands and escorted her to the ship and into the king and queen's dressing room. Morgan sat on a stool in front of a mirror so her friends could get her ready for the ball.

Trying to bolster their spirits, Morgan whispered, "I got letters from the boys, somehow."

The guardians made sounds of delight.

"I overheard King Eadric say he had gotten a batch of letters. I'm surprised he delivered them. How are they?" Bianca asked excitedly.

"He probably delivered them to taunt us. I don't understand why he's allowing us to remain captive in Furreshda." She paused before asking, "Can we read them?"

"I only brought Tristan's letter. I haven't read it yet." She pulled the crumpled letter from her pocket.

"Well, let's hear what he wrote," Bianca cheered.

Morgan smiled and read:

> Dear Morgan,
>
> I had to write this letter as soon as the courier arrived so you can get it tomorrow.
>
> Do you want to go sailing with me? That would be fun when I get back. If you do want to go, you have to do something for me. Don't run away. You're safe there. Our friends will never let anything happen to you.
>
> Unfortunately, I must make this letter a short one. We arrive in Airk tomorrow night. By the time you get this letter, it will be evening. Ichiban said we will have to fight for every inch to get near Furreshda. I'm so scared, Morgan, but I can't tell the others that. The men look to me for courage and guidance. They expect me to lead them to victory against impossible odds. I just don't know what to do.
>
> I need you and your strength, Morgan, more than I ever have, and we need our friends beside us. In every battle, I was always either defending you or the soldiers. I have never actually felt like I was invading another kingdom. I'm probably a coward for thinking this way. Please don't think any less of me. You, Rayna, and our friends are always on my mind and in my heart.
>
> > Love,
> > Tristan
>
> P.S.: This may be the last letter I can write safely. Do not write unless you hear from us first.

Morgan stopped reading.

Bianca asked, "What else does it say?"

"Nothing," she lied cheerily. She couldn't bring herself to read the next few sentences aloud:

> Morgan, you're always on my mind. You're the one who keeps me going. My mind often leads me to the day you showed me ocean berries. I could stay in that moment forever. I often wonder what could have been if we remained in that moment for just a bit longer. Yet these thoughts and the confession of your feelings confuse my heart. I'm afraid of the consequences of our world's law if we continue down this path.

When the dressing room door opened, the three girls saw Rayna standing there. Rayna gave a friendly smile. "Hey, are you working on Morgan's hair? Can I help?"

None of them replied. Rayna, a little confused at their silence, saw the letter with Tristan's signature in her sister's hands. "Hey, is that a letter from Tristan? Is it for me?" She walked toward Morgan.

The guardians put their hands on the hilts of their swords. Rayna froze.

"What's gotten into you guys? Why are you so cold?" she asked. "If that letter is from Tristan, then it must be for me. I've been waiting for him to write. He's my guardian, after all."

It was too much for Morgan. She stood, clenching her fists. "What the hell? Why are you acting so nice all of a sudden?"

"What do you mean?" Confusion raked Rayna's face. "I've been waiting for Tristan to answer my letters. That's his signature, so it must be for me. Why else would he write?" Rayna tried to grab the letter, but Morgan ripped her hands away quickly.

"What do you mean answer your letters?" Morgan's ire rose with her question. "You haven't written to him. I've asked you repeatedly to do so, but you just walk off and ignore my pleas. I'm the only one who has written Tristan in the few days he's been gone. In his return letters, he says he's saddened he hasn't received anything from you. You're a bitch, Rayna. Don't you ever lie about something like that. He still loves you, and you treat him like garbage when your so-called fiancé is around. Now, he is out there paying for your mistakes. I want to be out there to help him through his ordeal, and there you are out doing your own thing like nothing ever happened!" Morgan's chest heaved. She glowered at Rayna. "Leave, Rayna."

Rayna acted like she had something to say in her defense, but her mouth closed, and her eyes became watery. "May I please see the letter?" she asked quietly.

Morgan stared at her; fury raged in her eyes. "No, Rayna, you may not."

Tears spilled over Rayna's cheeks as she ran out of the room.

Chapter 14

From All Sides

vening had come, and Tristan's small fleet docked a mile outside of Airk. The soldiers exited the ships with the guardians, and Ichiban led them down a dark and muddy dirt road.

Anxiety threatened to overcome Tristan. His eyes continued to surveil the surrounding area for movement. Lazarus, however, seemed entirely at ease.

"So, what was the last thing you wrote to Morgan, Tristan?" he asked.

Tristan, Lazarus, and Zro agreed to each write Morgan a letter, thinking it would be nice for her to come home to. In case they didn't survive, they knew the letters would serve as their goodbyes. Tristan hesitated for a moment, unsure if he should divulge his confused feelings for Morgan right then.

"I don't think this is the time or place…"

"Of course, it is," Lazarus interrupted. "We are on the verge of battle—might as well. I basically told her goodbye. That I might not be coming back, that she was always like a big sister to me, and that I love her."

"Laz, those are some pretty heavy words," Tristan teased.

Lazarus took a deep breath. "She is a good friend. I always considered her family, given that I was around her so much. So what did you say to her?"

"The usual stuff, you know. I care about her, but I love Rayna."

Tristan hesitated a few beats before adding, "She says she wants to go sailing with me."

"Oh, and what made her say that?" Lazarus asked with a surprised glance.

A crimson flush crept across Tristan's face. He took the earpiece out of his ear, signaling Lazarus to do the same. "In my last letter, I told her how beautiful and serene the ocean is at night, and she said she wanted to go sailing."

"You sure that's it?" He gave Tristan a cocky smile.

"Of course, it is." Tristan broke eye contact.

"It's none of my business, but I think getting involved with a princess is what got us here in the first place. Just don't go making the same mistake twice."

"That's what I said." Caster's voice blurted through their earpieces. Tristan turned around to look at Caster. "That's right; my ears do more than just frame my face. Now, shut up, or you'll give away our position!"

"Look, it's not like that. I promise," Tristan said. His tone grew more serious. He didn't think Lazarus believed him.

"If you say so, my friend, but just remember that you aren't the only one paying for your mistake. If you hurt Morgan, I will break your legs."

"Shut up, you two, and stay focused," growled Ichiban.

As the army slogged its way through the mud, silence engulfed the world and put all the soldiers on edge. The only sounds were the scouts occasionally checking in with Ichiban through their radios. With no sign of enemy forces, the way was long and unnerving.

Finally, Ichiban addressed the men. "Advance slowly and keep low. We are almost there. Stay sharp!"

Tristan pulled slightly ahead of the other soldiers to get an unobstructed view of their path. They rounded a wall of trees and saw a trench where the scouts were located. Their vantage point allowed them to observe the town bordering the sea.

Ichiban whispered into his radio, "We're right behind you."

"Okay, sir. I'm going to advance a little," the scout said. He climbed to his feet and walked to the top of the hill.

Ichiban, in a panic, whispered after him, "Get down!"

Before the scout could drop for cover, dozens of turret guns from the village fired. Bullets shot through the scout for what seemed an eternity. From his location on the ground, Tristan watched the body roll down the hill. Dozens of Tristan's camouflaged soldiers appeared and climbed to the top of the hill to return fire.

Ichiban and Caster ran to the trench and yelled, "Advance and open fire!"

Immediately, Tristan rose to a crouch and advanced with the others. While his soldiers took cover next to him, Tristan crawled to the top for a better vantage point. The turret guns fired from the buildings in the village. Among the buildings, numerous enemy soldiers rallied and charged the long trench.

The water in the surrounding sea rippled violently. Three ships, each encrusted with gold and coral, discharged from its depths and quickly rose into the sky. Crusted in barnacles and algae, the ships appeared to have been underwater for quite some time. The ship's artillery cannons roared as they blanketed the trench with shells. Tristan saw the charging soldiers spread their lines even thinner to flank the Sorriaxian soldiers.

Tristan touched his earpiece and commanded, "Zro, take a small squadron of snipers and fall back to a spot where you can quickly take out the turrets and maybe put some fire on those ships!"

"I'm on it!" Zro said. He signaled half a dozen soldiers, left the trench, and fell back.

Tristan heard Caster shout in his earpiece, "We need to spread our lines, so we don't get out-flanked!"

"We hear you, Caster. We won't let them flank us! Laz, take half the men and spread them out down the trench. I'll take the other half and head up the other way!"

"Got it," Lazarus replied and then issued his own command. "Ichiban, tell your troops to cover us!"

Tristan ran, and men joined in behind him. Several of them dropped from gunfire as the trench did not provide much cover when they stood. Tristan created as large a barrier as he could to protect the surrounding soldiers. He yelled, "Spread the line thinner. We can't let them get around us!"

Tristan saw the enemy doing the exact same thing he had strategized. High winds picked up around Tristan; he saw one of the Furreshdian ships lower and hover in front of him.

"Rockets to the west. Fire!" Ichiban barked.

A dozen rockets, headed for the ship, flew from Ichiban's position. They exploded on impact, damaging the side of the vessel slightly. Artillery cannons rose, aimed at Ichiban.

"Keep spreading the lines!" Tristan yelled to his soldiers. In desperation, he cried out, "Come on, Angel wings. Where are you?"

It worked. His dirty white wings appeared once again. Tristan flew into the sky, controlling his wings with some difficulty. He unsheathed both of his swords. Bullets shot at him while he flew, only to hit his barrier. Tristan put his newfound power into his blade and swung it, unleashing a massive black wave of energy that split the ship in two upon impact.

Tristan stared at his weapons for a moment, amazed at what he was now capable of with just one swing of his sword. Beneath him, enemy soldiers swarmed out of the buildings—it was an ambush. He directed his power into the sword in his right hand until it emitted a bright black light. He stuck his sword into the ground on the enemy's side. The energy exploded and sent a shock wave that tore away at the ground and buildings.

The turrets ceased firing one by one as the snipers did their job. Zro started to glow with energy. He fired two rounds. The remaining ships in the sky exploded and showered the ground with their fiery debris.

Lazarus stood on the top of the trench, raised his sword, and yelled, "Forward!"

The soldiers charged out of the trench and headed toward the city. Tristan darted out of the sky and glided through the enemy soldiers. His sword encountered the first person who appeared in front of him. Tristan quickly approached the man and rammed his sword into the man's back. Gliding through the enemy soldiers, he cut them down one after the other.

"Culvac, guardians, meet Caster and me at the dock," Ichiban's voice crackled through Tristan's earpiece. "All soldiers, clear out the city."

Tristan retrieved his sword and flew toward the dock. Beneath him, he saw more rabbits scurrying away from the dock and head into the woods. Tristan stuck his feet out to land, but the force of his wings sent him tumbling forward past his group and into the side of a fish stand.

He heard a few of them laugh. Caster shouted, "I'm surprised you stayed in the air that long. Gotta stick those landings."

Tristan, slightly dazed, yelled back, "Shut up, Cas!" When he heard no retort, Tristan looked up. The others stared off into the ocean that stood between them and the islands. A bright glow emanated from the island's beach.

"What's over there?" Lazarus asked.

Ichiban took a deep breath before explaining. "Those are elemental magic users, mostly magic that has to do with nature. They can summon creatures out of the elements to aid them. Supposedly, if enough of them sacrifice their lives, they can summon what some people may say is one of the many Aeons they worship."

"Don't count on the gods to come down and help out these elementals," Caster added. "Tread lightly. Their magic should not be underestimated."

"I hope it doesn't come to that, but our last contact from this line said the elementals all remained neutral," Ichiban continued. "By the looks of things, that may have changed. There aren't many, but it seems that the real battle is still in front of us."

One of the camouflaged soldiers approached Ichiban. They saluted each other. "Greetings. I am Lieutenant Codwal. My men and I have orders to hold this line."

"I am General Ichiban. May I introduce Guardians Tristan, Lazarus, and Zro and Captains Culvac and Caster. Why were you lying in the ditch, lieutenant?"

"Observing the enemy. Just a few days ago, that position had never been fortified with this many soldiers and guns. We wondered if we had been discovered, and they were waiting for us to make a move. Then, you showed up," he explained. "It's like they knew you were coming."

"Yes. That does seem odd, but we have no time to worry about that now." Ichiban tried to hide his concern. "We have one large body of water to cross. From the looks of it, we will not be alone in the sea." All around the water's surface, fins, humps, and tails emerged, disturbing the surface's peace.

"There are only three ferries," Tristan pointed out. "We can't fit all of the soldiers into one trip."

"No, we can't," Ichiban said in agreement. "Maybe two hundred per boat. The first wave will be very vulnerable. The three guardians and I will be the first to try to hold off the elemental forces. Culvac and Caster, gather our men. We will head for the islands immediately."

Culvac saluted, and Caster nodded in agreement.

Soldiers boarded the creaky boats and mounted the usable turret guns. Sharks swam around the boats, waiting to capitalize on someone's carelessness. Each guardian boarded a different boat. Ichiban boarded the center boat while Culvac and Caster remained behind. The ships set sail.

Ichiban barked over his earpiece to everyone. "Except for the helmsmen, I want every person to point a gun forward. This will not be an easy ride to the other side!"

The soldiers prepared for the fight. Tristan, Zro, and Lazarus had their barriers ready to protect the ships. Sharks lunged at the vessels in an attempt to eat whoever was closest to the edge. In the distance, the glow on the islands drastically became more intense. A large, faint symbol was visible from the sea floor for a brief moment, and then everything fell silent. The sharks stopped attacking. The cannons stopped firing. The water in the distance in front of them rose as if something substantial were emerging. Tristan could see four gigantic bright orbs rising in the water. When they hit the surface, the water erupted and caused a tidal wave that towered above the ships.

"Guardians, raise your barriers!" Ichiban yelled.

When the water hit, it reflected off the barriers, falling back into the ocean. When the water settled, Tristan heard sounds that mimicked a whale's song. The noise, echoing across miles, shattered the windows on the boats. Horrified, Tristan realized that the orbs of light he had seen in the water were the glowing yellow eyes of a gigantic sea serpent. The enormity of the dark green, scaled creature dwarfed their boats. The creature's head and mouth were large enough to swallow all three boats at one time. A dozen tentacles danced around the water's surface. The serpent roared briefly but loudly. It was enough to make everyone cover their ears and cause some buildings on shore to collapse.

Tristan heard Culvac's quivering voice over the radio. "Sir, what do you want us to do?"

"We're right behind you," Caster reassured them.

Ichiban, shaken by the sight of the beast, hesitated to answer. "Hang back and find cover, Culvac. This isn't going to be pretty."

The guardians unsheathed their weapons; the soldiers raised their rifles. The beast roared once more into the sky, forcing the men to cover their ears again. The water's surface started to shift and bubble. A hydra head slowly emerged from the water. And another. And another. They multiplied as they emerged. One of the creatures lunged at Tristan's boat, grabbing a soldier and dragging him to the depths. The attacks soon came from all sides, signaling the soldiers to open fire on the oncoming serpents.

"Sir! Hydras all around you!" Culvac reported.

"Don't you think I know that!" Ichiban roared. "Fire on the large hydra. We need to buy some time to clear out these beasts. Caster, position the snipers to keep these hydras at bay!"

"Yes, sir!" Culvac shouted. "All troops, take aim!"

"You heard the general! Snipers, fire at will!" ordered Caster.

Soon, rockets and rifle rounds shot at the great beast.

"Remember, these are hydras," Ichiban yowled into his radio. "No head slicing! That goes especially for the guardians!"

The great beast roared again, and a large white beam shot at Lazarus' ship. He immediately created a barrier to protect the ship. The beam cracked his shield, forcing Lazarus to one knee, but he could still maintain his defense. The beast closed its mouth and observed the ships along with the powerful guardians they possessed. In the guardians' and soldiers' heads, a female voice spoke.

"I'm Hyperion. I am the Aeon of the Oceans, who watches over the entrance of Furreshda. Turn back now!"

"There's only one god I listen to, and she's not you!" yelled Zro. Zro raised his rifle and filled it with energy. Three rounds exploded on Hyperion's chest. The beast roared, signaling the hydras to continue their onslaught.

"Good job, asshole," Tristan yelled at him. "You pissed her off!"

A hydra came right for Tristan. Instinctively, he swung his blade, cutting through the beast's neck. Its lifeless head fell onto the deck, allowing gravity to sink the body. Momentarily, bubbles covered the surface, and three hydra heads reemerged.

Ichiban grabbed Tristan by the back of his armor and yelled, "What did I say? No head slicing!"

One of the heads went straight for Ichiban. The wolf smacked the beast's head aside and climbed across its neck to its body. He pulled out a small metal rod and pushed a button that extended into a spear. He drove the spear into the beast's chest. He extracted the rod after piercing the beast's heart. The heads came eye-to-eye with Ichiban. He lifted the spear, growled ferociously, and showed the beast its own heart. The hydra's heads slowly sank into the water. Ichiban raised his spear into the air and roared in triumph. Ichiban hopped off the corpse and back onto the boat. "That's how you do it, boy!"

Tristan smirked at his mentor and refocused his attention on the raging beasts surrounding them.

Hyperion screeched and summoned her power. Water cyclones rose around it, forcing surges of water to spin around them. Despite the boat's engines pulling them away, the force of the water drew them in closer. Hyperion's tentacles swarmed around the ships and stripped a few more soldiers from them.

Ichiban shouted, "Cut down the tentacles, or they'll capsize us!"

The men armed themselves with spears and axes, waiting for the next attack. Hyperion screeched and sent another cyclone toward Tristan's boat. Its energy swallowed everything in its path.

Before the cyclone's energy could consume Tristan, he summoned his Angel wings and took to the sky carefully. He started depositing all his power into his swords. Doing so, he lost what focus he had with his wings, and they vanished. Tristan fell, the fluttery feeling in his stomach hit him, and he lost some of the power focused into his swords. Feeling the force of the cyclone drawing near, Tristan regained his focus during the fall and refastened his grip on his swords. He swung both blades downward, unleashing a black wave and splitting the cyclone through the middle. The water spilled back into the sea. Tristan fell faster and faster toward the beast-infested waters. He emptied his mind of his swords and focused on his wings. Please come out; please come out! The screeches of the hydras below grew louder. "Screw it!" He shot his sword into his ship's cabin. He hit the button on his hilt to retract the blade and pull him to the ship.

A tentacle wrapped around Tristan's leg and dragged him below the water's surface, ripping the blade out of the side of the ship. He was pulled in and out of mouths while countless sea creatures snapped at him, narrowly missing each time. Behind him, Tristan saw numerous beasts in hot pursuit. Below him, legions of hydras swam for the surface. Then, Tristan located Hyperion. The magnificent beast's body touched the ocean's floor and coiled around. Its tail of tentacles reached for the surface. Running out of air, Tristan cut his way through the tentacle holding him. When the blade sliced through the scales, he heard Hyperion's garbled screech. The intensity of its grip waned, and Tristan slipped free.

Knowing the other beasts followed right behind him, Tristan swam as fast as possible. Other creatures snapped at his feet, barely missing. The water's surface glimmered above him. He desperately needed the oxygen that was only feet above him. His hand breached the surface and then his head. He gasped, sucking in all the air he could. When he started sinking again, a hand grabbed his.

"I've got you. Let's go!" a familiar voice said. "Keep moving, and don't let go of me, Tristan! The *Water Walk Spell* won't work if we stop."

Tristan raised his head to see Caster standing on the water. He managed to get his feet underneath himself in time to gain his bearings as they immediately ran toward the shore.

"What the hell is this, Cas?" Tristan yelled, trying to keep pace with Caster, who pulled him across the water's surface.

"*Water Walk*. It's exactly what it sounds like. Do not stop!"

Mouths of various sea creatures burst from the water's surface behind them, barely missing them.

"Don't look back. Just run!" shouted Caster.

Together, they sprinted as fast as they could. An enormous shark emerged in front of them. Unthinkably, they ran into the mouth of the shark. Caster's grip tightened, and cold splinters surged through Tristan for a fraction of a moment. Immediately, they reappeared on the water's surface. The smell of rotten fish clung to them.

"Trust my *Shadow Step Spell* and keep running!" Caster shouted.

They passed through multiple sets of mouths but remained unharmed. The water shifted violently, forcing the two guardians to divert their attention. Hyperion descended from above them, roaring her loudest yet. Her calls resonated painfully in Tristan's ears. Through his earpiece, the others yelled at them to run faster. The Aeon's damp breath stuck to his back.

"Run, you sons of bitches! Run!" Lazarus screamed.

Ahead, the soldiers on the shore frantically signaled for them to keep moving. Hyperion's mouth began to close around Tristan and Caster. Lazarus shot a yellow beam at Hyperion while Zro simultaneously fired multiple shots that hit the Aeon, blasting her back into the water.

A massive wave hurled Tristan and Caster onto shore. Breathless, they gasped for air and spat up sea water.

"You okay?" Caster asked through wheezes.

"Yes, thanks to you," Tristan replied. He stood up and shook off the water.

"Tristan, are you hurt?" Ichiban called through Tristan's earpiece.

"I'll live." He coughed up water. "Listen, you have a legion of hydras right beneath you."

"I see that, genius. Fly me to Hyperion. I'll attack it at point-blank range," Ichiban replied.

Still panting, Tristan asked, "Are you sure?"

"Yes!" Ichiban yelled. "Move your ass! I'm not sure how long the men can last."

Tristan stretched his damp wings and hastily flew to Ichiban's ship. Before Tristan could launch them both from the deck, Ichiban reached out and ripped one of the turret guns from the ship's railings.

"Ichiban, you're heavy!" Tristan groaned.

Ichiban snorted. Tristan banked around the side of Hyperion's face and dropped Ichiban on top of her neck. Ichiban hacked away at the great beast's scales and cut a large hole in her neck. Hyperion shook her head, trying to topple Ichiban. The wolf jammed the turret gun into the wound he created and braced himself. Ichiban pulled the trigger, and the gun ripped into Hyperion's neck. The beast's agonized roars echoed through the guardians' heads.

Tentacles twisted around Ichiban. Zro fired energy-filled rounds and blasted the tentacles apart. Hyperion's screeching amplified while Ichiban's turret gun pierced deeper into the Aeon. Lazarus fired three green balls of energy into the serpent's chest. Lazarus then filled his sword with energy and swung the blade. An unleashed massive wave of energy flew upward, hitting Hyperion and throwing her back into the ocean. Ichiban released his hold and fell toward the beast-infested water. Tristan swooped down to catch Ichiban before he was submerged in the raging waters. Tristan flew back to the ship, dropped Ichiban on the deck, and promptly crashed to his knees in exhaustion. His wings folded back into his body.

"Sir, is it over?" Zro asked through the radio.

"I'm not sure," he panted. "Don't do anything unless I say so. Keep your weapons ready."

The waters calmed, and the hydras vanished. The clouds above moved away to reveal a full moon. Ichiban growled, sensing the coming danger. A sphere of water containing Hyperion emerged and hovered in the sky. Tristan gawped at the beast and wondered what the serpent had in store for them now. Hyperion screeched. Several walls of water arose one after another from the ocean and headed for the three boats. Mustering his remaining strength, Tristan managed to reform his Angel wings and took to the sky.

"Tristan," Lazarus called through his earpiece, "get me to Hyperion."

"What do I look like, a carriage driver?" Tristan complained. He swooped down and grabbed Lazarus anyway. "I can't take you all the way up. We need to stop those waves. You're going to have to jump!"

Tristan stopped and put his hands under Lazarus' feet; Tristan used his magic and beckoned a whirlwind. He shouted. *"Turbite!"* The funnel of air shot Lazarus up to Hyperion.

Tristan unsheathed both his weapons, expanded his barrier, and dug deeper into his powers. He couldn't worry about his wings failing him now. He had to save his army. His shield swirled in gold and black and spiraled into a larger sphere with every second. It tore away at the first wall of water and then the second. The waves continued to pummel Tristan's barrier. He winced. "Laz, hurry. I can't keep this up much longer!"

The waves of energy Tristan emitted started to rock the surrounding body of water. Lazarus glided through the air and darted through the sphere of water. He created a barrier around himself so he could breathe and raced to Hyperion's body. When Lazarus reached her head, he filled his sword with energy. Then, he leaped off and floated in front of the beast. He swung his sword once, hit the serpent, and knocked her head to the side. He swung again, knocking it to the other side. Hyperion shrieked in agony.

"Hurry, Laz!" Tristan wailed. He was in pain, and his control was slipping.

Lazarus used his barrier to glide toward Hyperion, repeatedly thrashing his energy-filled blade. When the serpent fell to the bottom of the sphere, Lazarus lifted his blade and put everything he had left into his sword. Lazarus descended to Hyperion. He swung his sword, forcing her out of the sphere of water and down toward the sea. As the sphere disintegrated, Lazarus' sword slipped from his hand. He shot downward using his whirlwind. He caught his blade and aimed for the serpent. Hyperion hit the ocean, creating one last tidal wave that cleared out the water all the way to the floor.

Tristan watched, horrified that he could not offer any defense against the massive wave. He heard Zro's rifle fire. The explosions did nothing to slow the wave. When the wave approached, Tristan bellowed harder than he ever had in his life. Bolstering his barrier, he extended more energy than his body could handle. The wave hit Tristan's barrier, causing a massive explosion of water.

Lazarus, glowing like a falling star, plummeted to Hyperion. The serpent stretched out to consume Lazarus; Lazarus swung his blade. The sword and its energy sliced through Hyperion, splitting her in two all the way to the ocean's floor. Tristan watched Lazarus reach the ground with his blade triumphantly in hand as the serpent and water collapsed around him. Then, the massive tidal wave consumed him, too.

Chapter 15

The Ceremony

Morgan sat in her room, waiting for Rayna's new guardian ceremony and wedding. There was a knock at the door. When Morgan invited the guest to enter, she was surprised to see Ry and Mira enter, escorted by Furreshdian guards.

"We are here to escort you, my lady," Ry said sarcastically with an exaggerated bow.

"I'm glad it's you two," Morgan said as they exited her room.

"Always a pleasure, princess," Mira said happily.

Morgan asked, "Where are Bianca and Charity?"

"They're meeting us in the ballroom," Ry said through a stifled yawn.

"Tired?" jeered Morgan.

"Yeah. Don't get much sleep in a dungeon," Ry complained, rubbing his face with exhaustion. "But I do find it odd that they let us wander around freely like this during the day."

Mira chimed in, "Yeah, we've only slept a few hours over the last couple of days."

"They have nothing to fear from us. There's nowhere to run even if we could escape," Morgan said.

"It makes sense," Mira answered. "But I still don't understand why our king hasn't done anything to get us out of here. He's here, too. Is he conducting peace talks with Furreshda?"

"That does seem a little odd." Morgan paused a moment to think. "Maybe he's working for a bigger plan. He and Rayna haven't been the same since we arrived. If we were kidnapped, then why is my father here?"

"A little method to his madness, huh?" Ry asked a little sarcastically. "I don't know. Lately, I have trouble trusting your father's judgment. I know he is the king and all, but his orders have become unsound."

"I know." Morgan sighed.

When they reached the ballroom, the doors opened, and crowds of people turned to face Morgan and the two guardians. Before them, she saw Corriander's royal family standing alongside hers and the royal family from Furreshda. With Morgan's arrival, the only two people missing were Rayna and Ethan. Morgan walked down the red carpet to take her place next to her mother, Queen Christina. Ry and Mira stood behind Morgan and the queen next to Charity, Bianca, and the rest of the guardians. The door through which Morgan had entered soon opened again. Rayna stepped into the ballroom. She wore an elaborate dress and carried flowers in one hand and Ethan's staff in the other. Rayna reached her father and stood in front of both kings. She bowed her head.

"Will the new guardian for my daughter, please enter," King Eadric asked with a smile.

The door opened a third time. Ethan strode in, wearing black and red guardian-like armor. Fully suited and sans helmet, he approached Rayna and knelt before Eadric and his own father.

"You may rise to face my daughter," King Eadric proclaimed. "The wedding ceremony will now commence. If there are any objections, let them be known now."

Ethan stood and faced Rayna. Attendants took Ethan's helmet and Rayna's bouquet. Morgan's heart sank as she studied the delight on her sister's face.

"I object," Morgan interjected. "I thought this was a ceremony for guardianship. How can someone outside of Sorriax be a guardian? He isn't properly trained to be a guardian! No one said Rayna was getting a new guardian."

"It is final." King Eadric glowered at Morgan. "Their wedding vows will be used to complement their guardian vows. Anyone can be a guardian. Only my approval is required to say who can and cannot be a guardian. Ethan doesn't need training; he is of royal blood. His power is adequate to protect my daughter."

Morgan raised her voice. "But what about…"

"Not another word, Morgan, or I will have you escorted out."

Morgan kept her mouth shut but glared at her father and sister in silent protest. The king took a deep breath.

"Now," he continued, "without further interruptions, do you, Ethan, take Rayna to bind your life to hers? To rule this land and its people? To take your place among my fathers before me?"

"I do," responded Ethan as he smiled at Rayna. He slipped a ring on her finger.

King Eadric's mood lightened as he asked, "Now, do you, Rayna, take Ethan to bind your life to his? To rule this land and its people? To take your place among your mothers before you?"

Rayna smiled back. "I do." She slipped the ring on Ethan's finger.

The king announced, "With the Aeons as your witnesses, and by my power, you two are now pronounced husband and wife. Rayna, present the weapon with which Ethan will protect you."

Proudly, Rayna gave him the staff.

"Ethan, you may kiss the bride."

When Ethan leaned in and kissed Rayna, the crowd applauded. Morgan stood silent and still. "Get me out of here," she mouthed to Ry.

Morgan looked past Ry and saw the hooded goddess in the back of the room, playfully biting her fingernail. She waved at Morgan. Ry moved to regain Morgan's attention.

"Don't you think your father will…" he whispered.

"Please, Ry?" Morgan interrupted. A single tear streamed down her face.

Ry saw the anguish in Morgan's eyes and nodded his acquiescence. He signaled to the other guardians and then took Morgan's hand. Together, they walked out of the throne room with Mira,

Bianca, and Charity behind them. Morgan searched once again for the goddess, but she had vanished.

"Hey, wait!" a voice called out.

They stopped in the empty hallway to see Rayna rushing toward them.

"Hey, why did you leave?" she asked, smiling radiantly at the group.

"What do you mean?" Morgan asked, annoyed by her sister's ignorance. "Can't you see what you are doing? What about Tristan?"

"What do you mean?" Rayna asked, her light-hearted mood gone.

"Tristan, Rayna! You remember him, don't you?" Morgan yelled. She couldn't rein in her harsh tone. "The boy you claimed to care about so much that you begged me not to say a word? He's fighting for his life—for your life—as we speak. I know this is an arranged marriage, but you're not putting up a fight at all!" As much as it pained Morgan to convince her sister to reconsider what she was doing to Tristan, she didn't want Tristan out on the frontlines fighting for a reason that had been forgotten by the one he cared for.

"I care for Ethan. Did you ever think of that?" Rayna spat. Her face flushed an angry crimson. "Over the last few days, he has been wonderful. He's all I think about."

Rayna's remarks upset Morgan even more. Tears streamed down her face.

"Do you really care about Ethan so much that Tristan doesn't even matter to you anymore? You don't even mention him. He's out there facing this punishment because of your careless actions!"

"You heard Father!" Rayna yelled. "I'm not allowed to say his name!"

"You married him, Rayna, in front of our family and the entire kingdom!" Morgan cried indignantly. "You're such a selfish child. If your old toy gets broken or tossed out, you just go and find a new one."

"How dare you. You think that Tristan doesn't matter to me anymore?"

"No, I don't," Morgan explained. "He's out there fighting the world for you, and all you have done is abandon him."

"Well, at least he has you to come to his rescue, then, huh? Have fun with my old toy!" Rayna yelled back derisively.

Morgan scoffed, surprised at her sister's words and apathy. "Neither of us can comprehend what Tristan is experiencing and what dangers he is facing just because he loves you. Do you even know how lucky you are to have him love you the way he does?"

Rayna hesitated before she asked, "What does it matter to you, anyway? It's not like you could even understand love. No one would ever love you as Tristan loves me."

"I used to think you deserved his love." Morgan lowered her tone. "But now I know that Tristan deserves so much more than the love you won't give him." Morgan spun on her heel and stepped away from her sister and the waiting guardians.

Rayna gawped at her sister's back for a moment. Coming to her senses, she looked toward the guardians and smiled. "Well, you are all welcome to come to the reception. I wanted you to be there so I could spend some time with you. You are still my friends, right?"

"I'll pass. I'm sorry you ran halfway across the castle to be rejected," Morgan said coldly over her shoulder. Addressing the guardians, she said, "You may do as you please."

Morgan opened her door and walked through the entryway. She paused for a moment to see if the others would join her. One by one, the other guardians followed Morgan.

"Sorry, Rayna," Ry said, glancing over his shoulder.

Rayna had tears rolling down her cheeks as all her old friends walked away from her.

"Please," she whispered. She fell to her knees and cried into her hands as her only friends left her. "Please, don't leave me alone with..."

Chapter 16

Healers

Tristan opened his eyes slowly and discovered his vision was blurry. He repeatedly blinked to clear his eyesight. A wet washcloth wiped his forehead. He watched a dark-haired, pale woman in dark robes tend to him. Tristan felt like he had just awakened from a bad dream.

"Rayna? Is that you?"

The woman giggled a little. "No, I'm not your Rayna. I'm the village healer."

Tristan rubbed his eyes, and his vision cleared. The woman was decidedly not Rayna, and he couldn't comprehend how he'd made that mistake. The woman had a slight glow that emanated from her skin. She studied him with eyes that gleamed an odd, dark blue. He sat up and appraised the wooden building. There was no escape that wasn't through the healer.

"Where am I? Where are my men?" Tristan tried to stand.

"You need to lie back down," the healer said. She placed her hands on his shoulders and gently pushed him back down. "You are not fully healed."

He grew faint and stopped resisting the healer's ministrations. He lay his head back down. "Where am I? Where are my men?" His concern had not waned.

The healer stood and answered, "You are in the elemental village."

Alarmed, Tristan sat up and searched for his weapons. He challenged his memory to recall all he had ever learned about the elementals: they physically resembled normal humans, but their eyes had an inhuman shade of blue. The elemental's magic took on different forms of animals and other creatures. This trait was unique to them.

"Your weapons and your armor are with your Irkshdan leader," the healer said before Tristan could remember anything more. She placed her hand on his head, and his thoughts quieted. "Elementals are a peaceful people. You are safe. The few who did attack are a group of radicals who believe in stopping the Naughtrious family. Most of our people don't condone violence; our way of life does not revolve around death and destruction."

"No violence?" Tristan asked. He relaxed, knowing he wasn't in imminent danger. "That wouldn't be a bad way to live."

"No, it isn't," the healer said, smiling.

Tristan rubbed his eyes again. He couldn't seem to keep his vision clear. He stretched and felt a stiff pain in his back. "How long have I been asleep?"

"Your leader brought you here two days ago. You have been asleep for quite a while."

A sudden urge hit Tristan. "Where is your…"

"Right over there." The healer pointed behind her.

Tristan could hear the woman's laughter as he unsteadily scurried over to the small restroom. When he returned, Zro and Lazarus were there waiting for him.

"Damn, man," Zro said. "Put on some clothes."

Tristan blushed when he realized he was only wearing his undershorts. Apologizing, he hurried to his bed, where a clean set of clothes draped across the footboard. Tristan shouted excitedly. "Lazarus, you're alive! How?"

Lazarus had a look of befuddlement on his face. "I remember very little of the moment. Hyperion's body collapsed around me, and I think it absorbed the brunt of the force of the water. While I was under water, the only thing I remember was a dim glowing hand."

Tristan joked. "And you say I sound crazy when I'm hit in the head."

"So, doctor, is he going to be okay?" Lazarus rolled his eyes.

"I am a healer, not a doctor." She glared at the guardian. "Yes, he just had a case of exhaustion, nothing more. With a good meal and a little more rest, the boy will be as good as new."

"That's damn good to hear." Lazarus slapped Tristan on the shoulder. He left his hand on Tristan's shoulder and squeezed. "Ichiban wants to move out in the next few days and head for the entrance to Furreshda."

"Tristan, you may now get out to stretch your legs for a bit and have a little dinner. I want you back in bed by nightfall. In the morning, I'll give you one last check-up to make sure you are fit to depart." The healer left them.

"Thank you," he said, nodding his head in acquiescence.

Dusk had arrived; Lazarus and Zro escorted Tristan outside once he was fully dressed. Tristan stopped for a moment and admired how peaceful the village seemed. He saw some elementals farming while others instructed children about their powers. All around him, Tristan could see the elementals' spells take the form of various animals. He saw children playing with elemental wolf cubs. The serenity of the elementals was soothing after so many days of battle.

"Not a bad place to live at all," Tristan muttered.

Zro asked, "What?"

"Nothing. Nothing at all." Tristan shook his head.

"Come on," Lazarus said. "We're supposed to meet Ichiban in the dining hall they've set up for us."

The three guardians entered a large building where soldiers were seated at hundreds of tables. Several soldiers greeted Tristan as he passed by; the soldiers shouted praise and shook his hand.

"Since when did you become so popular?" Lazarus mocked Tristan. "They act like you were the one who killed the Aeon."

"Aw, don't be like that," Tristan replied with a snarky tone. "You know I would have killed that Aeon if I hadn't been so busy helping your heavy ass get there. But saving everyone does have its perks." Tristan accepted a glass of mead from a soldier.

Tristan was about to take a sip when Culvac walked by and took the glass away from him. Culvac escorted them to the front, where Ichiban and Caster sat at a table with four empty chairs. Tristan said hello to some of the soldiers he recognized as he passed by them. When they reached their table, Caster stood to hug Tristan.

"I'm glad you're okay," Caster murmured close to Tristan's ear.

"Thanks to you." Tristan hugged him back. Together, they sat down.

"It's about time you got up, boy," Ichiban growled.

"Nice to see you, too, Ichiban."

Elemental chefs brought out a feast: whole-cooked turkey, a plate of cooked griffin eggs, salad, potatoes, and a pitcher of water. They placed it all on Tristan's table.

Before taking a large bite out of a turkey leg, Ichiban said, "In two days, we pack up camp and head through the islands to the road to Furreshda. A guide has agreed to take us there and let the other villages know that we mean them no harm as long as they don't attack us."

"What should we expect when we get there?" Zro asked.

"I don't know," Ichiban answered through a mouthful of meat. "I've never seen it. I expect that it will be a cavern of some kind."

"My people always said it was a road," Caster explained.

"So, what happens afterward?" Tristan asked.

Ichiban tilted his head a little and asked. "What do you mean?"

"If we accomplish our mission and make it out of Furreshda alive, then what?" Tristan shoved a spoonful of his food into his mouth.

"A little optimism never hurt anyone. I imagine we will go home, Tristan," Ichiban said and laughed.

"Home?" Tristan looked down at his plate. He contemplated the word for a moment before saying, "I think we should keep going."

Everyone stopped eating. Lazarus stared at him like he had gone mad. "Why? If we finish what we set out to do, why would we keep going? Don't you want to see your family again? I do. What about our friends or Rayna, even?"

Tristan permitted himself to think about Rayna's smiling face for a moment. Thoughts of her comforting embrace and her warm lips pressed against his after he'd become her guardian flooded his head. Just as quickly as the pleasant memories came, images of Rayna brushing past him and embracing Ethan slammed into his mind. Tristan recalled the feel of Morgan's hands restraining him from assaulting Ethan that night. The thought of her hands confused the memory and brought him back to his senses. He shook his head.

"The more enemies we eliminate, the fewer they have to fight, and the closer we are to the end of the war," he explained. "That's our goal, isn't it? To win the war? From what was said, we were set up back in Airk. If we keep going, we might catch the enemy off guard."

Caster shared a glance with Ichiban. "He has a point."

"Well, if we survive," Ichiban replied, "we'll talk to the men about it and let them decide whether they want to go home."

"You're actually considering this?" Lazarus asked, stunned.

"Tristan does have a point," Ichiban answered.

Lazarus took a deep breath and went back to his meal. Tristan stood up and tapped his glass to get everyone's attention. When all eyes were on him, he continued. "I will only take a moment, and then I will let you get back to this amazing meal our friends, the elementals, have prepared for us." Tristan raised his glass. "To our gracious hosts for inviting us into their homes and treating us as guests."

Tristan sipped his water while some soldiers chugged their mead. Tristan slowly lowered his glass and stared out at his men. "I want to thank you all for your bravery. Every one of you. The last battle was pretty crazy."

One of the soldiers stood up and shouted, "Yeah, you killed a damn ocean goddess!" The room roared with cheer.

Tristan laughed at Lazarus shaking his head. The room quieted. "Actually, that credit goes to Lazarus. He killed Hyperion." Tristan regained his composure. "Can you believe what we accomplished together? We killed the Aeon. We killed a goddess. We are unstoppable. If a goddess cannot stop us, then who can?" The room cheered once more. Now that Tristan felt he had their full attention, he worked up the courage to say what he really wanted. He took a large gulp of mead and set his glass down.

"All of you have fought and displayed magnificent courage. Our army is incomparably strong, and we are a force to be reckoned with! We are the hammer that shatters the anvil! When—not if—when we accomplish our mission, take Furreshda, and save our princesses, I want to ask you to continue with me." His words were met with silence. He walked among his men into the center of the room. "Isn't this the goal? To end the war? If a god cannot stop us and a kingdom cannot stop us, then what can?"

"What about our families?" a female soldier shouted. "What about my children?"

Tristan stared across the room and met her eyes. He nodded. "I will not force any of you to fight longer than our king has demanded of us. You may go home. Go home to your kids, your families. I'm sure your loved ones are aching to see you. I know why you are here. You are here because of me, and I would want nothing more than to be at home. I want you to be home with your families. But the second we get home and the war continues for years and years to come, the point will come where our children will fight, where our children will die for it. Let us be the ones who end it. Let us be the ones who fight so our children won't have to. Let our sacrifice be known so the ravages of war will no longer consume the rest of the world. Now I ask you, my brothers, my sisters, will you walk with me into hell?"

Once again, there was silence.

"Aye, brother," Caster said. Tristan turned and saw Caster standing behind him.

"Aye!" Ichiban stood up.

"Aye!" Culvac slammed his hands on the table as he shouted. Pushing back from the table, he nearly spilled his ale.

Lazarus and Zro stood silently, nodding at their friend. Slowly ayes erupted around the room until every soldier was on their feet, roaring with pride and cheer. Soldiers hoisted Tristan onto their shoulders, cheering for their guardian.

When the celebration stopped and everyone returned to their meals, Tristan finished his food, said his goodnights, and made his way back to the healer's cabin to return to bed. The short excursion to dinner had exhausted him.

Tristan gazed into the black void from the comfort of his bed. A quiet and gentle voice echoed from the darkness. "Good night, my Angel," it whispered.

Tristan fought sleep for a moment, trying to determine where the voice could have come from. In the back of his mind, he knew it was the hooded woman.

≈

Tristan woke up to find Caster closing the door to his hut. "Time to get up. We have work to do."

Tristan rolled over and covered up with blankets. "I'm on the mend, Cas. I shouldn't be doing anything."

Caster walked up to him and touched his foot. "Time to get up."

Tristan rolled out from under the bed and dressed. "What are we even doing?"

"We are going teach you to fly."

Tristan was a little excited about this but had his doubts about Caster's knowledge. "Do you know how to fly?"

Caster retorted. "Do you?" Tristan shook his head. "We will figure it out together. We may need those wings before this is all over." Tristan and Caster went outside to the main roads between a few cabins. "Now, show your wings."

Tristan looked over his shoulder at his back. "Wings! Wings come out!" Nothing happened.

Caster shook his head. "It's a reflex. I want you to flex your back and call upon them with your mind, like how you would use your hand to grab a cup of water without thinking about it."

Tristan took a deep breath and flexed his back. He pictured his wings emerging from his back. He opened his eyes and looked over his shoulder to see them there. Tristan looked up at Caster to get his approval.

Caster nodded. "Good. Up until now, you have been solely using and calling upon your wings based on instinct. This needs to change because you can't pick up a random set of wings and automatically know how to use them. That's just not realistic. Flap your right wing." Tristan instantly flapped his left wing, but it threw him off balance into a wall, headfirst. Caster roared with laughter. "I said right wing, you dunce." Tristan glared at Caster out of the corner of his eye. His head throbbed. "Get up, try again."

Tristan dragged himself to his feet and stared at Caster. Several insults ran through his mind, but he couldn't decide which one to use.

Caster looked at him with fleeting patience. "Again!" Tristan flapped his right wing this time. "Good. Now the left one." Tristan closed his eyes tightly and tried forcing the left wing to move. "Your face looks like you're constipated. Just move your wing."

Tristan shouted back. "This isn't easy, you know!"

Caster calmly said, "I doubt it is. But our time here on this island is limited. You need to be a quick study." Tristan flapped his left wing. "Very good! Now, flap them back and forth one at a time until you have complete control over them." One at a time, Tristan flapped his wings for a few minutes until he had control of his wings.

Caster nodded. "Now, flap them both at the same time." Tristan took a deep breath and flapped both wings. He felt a small lift. Caster chuckled. "You didn't fall on your ass. You already show improvement. Now, I'm going to clap my hands in a rhythm that will get faster. Flap your wings to match it." Caster started to clap slowly. Tristan flapped his wings again and again. He felt his feet leave the ground until he was hovering. Caster shouted, "You're doing it! Amazing!"

After two days of Caster's training, Tristan could control his wings, but the effort was exhausting.

When Tristan awoke from a long-needed rest, the healer was already in his room, prodding and examining him.

"Good morning!" she said. "How do you feel?"

Tristan saw his armor and weapons on a table and remembered the cheers of his soldiers.

"Rather good," he answered. "And you?"

"I am well. Thank you for asking," she answered with a smile. "You are free to go. You seem rested, and your heart rate is normal. My work is done. Just don't overdo it like that again. Your body may quit on you permanently. I'm sure your Rayna wouldn't want that."

"Thank you, again," he said, bowing to the healer with respect.

He dressed and thought about holding Rayna underneath their tree and how soft she was. Lately, Morgan crept into his mind whenever he thought of Rayna. He couldn't help but remember falling on top of Morgan beneath the Almboch tree, the way her soft body conformed to his own, and the way her eyes begged him to stay. Taking a deep breath, Tristan regained his composure. He stepped outside, dressed in his armor and his weapons sheathed on his back. The sun was blinding, so he pulled his hood up to shield his eyes. He watched the soldiers gather at the border of the village where Ichiban rallied them.

Tristan saw Zro rejected by a group of elementals. They both headed toward the crowd of soldiers.

"Spreading the good word about Aerra?" Tristan asked, approaching his friend.

"You know me. Wolf is the best goddess," Zro said with a shrug.

Tristan smiled in admiration of his friend's faith. "You'll never convert these people, Zro, and I can tell you why."

"Oh, yeah? Enlighten me, wise one."

"How many Aeons have you met?" Tristan asked.

"I met Hyperion," Zro replied hesitantly. He gave Tristan a wary glance.

"You see all these people?" Tristan gestured at all the elementals around them. When Zro nodded, Tristan continued. "Hyperion came to their aid when they called to her. Have you ever seen Aerra come to our aid? Have you ever met her?"

Zro stopped in his tracks, experiencing a moment of realization. He caught up to Tristan and smiled. "Wolf is the best goddess." He smiled as Tristan shook his head and snickered.

As they approached the crowd, they heard Culvac say to Ichiban, "We are all accounted for, sir."

Ichiban took note of Tristan's and Zro's arrival and nodded. He turned to the guide, a skinny, seasoned elemental man with a long, graying beard. "We will follow you."

The guide nodded and led the soldiers down the road away from the village.

"Unit 112, let's move out!" Ichiban's booming voice growled.

≈

Along the beaten path, the soldiers marched. Tristan saw countless elementals with their creatures and beasts. Some creatures took the form of small insects; others were the size of large dragons. Some were monstrous and intimidating, while others displayed beauty comparable to the most delicate of flowers. They traveled from island to island using small boats.

Dusk came swiftly, and the guide led them to a beach on the center island. "Here is the entrance to the road," the little man said.

"What do you mean? I see nothing." Tristan scanned the beach for a cave of some kind.

The guide pointed to the ocean and explained, "The road is in the water."

The guardians and soldiers stared into the water. An unidentifiable force in the water separated the sea, creating two walls of water thirty yards apart.

"Is there no other way?" Ichiban asked, frustration and outrage crossing his face.

Tristan stood behind Ichiban. He understood Ichiban's reluctance to head back into the water because he felt the same apprehension crawl over his skin.

The guide simply answered, "Not unless you want to swim to Furreshda."

"We will be surrounded at all times," Ichiban growled. He shook his head, recognizing it was not the fault of the guide. "Thank you, sir. Your services are no longer required."

The old elemental bowed and headed back the way they had come.

Ichiban barked, "Set up camp. We will start down this path in the morning."

Tristan set up his tent with ease. He walked to the water's edge and looked down the darkened path that led to the depths of the ocean.

"Kind of eerie, isn't it?" asked Culvac.

Tristan noticed that Culvac had joined him. "Yeah, but we'll be alright," he said to ease himself as well as Culvac.

"It is appreciated," said the captain, smiling and shaking his head, "but you don't have to put up a tough front around me. Like the men, I know that tomorrow we may lose a lot of soldiers down there in the depths. Then, after the exhausting fight to get to there, we'll have to go against its army and the royal family with whatever soldiers we have left."

Tristan took a deep breath and stared down the path. "We won't lose anyone on the way there, Culvac. I'll do everything I can to keep the men alive."

"I know you will, sir. Don't forget that we are here to do a job, and so are you. None of my men can fight the royal family members on equal terms. You, Lazarus, and Zro are our only chance of winning—you three cannot wear yourselves out tomorrow defending us," Culvac explained.

"Don't be foolish. If we don't…"

"I mean it, Tristan." Culvac's tone turned serious. "You may be my commanding officer, but I do have more battle experience than you. We're going to need the three of you at your best if we expect to come out victorious. So, sir, get some rest and leave the trip to us. We will make sure you and the other guardians get there in one piece."

"Thank you, Culvac." Tristan respectfully pulled back his hood and made eye contact with Culvac. For the first time that day, he let the sea air blow through his hair. "Just watch yourself out there."

≈

Tristan woke up to a disturbance near his tent. He peeked out only to see a large family of crustaceans with sandy-colored shells and claws. They were boulder crabs, some of which were four feet tall and probably weighed three hundred pounds. Some of the crabs grabbed soldiers in their sleep and dragged them to the sea.

"Hey! Wake up!" yelled Tristan. He grabbed one of his swords. "Wake up, everyone! We're under attack!"

Tristan ran and climbed on top of one of the crabs that had a soldier in its claw. He stabbed the crab, running his blade through its shell. Tristan shot the blade through the crab's body, and the blade stuck in the sand. All around, soldiers awoke and helped those in danger of being dragged into the water. Zro fired his rifle nonstop to keep other crabs from emerging from the ocean. Ichiban charged at a crab that had reached the water's edge with a live soldier in tow. Ichiban grabbed the claw that gripped the soldier and ripped it from the beast's body. He grabbed the stalks that held its eyes and pushed the creature onto its back. He rammed the claw into the crab's underbelly.

Tristan observed in horror as a mother crab with hundreds of babies on its back emerged from the water. The babies ran off its mother's back and headed straight for the closest soldier. The man shouted and pleaded for help as he was overrun and dragged into the water. The soldier pulled a grenade from his waist and pulled the pin just as he went under. The blast filled the ocean with blood. The explosion, however, was enough to frighten the rest of the crabs away.

In the calm that followed, Ichiban shouted, "We're leaving. Pack everything!"

Tristan jogged over to Ichiban and asked, "Don't you think we should give the men some time to recover?"

"No." Ichiban studied the sea in front of them. "They know we are here. It will only be a matter of time before they send a larger wave of creatures to pick us off one by one. We cannot stay in one place for too long. From the first moment we stepped onto this beach until we enter the city, they will watch us and send their sea pets after us."

"Why don't they just come out to face us?" Tristan asked.

"They are using the sea life to diminish our numbers, maybe even get lucky and kill one of you guardians." Ichiban addressed the soldiers in his gruff voice, "When we step onto that path, we will travel in groups of twelve. No one goes anywhere alone. Is that clear?"

The soldiers shouted in unison, "Yes, sir!"

"Good. Now, let's move out!" Ichiban shouted.

Chapter 17

Bottleneck

The sun had risen to the middle of the sky; noon had arrived. Tristan, along with his soldiers, had walked down the path to Furreshda for hours. The rising walls of water grew with each step. Razor-sharp rocks, coral, and sea plants surrounded them on the paths. The water was clear from the sunlight, allowing them to see fish swim on all sides of them.

Tristan stood in the middle of his group of soldiers for protection. A little water sprinkled on him. Above his head, he saw a group of dolphins sailing over the gap between the water walls. Everything looked brilliant. Tristan thought it was a little funny that Ichiban was so on edge. He had claimed they would be surrounded by creatures and have to fight for every inch. What was he talking about? This place was beautiful, calm, and peaceful. There couldn't possibly be any danger lurking in here. Tristan smiled at his surroundings and closed his eyes for a moment. Enjoying the rising water, Tristan felt at peace; the push and pull of the ocean put him into a comfortable trance.

≈

Night had fallen, and a thunderstorm brewed overhead. The water turned black and opaque. The army marched on. Lightning on Tristan's left illuminated the ominous sea. He saw a family of whales swim just inches from the wall of water. The soldiers lit torches to navigate the treacherous terrain.

Over the radio, Ichiban told Lazarus, "This is a bad idea. We're giving away our position."

"Maybe so, but the men can't see. Some of them are getting hurt on the rocks."

"Well, now that you all can see, the enemy can see us," Ichiban growled. "Keep your guard up. Anything can happen."

"Nothing has happened all day, Ichiban. Maybe they are waiting to hit us full force when we arrive at the kingdom," Tristan suggested. The calm of the day had him wondering about the enemy's tactics.

"Unlikely. Even if they were, they know where we are now," Ichiban snarled. "They can see the light for miles, especially when it's pitch black like this."

At the water's edge, he saw a soldier stick his head into the water to wake himself up.

"You fool. What are you doing?" yelled Ichiban.

A large shark popped out of the water, sucking half of the man's body into its mouth and dragging him deep into the water. Two tentacles reached onto the path, grabbed two more soldiers, and pulled them into the sea.

"You see!" Ichiban screamed into the radio. "Everyone, backs to one another!"

The groups of soldiers put their backs to each other and stood in circles. The light from the torches reflected off the surface: it was impossible to see into the water. The men around Tristan trembled. A few of the soldiers took deep breaths to try to calm themselves.

"Steady, men. Calm down," Tristan reassured. "Nothing good will come from panicking."

"I want complete silence," Ichiban whispered into his radio. "Those who have flare guns, prepare to shoot into the ocean. Do so, on my mark—now!"

Red balls of fire shot into the water. Red light filled the ocean, exposing countless sea creatures: serpents, krakens, crustaceans, sharks, hydras, and others Tristan couldn't identify. All stared beady-eyed at the soldiers.

Tristan stared and focused on the horde in front of him. His breath became shallow, and his heart pounded against his chest.

"Fire at will!" Ichiban roared.

The torches all dropped and immediately burned out. Gunfire lit up the path when the sea creatures charged the soldiers.

~

In Furreshda, carriages gathered from all over the land; the kingdom hosted a ball to celebrate Rayna and Ethan's return from their honeymoon. The guests gathered in the royal ballroom, where everyone waltzed in unison. Morgan paired up with Ry, while Charity, Bianca, and Mira danced with a few high guardians. The guests of honor, Rayna and Ethan, danced in the middle.

"I know Tristan has been writing to you. Have you heard anything lately?" Ry asked Morgan.

"No." Morgan sighed. "He said not to write until I hear from him first. I can't help but think he and the other guys are in danger." Morgan shot a look at her sister, who smiled at her new husband and their guests without a care in the world.

"I have the same feeling," Ry explained. "I wish there was a way to find out if he's okay. Little Miss Instantly-Moves-On seems to be having an enjoyable time."

"He'll be fine," Morgan said to comfort Ry. "When they have taken Furreshda, he will find us."

Her words had the opposite effect, however. "Yeah, after Furreshda," Ry said despondently.

When the song ended, everyone stopped dancing to clap. The king stepped up to the podium where the orchestra played. "Can we have the floor cleared, except for the newlyweds?" the king asked cheerily.

All the other guests left the floor. A well-paced song played while Rayna and Ethan waltzed, spinning around the dance floor.

≈

A boulder crab dove at Ichiban. He rolled over on his back, firing his rifle as the crab soared over him. Tristan and Lazarus ran next to Ichiban and fired their rifles, suppressing the creatures while Ichiban rose. A loud roar came from above; water splashed around on the surface of the ocean. The three saw an enormous glowing pearl-blue dragon bear down on the soldiers.

"Sea dragon!" Ichiban shouted. "Take cover!"

The soldiers around them hid behind a group of rocks, but Tristan, Lazarus, and Ichiban ran down the path. The dragon emitted blue energy, illuminating the area. Large shards of ice shot out of the ground in an attempt to pierce them.

One of the ice shards caught in the wall of water and rose to the surface. Lazarus jumped onto the chunk of ice, rising to face the oncoming dragon. He vaulted off the ice, dove toward the flying beast, and thrust his sword through the dragon's neck. They tumbled to the ground together. When they hit, Tristan charged at the dragon, swinging his sword. He cut through the sea dragon's skull to deliver the final blow.

≈

Rayna swirled around the dance floor a little faster as the song's pace picked up. Ethan twirled her in a circle and then tucked her closer to his body. They spun away from each other and then back in, repeating this configuration a few times. They twirled toward each other, grabbed each other's arms, and sidestepped clockwise in a circular pattern.

Morgan glowered at the two, dancing perfectly in sequence. Anger consumed her as she observed how happy they seemed to be with each other.

≈

Tristan grabbed Culvac, forced him to the ground, and shouted a warning at the soldiers. Three large turtle dragons poked their heads out of the water. Their heads were large enough to consume a person with one bite; their shells were more massive than a two-story building. Their four legs easily supported a few dozen tons. The turtles inhaled briefly and exhaled beams of ice onto the path and at the walls of water. The waves froze everything in their path, including a few of the soldiers. The water rose, forcing the ice into the air. Over their heads, Tristan saw the falling ice. He pulled Culvac up from the ground and started to run. Shards of ice fell where they lay, shattering into hundreds of jagged pieces.

≈

Rayna and Ethan stepped around each other with their backs to one another in a square pattern. Other royal couples joined them, dancing in sequence. They all stopped in front of their partners and extended their right hands to them. They stepped left, spinning their bodies. They stepped right and left again. They pulled themselves closer to their partners with their backs to one another and then side-stepped around each other. They repeated this in the opposite direction. Their hands met after the second lap, and they pulled themselves to one another. Their eyes met, and the lights dimmed.

≈

Tristan stopped in the center of the fight. Caster appeared next to him. Above them, large jellyfish tentacles appeared over the top of the water walls. They started to shower the soldiers with electric charges. Caster and Tristan exchanged a quick glance and nodded at each other. Tristan expanded his wings and flew to the top of the wall. He chopped off a tentacle. Caster passed through the shadows and severed a tentacle from the opposite side. Darting from side to side, flying, and stepping through the shadows, they slew the tentacles as they appeared.

≈

Rayna had her back to Ethan and reached behind to grab his hands. She pulled his body into hers. Her hips swayed rhythmically against his waist. With one hand still on her hip, he grabbed her hand and spun her around to face him. He pulled her in to spin her away again. With their arms outstretched, Rayna twirled Ethan back into her. Their hands and eyes locked once more.

≈

Tristan pulled the pin of a grenade and tossed it into a hydra's mouth when its head came out of the water. The hydra pulled its head back into the wall before it exploded, splashing blood all over the path. Three more hydra heads popped out of the water. Zro ran across the path to the hydra. One of the heads snapped at Zro.

He shoved his gun into its mouth and shouted, "Good night!"

Zro recharged his gun with his power and shot another round, forcing the massive beast to explode.

≈

Ethan twirled Rayna once more, ending with a dip. He gazed into her eyes and kissed her. He put his hand on her cheek and caressed it with his thumb. Morgan and Ry were close enough to hear Rayna whisper, "I love you, Ethan." Morgan couldn't believe it. Her sister really had moved on from Tristan.

"I love you too, my princess," Ethan replied, kissing her again. He twirled her three more times, a little faster after each rotation. He pulled her in, and their hands met. In sequence with the other couples, they took large steps, dancing around the open area. When Rayna smiled at him, her eyes glimmered. He pulled her in, and she rested her head on his shoulder. They began to dance slowly, falling out of sequence with the rest of the dancers.

Morgan stopped dancing with Ry and strolled over to the bar to grab a glass of ale.

"Enjoying the party?" asked Rayna, panting from the dance. She gulped down a glass of water with such haste, Morgan was surprised she didn't start licking the condensation off the sides.

Morgan stopped sipping her mead to answer. "Not really, to be perfectly honest. The music is droll. The company is poor, and the mead lacks flavor."

"Well, we are in Furreshda, after all. I imagine the beer would be a bit salty for our taste," Rayna said, ignoring her sister's criticism.

Morgan diverted her attention to the dance floor. Rayna extended her hand. "Would you like to dance with me, sister?"

Ignoring the proffered hand, Morgan replied, "No, Rayna. I don't want to dance with you."

Rayna retracted her hand to her chest as though wounded. "Did I do something wrong?" she asked innocently.

"You've done enough, Rayna."

"Sister, you should be thanking me." Rayna's voice hardened. "Tristan is yours now. You are with the boy I love."

Morgan set her mead down in frustration. She watched the physical changes roll over Rayna. She studied her sister's eyes. Morgan could see the forced smile on Rayna's face, but her tears seemed real.

"The boy you love? Are you kidding me, Rayna? Why don't you leave then? Why don't you go back to him? If that's what it takes for you to see what you're doing, Rayna, I'm willing to give him up for you."

"They won't let me—she won't," said Rayna. She sniffled through her smile, and her face went blank while she stared into the ground.

"Who won't let you, Rayna?" Morgan took a tenuous step toward Rayna. "The hooded woman? Who is she?"

Two guards approached the two princesses. "Come, princesses," one said forcefully. "We are here to escort you and your guardians to the dungeon. An attack on the kingdom is imminent. We do not want you to aid the attackers in any way."

Rayna's eyes met Morgan's. Morgan knew the eyes looking back at her were not the eyes of her sister. The lights flickered violently.

Rayna spoke in two different pitches simultaneously. "The end will begin with ash."

Chapter 18

The March to Farreshda

Tristan pulled his sword out of a boulder crab and watched the sunrise illuminate the walls of water that lined their path. The sea creatures retreated, leaving the bodies of their dead and wounded. Tristan fell to his knees in exhaustion, along with most of the soldiers around him. Forced to fight all night, the soldiers of the 112th were tired, hungry, and physically immobile. Tristan saw Ichiban walk by.

The wolf, out of breath, barked into his radio, "Everyone, get up. We cannot stay here. We have to keep moving!"

"Ichiban, we need to rest. The men can't move," Lazarus protested through his earpiece.

"Don't you think I know that?" He studied the soldiers. "The enemy knows where we are. We need to get a few miles from here, and then the men can rest for a few hours. Believe me, Lazarus, I'm tired, too." Ichiban walked past the guardian and barked into his radio, "On your feet! We only have a few miles to go. Then, we can rest. Now move!"

The soldiers slowly and grudgingly stood and followed their seemingly tireless leader down the path, leaving behind the previous night's death, destruction, and carnage. Each step took its toll. Some soldiers fell to their knees; other soldiers carried their wounded comrades and helped bear their burdens. Tristan stared straight ahead, lost in his lethargy. He concentrated on simply placing one foot in front of the other. He didn't notice when he veered from his straight line and skimmed the wall of water to his right. Merely a foot away, a white shark tracked Tristan through the water. The shark was so giant its mouth could swallow Tristan whole.

Tristan stopped to study the fish. He slowly pulled his sword from a sheath on his leg. When the beast glanced at a passing soldier for a brief second, Tristan brought the sword down through the water and pierced the shark between the eyes. He pulled the giant fish out of the ocean onto the path. Ichiban approached him and appraised his catch.

"This is as good a spot as any to rest," Ichiban said. "It's almost noon. We have walked far enough—plus, you caught us some lunch!"

"I hate fish." Tristan rolled his eyes and pretended to gag.

The soldiers stopped marching and dropped to the ground in exhaustion. Tristan managed to start a fire and got comfortable around it while a soldier cooked the large fish. Ichiban, Culvac, Caster, and the rest of the guardians joined Tristan around the fire.

Culvac said, "You three need to get some sleep."

"So do you, captain," Zro said.

"I'll be fine," Culvac argued, "but you guys need to rest, even if it's just for a short while."

"He's right," Ichiban added. "Don't worry. We'll keep an eye on everyone."

Tristan scanned the unit and saw all the soldiers passing out along the path with nobody left to pull guard duty. He yawned, laid his head down, and immediately fell asleep.

≈

"Hey, Tristan, get up." Zro stood over him. He nudged Tristan with his boot. "Hey, it's time to go, buddy."

Tristan woke up startled and reached for his blade. The sun was no longer overhead. He heard Ichiban's voice echo in his earpiece.

"It's been four hours," he said. "It's time to move out. We need to reach the city before nightfall."

Tristan heard Caster add, "I know we're all tired, but we cannot afford another battle like we had last night."

Somewhat refreshed yet still exhausted, Tristan trudged with his soldiers along their path, undisturbed for hours. After a while, the path began to curve and slope downward more steeply than before. In the distance, two torches lit the entrance to the underwater city. Tristan, Zro, and Lazarus took the lead and gestured for their soldiers to follow with caution. Turrets from within the walls of water fired into the advancing soldiers. Tristan, fed up with holding back, shouted and expanded his barrier to protect the soldiers from the oncoming bullets. The barrier stretched out so far that its energy forced the turrets to malfunction and blow up.

"Let's take the city!" Tristan shouted. Tristan charged through the threshold of the city with his soldiers at his heels. Tristan looked at the city sitting at the bottom of the ocean, surrounded by a wall of ocean that must have been a mile high. Along the wall of water encircling the city were the green orbs that produced mana. The idea of being at the bottom of the ocean while completely dry and breathing oxygen kind of messed with Tristan's head a bit. He looked up and saw the sky. He felt the ocean breeze on his skin. Hundreds of Furreshdian soldiers met them. Tristan raised his swords, and his power erupted with beams of light that shot from the ground, blasting the enemies aside. Gunfire came from within the buildings while the soldiers ran into the streets and found cover.

"My men will get you to the castle," Tristan heard Culvac radio Lazarus.

Tristan raised his hand and fired a ball of black energy at a building filled with enemy soldiers, destroying it. "No, my men will not get you to the castle, but we guardians will. Just make sure you don't let anyone in after us!" Tristan replied.

Lazarus swung his sword and unleashed a wave of energy, knocking down two more buildings. Tristan glanced over his shoulder to see ships rise out of the ocean. A shockwave of power erupted from the castle, hitting the walls of water surrounding the city. Moments later, sea creatures that were able to move on land poured out of the walls of water around the city.

"All forces get to the castle," Ichiban shouted over the radios. "The queen summoned an army of beasts. Do not stop for anything. The guardians will clear the way!"

Zro shot his bullets into the sky, covering the troops from the attacks above. Tristan and Lazarus sent wave after wave of energy, destroying the buildings around them to help their army move forward to the distant castle.

"Save it!" Culvac yelled as he tossed Tristan a rifle.

Tristan sheathed his swords and held the rifle tight. In the distance, he could see the magnificent castle nestled deep in the city. Tristan ran by other buildings; he saw civilians witness the fight from their windows: women, children, and the elderly.

Lazarus shouted into his earpiece, "Leave the civilians out of the fight!"

Tristan nodded his head in approval. While they ran, Tristan got separated from the other guardians. He found himself with a group of soldiers when a high-powered machinegun fired at them from a nearby building. They ducked into another building for cover. Bullets whizzed by from all directions, drawing the attention of the surrounding soldiers. No one seemed to have noticed Tristan's small pinned-down group.

"Are any of you snipers?" Tristan asked. When none of the soldiers stepped forward, he swore. "Fine. You with the rocket, come here!"

A man wearing a rocket launcher on his back trotted to Tristan.

"Listen, you only get one shot. I'm going to run out there to get his attention. You have a few seconds to aim; make sure you hit that gun nest, understand?"

"Yes, sir!"

Tristan readied himself with a deep breath and stepped out into the street. A giant thrashing serpent burst from the building next to him.

"Keep going, sir," one of the soldiers yelled. "We'll handle it!"

The soldiers opened fire on the beast while Tristan continued into the street to draw the machinegun fire. The rocket soldier stepped out behind him. Tristan hoped the man's aim was accurate. He fired his rocket, but Tristan's distraction wasn't enough. Behind him, the soldier's body fell to the ground, riddled with bullets. The rocket hit the small nest, causing its roof to collapse and clear the path down the road.

Seconds later, the serpent collapsed, and the soldiers climbed up its body, stabbing and shooting it. When the serpent was clearly dead, they jumped off to follow Tristan down the street. At the end of the street, Tristan came to a four-way crossing. When he peered down the next road, large tentacles flailed from every direction. He saw Culvac with a large squad suppress the creature with gunfire. Tristan studied the scene to find enemy soldiers on the rooftops, aiming at his comrades. "Fire onto the buildings!" Tristan yelled.

Tristan and his soldiers fired a barrage of bullets, causing the Furreshdian soldiers to take cover and provide Culvac's group the chance to take down the sea creature unhindered. The kraken carried several live soldiers, while others fired at it, trying to slow it down.

"Grenadiers coming through!" said two soldiers, carrying grenade launchers.

Tristan shouted, "Give them some cover!"

They ran in front of Tristan. They shot multiple rounds that destroyed the top floors of the buildings. Some of Tristan's soldiers fired at the monster; others continued to focus on the surrounding Furreshdians. One of the grenadiers reloaded his gun and charged the kraken. The grenadier climbed onto one of the kraken's tentacles, using only one hand. The tentacle danced around like a live wire, trying to shake the soldier off. When the soldier climbed high enough, he aimed the grenade launcher at the kraken's body and fired repeatedly. Immediately, the tentacles dropped to the ground in resonating thuds. The soldiers freed themselves from the kraken's grip and scaled down the massive monster.

Once the noise died down, Culvac shouted, "Everyone, keep pressing forward!"

The soldiers all shouted while charging over the dead kraken. Tristan glanced over his shoulders to find that more sea creatures had closed in behind them.

"Keep moving! Don't stop!" Tristan yelled, ushering the soldiers out of danger.

The soldiers began to run, firing back on the sea creatures and enemies alike. They only stopped fighting when they reached the castle. There, Tristan met up with Lazarus, Zro, Caster, Ichiban, and the remnants of the army. Together, they cleared out the defenses around the castle and set up a perimeter to hold off the remaining forces. Tristan and the men following him huddled behind the small barricade.

"You and the other guardians need to get into that castle," said Ichiban. "Now!"

"But what about you? There are so many of them!" protested Tristan.

"Go!" Ichiban barked. "We can hold them! Go!" Ichiban grabbed Tristan and shoved him toward the castle.

Caster pulled his rifle back to reload and looked intently at Tristan. "We can handle this. You need to go. This is what you've trained for. Now, go!"

Tristan nodded his head at Caster and then took a long hard look to size up what was left of the enemy. "Lazarus, Zro, get to the entrance of the castle!" Tristan took off, shouting into his earpiece.

Tristan reached the entrance first and broke it down. He saw one large corridor completely lined with soldiers aiming guns at him. Four shots fired from behind Tristan and erupted in explosions throughout the entire hallway.

"Let's go!" Lazarus ran past Tristan.

The three guardians ran down the hall. They came to a large room with dozens of different paths leading away from it. The sounds of soldiers closing in on them from all over the castle reverberated off the stone walls. Tristan sprinted down the closest hall with the other two guardians behind him. Soldiers began to swarm them. Tristan emerged from the hall to find a large door surrounded by soldiers.

Lazarus pushed Tristan forward and yelled, "Keep moving!"

The guards charged. The guardians raised their barriers and smashed their way through the soldiers, forcing them aside and bursting through the door. Lazarus turned, raised his hand, and fired his energy into the ceiling, causing it to collapse. The impact closed the entrance behind them.

When the dust settled, Tristan saw three boys, each holding a sword. The youngest boy didn't look older than twelve, and the oldest couldn't have been a year older than Tristan. The three boys were shaking; they looked clean-cut and formal, like they had never seen a fight before.

Tristan knew that it was time for him to play the part he was born for, the part he had trained his whole life for. He lowered his voice and said in a harsh tone, "Drop your weapons and walk away."

"No! We are here to defend our mother!" the eldest boy shakily said.

"You don't know what you are doing, boy!" Tristan narrowed his gaze. "You're shaking at the mere sight of us. You don't know the stench of blood or the weight of your own weapon. Walk away."

"Who are you to talk to me this way?" the eldest asked. "Do you know who I am?"

"Just by looking into your eyes, I can tell who you are," Tristan said, smirking. "You're a pampered boy who has had everything handed to him. Your mother has always stuck up and spoken for you. Sadly, you will never know how to do anything for yourself."

This seemed to strike a nerve in the boy. "Shut your mouth, guardian! Your power does not compare to ours. You have no right to talk to us this way!"

Tristan surrounded himself with a transparent black barrier and walked toward the three princes. "I am going to tell you one last time: drop your weapons and leave."

"We will not abandon our mother!" the youngest boy yelled and charged Tristan.

Tristan swung his first sword, knocked the kid's blade from his hand, and then rammed his second blade through the youngest prince's stomach. The eldest prince screamed out in a combination of anguish and rage and then charged at Tristan. The guardian tossed the boys aside.

"Zro, maintain constant fire on the oldest. Lazarus, go!" Tristan yelled.

Zro immediately fired energy-filled bullets that exploded against the eldest boy's barrier. Tristan and Lazarus ran at the second-youngest prince. The boy swung his sword, unleashing a wave of water at the guardians. The young prince, unable to control the power of the weapon, found himself blasted back into a wall by the water's force.

Tristan rushed the boy while the water crashed against his barrier, threatening to push him back. He forced his way through. When he reached the young prince, Tristan swung his sword, trying to connect with the other blade in order to knock it out of the prince's hand. Tristan missed. At point-blank range, the prince raised his hand and unleashed a wave of energy aimed at Tristan. The blast rolled off Tristan's barrier and demolished the wall behind him. The young boy stared into Tristan's eyes, but the prince couldn't hide his fear behind his anger.

When the dust cleared, light peeked through a small crack in Tristan's barrier. Dark power emanated from his fingertips and tried to consume him. Anger engulfed Tristan. He grabbed the boy, and with the help of a whirlwind, he tossed him upward.

Tristan yelled, "Laz, now!"

Lazarus leaped high into the air over Tristan and brought his sword down on the boy's hand. The prince's hand fell, and his weapon clattered to the floor. Lazarus thrust his sword again, ramming it through the young prince's chest.

Lazarus extracted his blade. He and the fading boy fell to the ground. The eldest brother raised his hand, shot a wall of energy at Zro, and knocked him off his feet and into the wall behind him. The boy ran to his dying brother and held him in his arms. Tristan and Lazarus walked to him, watching him weep as the younger brother slowly shut his eyes.

"You don't have any fight left in you." Tristan lowered his swords to give the boy a chance for mercy. "You're too distraught. Give us your sword, and your life will be spared!"

The survivor screamed. Beams of energy rose from the floor and shredded the room around them. Waves of energy emitted from the prince, forcing the guardians backward.

Tristan pulled out his sidearm and aimed it at the last prince. He pulled the trigger. The destructive energy vanished, and the last prince fell to the floor—dead.

"How did you do that?" Lazarus asked in astonishment.

"He didn't have his barrier up. Grab their weapons!" Tristan answered simply. "One more left."

Each guardian grabbed one of the princes' swords and walked to the end of the room where a large door stood. Tristan opened the door. Waiting at the end of the long room, the queen perched on her throne.

Chapter 19

Facing the Queen

The guardians approached the queen slowly. They all had their weapons ready for her inevitable attack. Tristan scanned the room to try to ascertain what her strategy was going to be. He couldn't hear any other approaching soldiers. She was the last defense of her kingdom. She stared down at them, her gaze haughty and detached.

"What business do you have with me, guardians of Sorriax?"

"You know perfectly well why we're here," Tristan said, ending on a sharp laugh. He shook his head derisively.

Tristan watched a single tear escape the queen's eye and spill down her face. "And what of my sons?" she asked in an icy voice.

"Dead," said Tristan calmly.

"Only a hag such as yourself would send her children to defend her when they can't even defend themselves!" Lazarus yelled.

The queen brushed a tear from her cheek. "I asked them to escape! They were just children! You heartless monsters must have hunted them down and killed them when they didn't expect it."

"You sent them away?" Tristan asked. He cocked his head in question. "They were standing right outside your door. I'll make you the same offer I made them: give us your weapon, and you can walk away."

Fury grew in the queen's stony eyes. "If my sons fought you to the death, what makes you think I would give anything less?" She unsheathed her sword and stood up.

"So be it. We will show no mercy," Tristan said.

The queen raised her voice, "Nor will my Falperion!" She screamed and swung her sword. Water erupted from the ground, quickly filling the room. The guardians erected barriers that encircled them and adopted defensive stances. The water reached the ceiling. Tristan hoped their barriers would provide enough oxygen to last throughout the fight. The queen raised her hand— white jets of water shot at the guardians. Dodging the streams, Tristan glanced over his shoulder to see that her attack had left holes in the walls. Tristan yelled while he ducked and spun around three different jets of water. "Don't let them hit you!"

"No, shit! Forget this!" Zro shouted. He lifted his rifle and fired three rounds. Two of the streams sliced the bullets in half; the third bullet headed for the queen. Wave after wave of water rushed at the remaining bullet, forcing it to slow down so much that it eventually sank to the floor.

The queen delivered her most powerful stream yet, crashing through the stone wall. Though the wall had been blasted away, none of the water escaped. The room remained in its cubicle form.

Tristan got the other guardians' attention and pointed at the queen. He formed his Angel wings and glided toward the queen. The three guardians moved quickly, dodging the streams of water. When they got closer, the pressure of the water pushing them away intensified—almost bone-crushing.

Tristan aimed his sword at the queen and shot his blade at her; the blade collided with the queen's barrier. Tristan retracted his weapon when a large force of water pushed him back across the water-filled room. Zro, struggling against the water pressure, raised his rifle once again and fired his energy-filled magazine into the queen's barrier, causing five minor explosions. The barrier didn't crack. The force of the water slowed the bullets down so much that their impact revealed no devastation. Zro pulled out the empty magazine and reached for another, finding that he had only one left. A geyser of water shot from underneath Zro, forcing him to the ceiling.

Lazarus charged at the queen while fighting the force of the water. He raised his hand and fired multiple orbs of green energy at the queen's barrier. The temperature of the water dropped dramatically; soon, shards of ice shot up from the ground. Lazarus danced around the shards and continued firing the orbs at the queen. A crack formed in her barrier; she glided backward with her eyes wide open, concern stretching across her arrogant face. A wall of ice formed between her and Lazarus.

Zro rolled out of the geyser and took cover behind some debris. He heard Lazarus' voice roar from his radio.

"Save it, Zro," Lazarus said. "Put everything you have into your last shots when you get a clear opportunity at her barrier!"

Lazarus started to summon his power. He filled his sword with his energy and pointed it at the ground. Mimicking Morgan's powers, he raised his sword into the air, and beams of energy rose from the ground under the queen. The energy shattered the ice and tore away at the queen's barrier. Shards of ice shot through Lazarus' barrier, hitting his legs, shoulders, and stomach. So much blood filled the area around him that the water turned red. A blast of energy shot Lazarus out of the cube of water. Breathlessly, he said, "Now, Zro!"

Zro yelled in fury and fired one large beam containing all five rounds, covering the queen. The beam dissipated, and Zro fell to his knees and dropped his rifle. The queen's barrier shattered and collapsed. She faced Zro with a mother's rage in her eyes. She raised her sword and pointed it at him. A small beam shot from the tip of the sword, disintegrating Zro's barrier and piercing his shoulder. Zro could not breathe, nor could he swim because of the wound in his shoulder—he could barely move his arm at all. Tristan rose to his feet. His eyes turned red, and dark energy surrounded him. The castle quaked beneath his feet.

"Executioner!" screamed Tristan.

Energy erupted from all directions, causing the water to roil; pieces of the castle collapsed. Beams rose from the floor and swiftly moved toward the queen. The beams moved through the queen, and she shouted in pain. The beams quickly combined and then vanished. She stood on weakened knees; her body shivered in defeat. Her fingers lost their tenuous grasp on her sword. Tristan lunged at her and swung his first blade. The force knocked the queen's sword from her hands. It landed with a resounding clang. After the water collapsed onto the ground, Tristan heard Zro and Lazarus gasp for air behind him. Tristan ran his second blade through her chest. He pulled it out, and she collapsed violently. Her body slumped toward Tristan. He dropped his weapons and caught her. She coughed up thick blood that landed on his armor.

"You managed to defeat me," she whispered.

Tristan's eyes lost all trace of red, and he spoke gently, "Yes, we did. I'm…"

"It's not your fault, child," she said breathlessly. "You have done what you were born and bred for."

"I'm sorry! I'm sorry!" Tristan cried, realizing what he had just done. "Oh, Aerra, I'm sorry!" He dropped to his knees and cradled the queen on his lap. She put her hand on his cheek and wiped away a tear.

"There is nothing wrong with using your heart, child."

"Please don't die. Please. Forgive me," whispered Tristan. Tears formed in his eyes once again. Thoughts raced through his mind: this was his first invasion. This was the first royal family he himself had killed. He ended a child's life. All of these emotions of right, wrong, and duty flooded his mind.

"It's okay," she whispered through labored breath. "Your princesses are in the dungeon. I can be with my family now…" The queen's body released one last shudder until her body grew limp in Tristan's arms. His shoulders slumped with the grief from what he had just done.

"Tristan, grab the queen's sword," said Zro from behind Tristan. He gestured at Lazarus' motionless form. "We need to get Lazarus to a medic. He's lost a lot of blood."

Tristan set the queen on the ground while wiping a few tears from his eyes and grabbed her sword. "Get Laz to Ichiban as fast as you can. I'll head down to the dungeon to get Morgan, Rayna, and the others."

Tristan hurried out of the throne room and found the stairs leading beneath the castle. He found himself in a musty, dark corridor with no barred cell doors. Instead, he found wooden doors with heavy locks on them.

"Rayna! Morgan!" Tristan shouted. "Call out to me so I can find you!" Tristan heard a shout from the doorway on his right.

"Tristan, I'm in here!" Morgan's voice called.

He pointed his hand at the lock and blasted it with his energy. The door opened. She immediately ran into his arms. Tristan embraced her but quickly released her to inspect for injuries.

"Are you okay?" he whispered.

Morgan pulled him back into her arms and hugged him tighter. She breathed in his scent deeply.

"Thank you for saving me," she murmured against his chest.

He gazed into her eyes and put his hand on her cheek. He gently stroked her face with his thumb. "There's nothing I won't do for you. Come on, let's get the others."

Morgan nodded. They ran out of the room and proceeded down the hall.

Tristan shouted again, "Call out so I can hear you!"

Four more voices came from the next room. Tristan broke the lock once again, and he came face to face with Ry, Mira, Bianca, and Charity. They huddled around him in excitement. Tristan tried to settle them down.

"Let's find Rayna and get out of here. They are still fighting outside," he explained. They agreed and followed him out the door.

From the end of the hall, Rayna's pleas filled their ears, "Help, Tristan! Please help me."

Tristan barged through the door and found Rayna glowing with black and red energy. Behind her stood Ethan with his arm on her shoulder, and the hooded woman stood on the other side with her hand on Rayna's other shoulder. Rayna's head slumped into her chest, and she appeared catatonic.

"Help me, Tristan! Help me," the hooded woman mocked in Rayna's voice. She laughed. The goddess addressed Ethan, "Go back to Sorriax. You are no longer needed here. Wait for further instructions and keep Rayna under control."

"Yes, my goddess," Ethan acquiesced and bowed. He stepped back into a portal made of black energy and disappeared along with it.

"What are you doing with her?" Tristan asked.

"You're so demanding, little elf," the goddess laughed. "Keep calm, Tristan. I plan on letting her go."

"I'm not messing around!" Tristan shouted. "What are you doing to her?"

"I'm keeping this dog on a leash!" the goddess snapped back. "Rayna's abilities make me question my own limitations. Rayna is under my and Ethan's control. She is the prime candidate to wield Rephalas! Show them!"

Rayna's wings expanded, and the force caused the walls around them to crack.

"You see that?" the hooded woman excitedly asked. "That's even without her sword. She's an Angel with royal blood who wields power great enough to make gods question their place. She is the one to make Rephalas bend to her will."

"How long has she been under your control?"

The goddess laughed. "How long? Tell me, my elf. When you laughed together as children, was it her?" Tristan felt his lip quiver with rage. "When you talked and wrestled by your little tree? When she fell asleep in your arms? Do you think it was her?"

Rayna sniffled loudly. She looked up at Tristan with tears streaming down her cheeks.

The goddess looked at her and then back at Tristan. "When we made love, do you really think she was in control? Feeling you, kissing you, loving you. Was it her? Tell me, Tristan."

Rayna's mouth opened. "I love...you...Tristan." She struggled to get the words out.

The goddess smiled. "Don't worry, she experienced everything, too. I'm not that greedy." The goddess turned to Morgan, "But it is you, Morgan. You are the one she looks to for salvation. It is you who has failed her!"

Morgan shouted. "How could I have failed her? I'm here! Right here beside her!"

A smile formed on the goddess. "Are you not in love with Tristan? Are you not trying to steal him from her?"

Morgan hesitated. "I would never!"

The goddess raised her hand and forced Morgan's head to look at Tristan. "Look into his eyes, those beautiful elf eyes, and tell him you don't love him!" Their gaze met, and Tristan could see the tears form in her eyes. Morgan hesitated and struggled.

Rayna cried out, "Sister, fight it!" The goddess lowered her hand, releasing Morgan.

"Enough! Rayna is not some tool for you to manipulate for your own selfish ambitions," Tristan shouted.

"Yes, she is. You all are. I see nothing in front of me but pawns in this grand game. You are such small, insignificant creatures. You have no idea what is coming. With the forging of Rephalas will come the salvation of all, and all shall become Dividers." She shoved Rayna toward them. A black portal formed behind her. "Before you make more unreasonable demands, take her. My work is completed. Go, my pawns. Protect and die for your king." Rayna became catatonic again.

The hooded woman disappeared through the portal in front of them, leaving them all confused. Morgan retrieved the hollow Rayna, and they made their way to the entrance of the castle, meeting back up with Lazarus and Zro along with the rest of their army. When the door opened, they all left. Around them, the fighting continued.

Breathlessly, Lazarus spoke, "Tristan, let them know we don't wish to continue this battle. We have done what we came to do. Please end it."

Tristan left Lazarus' side and approached the castle's barrier. He took a deep breath before he stepped over the small barricade. He continued into the middle of the battlefield and surveyed all the bodies on the ground. Around him, Tristan saw the Furreshdian soldiers and civilians in the roads and surrounding buildings, all staring at him.

He unsheathed Falperion, the queen's sword, and raised it above his head. "People of Furreshda, your queen has fallen in battle, as has the rest of your royal family! To face the ones who have slain your mightiest is fruitless. We do not wish to continue this fight. It is up to you: either allow us to leave, and we will spare your lives, or do not, and we will force our way through. Either way, we leave this city!"

Tristan heard arguments among the enemy soldiers about whether to continue the fight or not. He watched most of the people hurriedly retreat into their homes. Only a handful of the soldiers stood their ground, ready to charge at Tristan at any moment.

One Furreshdian soldier yelled, "While the rest of you act like cowards, we will not allow our queen to die in vain, nor will we allow her to die alone! Mark my words, guardian, I shall have the stench of your blood on me before I leave this world. For the queen!"

The remaining Furreshdian soldiers charged at Tristan.

Tristan glanced at the soldiers one last time. He closed his eyes to hear shots fired from the soldiers behind him. Bodies collapsed all around him. After Tristan opened his eyes, he saw the last of the true Furreshdian warriors lying on the ground. Tristan walked up to the one who had spoken. The man gasped for air. He knelt next to the dying soldier and produced a knife from his belt. Tristan turned away from the man, taking a deep breath.

"Go ahead, finish me, guardian," the soldier said, staring up at Tristan.

He looked back at him and said, "You're a brave man. The only thing that surpasses your courage is your honor."

"Don't think your words will allow me to forgive you or justify the slaughter of my men." The soldier laughed.

"I can't imagine they would, but I will not allow you to leave this world and enter paradise as a liar." Tristan cut his hand with the knife and placed his bleeding hand on the soldier's head.

"Will I see my family and my soldiers in paradise?" the soldier asked through a cough.

"Yes, you will, and take comfort in knowing that I and all whom I know and care about will never see heaven," Tristan said. He closed his eyes and acknowledged the harsh truth about himself.

The soldier exhaled his last breath, dying in Tristan's hands.

Through their crackling radios, Ichiban's tired voice gave the new directives. "I want another squad to grab a third ship. We will load all of our wounded onto it. Culvac, I need you and Caster to take your two ships to cover us and make sure there are no surprise attacks. We will head back to the islands to recover."

While some soldiers stood guard, most of them carried the wounded onto the ship when it landed. Tristan stood next to the ship, staring back into the city and at all the dead on the ground—his soldiers and the enemy's. The profound loss ached in his bones.

Chapter 20

Into the Darkness

Three days later, Tristan woke up to the sun rising on the beach. Near the water, he saw Lazarus exercising. The island where they had been resting was very peaceful. No one had bothered the recuperating soldiers. Occasionally, the local elementals would deliver supplies to aid the battered soldiers while the elemental healers nursed the guardians' wounds.

As day broke, the entire camp swarmed with life, and everyone got on with their daily tasks. After breakfast, Ichiban called a meeting with Guardians Caster and Culvac. They sat around a fire while a brisk morning breeze blew around them.

"I want to know when the rest of you think we should move out. I'd personally give the soldiers a day or two longer before we decide to leave. Lazarus, how are you feeling?" Ichiban asked.

"I'm fine. I don't think there are any other wounded soldiers."

"My men are all at one hundred percent, sir," answered Culvac. "We are ready to move our forces whenever you make the call, Ichiban."

Tristan asked, "Where are we going first?"

Ichiban observed the chaos around the camp.

"The other guardians and the princesses are still sleeping. They have been through quite enough. Let them and the men rest. I thought we should head north to parlay with the Irkshdan and allow them to agree to surrender. But for now, tend to your friends and rest up. I shall prepare a feast tonight to celebrate our victory."

Just when the guardians dispersed, Ichiban cleared his throat. "And guardians," he added, "well done."

They all nodded at the praise.

≈

Night had fallen, and the ships formed a circle around the camp. With conversation and mead, the soldiers celebrated their victory. Tristan sat alone in front of the fire and stared into its flames, quashing the darkness about to consume him.

On his right, Morgan sat next to him with a plate of boar meat and some sliced apples. He glanced at her as if he had something to say, paused, but stared back into the fire.

"What is it?" Morgan asked.

"It's nothing. How is Rayna?" He did not want to bring up any hurtful memories.

"She has been asleep in one of the captain's cabins ever since we set up camp. The healers say there is nothing wrong with her, but she won't wake up. We have guards outside her door to keep her safe. Now, tell me," she insisted. "Get it off your chest."

Tristan took a deep breath and spoke softly, "I'm sorry for Rayna. I'm sorry I couldn't get there faster. I'm sorry for everything."

"It's not your fault, Tristan." Morgan intentionally stared at the food on her plate. "None of this was your fault."

"Yes, but if I had never acted on my feelings, we wouldn't be here. Rayna wouldn't be unconscious. A lot of bad things happened because of me." Tristan sighed. "I believed in our choice to be together so blindly that I couldn't see anything going wrong. I'm a fool."

"No, you are not," she said softly. "I believe a lot of bad things didn't happen because you were there, Tristan. One way or another, this was going to happen. The goddess had intended it. It only went right because you were there."

"It doesn't feel like it went right. What about Rayna?"

"She's changed. Whatever the hooded woman did to her is making her unstable and unpredictable." Morgan took a bite of boar.

Tristan nodded his head. The dark anger welled up inside him again. He breathed slowly to control himself. "Yeah, I noticed. A few months ago, a slight feeling came over me, and it has slowly grown, but no one has noticed anything different about me."

Morgan surveyed his face. "You don't seem different: your eyes are still gentle and kind, your face is calm and beautiful, and your body doesn't seem battle-worn. Well, not to my knowledge, at least. She tucked his hair behind his ears and touched his cheek. "You have such a beautiful face."

Tristan blushed and turned back to the fire. Morgan set her plate down and scooted in closer to Tristan. She took his hand and lifted it into her lap. She inspected the golden armband that he had not taken off since she had fastened it on him. She caressed it.

"It doesn't even have a scratch on it. I'm surprised. With all the action you've seen, I was afraid it might have broken."

"I've tried to take care of it," Tristan shakily said.

"What now?" Morgan brought his hand up to her face and rested her cheek in it and closed her eyes.

"What do you mean?" He sat up a little straighter. He felt unsure.

Morgan turned her head in his hand and kissed his palm.

"What do we do now?"

She kissed his wrist. She moved to his bicep and then to his shoulder. Morgan gazed wistfully into his eyes. "Aren't you going to kiss me, Tristan?"

Tristan's heart slammed erratically against his ribcage. Contradicting thoughts of what got him into this mess in the first place flooded his mind.

"Morgan, we shouldn't. I…"

Morgan stared into his eyes. "I know you feel this, too."

"I don't know what to say," he said when words escaped him. The weight of his body vanished, and his head slowly twisted in circles.

Morgan leaned in so closely that their lips brushed. "Then, don't say anything," she whispered against his lips. She kissed him gently. "Let this happen."

She kissed him again. Tristan only hesitated for a moment before he returned her kiss. He wrapped an arm around her waist. With his free hand, he cupped her face. Breathless, Morgan pulled away and grabbed his hand. She stood up, and he followed behind her. They glanced around to make sure no one had noticed them leave together.

Morgan led Tristan to one of the ships. She took him into the captain's cabin and locked the door behind them. Morgan, taking the initiative, slowly removed Tristan's shirt and kissed his shoulder. His collarbone. His neck. Tristan traced her stomach with his fingers as he walked behind Morgan, unfastening her belt and removing her blouse. He wrapped his arms around her, kissed her shoulder, and moved to her neck. She put her arms around his. Over her shoulder, she locked eyes with him and begged him to kiss her once again. Still in his grasp, she angled her body to his and pulled him toward the bed. She backed herself onto it. Tristan crawled on top of her; their kisses never ceased.

Morgan looked into his eyes, breathing heavily. "Tristan, I care about you," she said with a shy smile. She looked into his eyes, not expecting him to say anything. "I think I always have."

"I…" Tristan hesitated, cutting himself off. He lifted himself off her body, suddenly feeling the significance of what he was doing. He looked down at his bracer with the ring embedded in it. He looked back into Morgan's eyes and their fiery passion. He took off the bracer and let it roll onto the floor.

He opened his eyes and put his hand on Morgan's cheek. He pulled her lips to his and kissed her fiercely. He looked at her. "I care about you, too." She pulled him down onto the bed with her.

≈

Tristan awoke in the middle of the night, unable to sleep. Thoughts of everything that transpired in the last several days inundated his mind. He saw Morgan lying next to him. His heart was confused. He didn't want to put his friends at risk again because of his actions. Seeing her body covered in goosebumps, he draped a blanket over her. He stood up, put on his pants, walked to a window, and stared up at the moon. It gleamed so brightly it lit up the entire area. The night air and the calmness of the gentle breeze assuaged the uneasiness in his mind and heart. He was scared to tell Morgan that they planned to keep going without her. Two arms wrapped around Tristan's waist. Warm lips gently pressed against his back and moved up his neck. His body tensed, and his hands balled as he readied himself to walk away.

"Come back to bed," Morgan whispered in his ear. "Please, Tristan." She trailed kisses down his neck. Her fingers flexed against his abdomen, and heat flushed over his body. Unable to resist her persuading touch and pleas, Tristan leaned his body against hers and slid his fingers between hers. She took his hand, and he let her lead him back to the bed.

≈

The morning sun beamed through the window. Morgan extended her arm, reaching out for Tristan. He wasn't there. The sheets were cold beneath her fingers. She immediately climbed out of bed, dressed, and ran out of the captain's quarters to find soldiers hard at work, readying the ship for takeoff.

"Excuse me. Where are the guardians?" she asked the nearest soldier.

The soldier gave a quick bow and replied, "Princess, they are with Ichiban right now, going over their next destination. He should be over in the central ship."

The answer confused Morgan. She smiled her thanks at the soldier. She rushed to board the main ship and found them conversing at the helm. She quickly approached. The guardians, Ichiban, Caster, and Culvac all stared at her when she interrupted. She made eye contact with all of them but stopped when she got to Tristan. He kept looking at the ground. She could tell he was avoiding her eyes. Was he ashamed of their night together? "I thought you were coming home with me." She tried to hide her disappointment.

"Though it was Tristan's idea, the men took a vote, and we have decided to keep moving forward as much as we can," explained Ichiban. "Those who are unable or do not wish to continue will accompany you and Rayna back to Sorriax. Ry, Mira, Bianca, and Charity will join you. Keep your guardians around you at all times."

"That's bullshit," Morgan forcefully said. "I demand that all of you return to Sorriax with me at once."

"I have never disobeyed you, my princess," Lazarus said. "But this one time, I must. The more we fight, the less you have to, and that is a burden I gladly bear for you."

"Then, let me come with you. I can help!" Sadness and anger crossed her face as she knew her fight was a lost cause.

"You don't have your sword." He looked down at the floor rather than at her face. "It would be easier for us to fight if we didn't have to worry about your wellbeing."

Morgan protested, "But I can take care of myself!"

"Your highness." Ichiban recognized her sadness. "You must understand that if you stay out here with us, you will most likely die."

Morgan glowered at all of them. Tristan received the worst of her glares. The sting of tears lessened their ire. She refused to let them fall. "I don't care if I die. I want to be out here to help you."

Caster took a few steps toward her and said, "You must go back. You need to relay the message to the king that we have won our battle and wish to continue. The soldiers' families need to be notified of who was lost and who is still alive—we have made lists. Most importantly, we all care an awful lot about you."

Catching Morgan's eyes, Caster pointedly stared at Tristan before saying, "We need someone to return home to."

"How will we get home?" Morgan understood what Caster meant.

Culvac said, "My men are readying a ship for you and your soldiers as we speak."

"What if I run into trouble on my way back?"

"We will stay here until you reach Sorriax so that we won't be too far away," Zro answered.

"When you get back," Lazarus instructed, "things may not go the way you want or the way they should. Just lay low."

"Lay low?" Morgan yelled.

Before she started another rant, Lazarus interrupted, "You may not like it, but you need your weapon, and we need you at your strongest. Placate the king a little and get that sword back."

A soldier approached them from Morgan's ship and said, "General, we're ready to go."

"You may want to say your goodbyes now," Ichiban said to Morgan. "You need to start making your way home."

Morgan couldn't hold back her overwhelming sadness. Lazarus walked up to her and embraced her tightly.

"Don't worry about us," he whispered against her head. "We'll be okay. I'm doing this for you, princess. I don't want you to fight anymore."

"Laz…" Morgan pulled her head from his shoulder to look at him.

"Everything will be fine when we come back. I promise," he said and then let go of her.

Zro walked up and hugged Morgan as well. "Goodbye, princess. I hope you have a safe trip home. May Aerra walk with you."

Morgan looked at Tristan, who stared at her. She waited for him to approach.

"Goodbye, Tristan," she said and waited for a response.

"I'll be back," Tristan said to Ichiban. "I'm going to escort the princess to her ship."

"Don't be too long," the general said with a nod. "We have a lot of planning to do."

Tristan grabbed Morgan's hand and walked her up the ramp to the deck.

"Is Rayna on board?" Morgan asked one of the deckhands. After he nodded his response, she said, "Good. Please keep an eye on her."

The soldier saluted her and went on about his duties. Morgan returned her focus to Tristan. They stared at each other without saying anything for some time. Tristan started to take off the armband. "You need to take this back, Morgan."

Morgan closed her hand around Tristan's to stop him from taking it off. "No, I gave that to you, and you promised to give it back when you saw me again."

"I did see you again, so please take it."

"We aren't safe in Sorriax. When you get home, Tristan," she begged, "give it back then, please. I want you to hold onto it for me."

"I can't, Morgan." He tugged Morgan's hand away from his bicep.

"Please, wear it," Morgan pleaded once more. "Whenever you look at it, I want you to think of returning to me."

Tristan hesitated one last time but answered, "Very well." After he had refastened the armband, Morgan stepped closer and put her arms around him. He hugged her, squeezing tightly. She angled her face toward his and moved to kiss him.

"Please don't," he whispered against the side of her head.

"What's wrong?" She stepped back from him.

Tristan said, "It's best if you didn't."

"But why?" Morgan's voice cracked.

"I can't do this to my soldiers again. I can't put them at risk because of what I do. What if I don't come home?"

"Goodbye, Tristan," Morgan spoke with a sense of finality. She wiped the tears in her eyes and walked away from him.

Tristan knew this would happen. What he wanted and what he needed to do could never be the same. Unable to control himself, a tear fell down his cheek. Morgan walked into her cabin and slammed the door. Tristan stood there, struggling with his emotions. His hands trembled terribly. Suddenly, he knew what he wanted. He raced after her. He threw open the door and slammed it behind him.

Morgan looked at him with anger in her eyes. "What do you wa…"

Tristan ran up to her and embraced her in his arms. "I'm so sorry. I'm sorry for everything I said. I don't want to lose you. I can't lose you." Tristan twined his fingers through Morgan's hair and pulled her into a crushing kiss. Morgan's anger faded into bliss.

Not wanting to break their kiss, Morgan whispered against his lips, "You will never lose me."

They held each other tightly, neither one wanting to be the first to let go. She softly touched his face and kissed his forehead. After a few minutes of silence, Tristan loosened his grip on her and stood up, pulling her with him.

"I don't want to leave you." She leaned her forehead against his. "Come back to me safely, and I'll make sure you have a home to come back to."

"I will," Tristan whispered in her ear. He kissed her cheek one more time.

She let go of him, and he walked off the ship. At the end of the dock, he turned to face Morgan. Their eyes locked. He watched the ship lift off. When it started to move, Morgan ran down the ship's deck to keep a clear view of Tristan. She lost sight of him when she reached the end of the ship. Nothing but clouds surrounded her.

Tristan stared off into the clouds. From behind him, he heard someone approach.

"My Angel," a voice echoed inside his head.

Tristan spun around. The hooded woman stood at the edge of a dark forest. She signaled with her finger.

"Come, let me show you the end," she whispered into his thoughts once more.

Tristan gazed at her for a moment, shedding himself of any fear or reservation, and followed her into the darkness.

Acknowledgments

Tremendous thanks to my publisher, Patricia Landy, for her patience over these last several years and her tolerance for my stubborn yet squirrel-like attitude. Without her I'd be lost. My army of editors. Malory Wood, Stacy Long, and Claire Shepherd. You have taken my story, elevated it, and made it so much better. The time Claire took to sit down with me, not only made my story better, but improved me as a writer as well. It took gallons of coffee, but we got there. I'd like to thank Ryan Durney for the cover illustration and Deanna Estes for the cover and inside design of this book. None of this felt real to me. It never hit me that one day I could see my book on a bookshelf in a store until I saw this beautiful cover. Thank you for giving my vision a face and bringing it to life. None of this would be possible without this wonderful team. Thank you for your patience and your belief in me. Not many believed in me, but you did. You saw what I wanted to do and took a chance on me. I appreciate you all.

I would like to thank some of my oldest and best friends Matt Schafer and Matt Robles. You two know how long I have worked on this story—all the way back to developmental stages. Thank you for checking in on my progress and making sure I was always on track. I would like to thank Travis Miller as well. From when we were children until high school, it wasn't a good era to be a nerd. It was highly frowned upon. You were more supportive of my creativity than any other of my childhood friends. Last but certainly not least, I would like to thank Shawn Roybal. I never knew music without you, nor would I have this deep appreciation I now have. Something that has always stuck with me—*Star Wars: A New Hope.* George Lucas submitted the finished film to all the film executives. They hated it. They told him to fix it and do several reshoots. George Lucas went back to editing and made one simple change. He brought the film back and the executives loved it. They asked what he did differently. He added music, that's it. Thank you, Shawn. You gave my story a pulse.

To all the beta readers who took the time to help me. Preston Stansbury, Kassidi Cline, and Nevaeh Martin, your insight of what to do and what not to do was invaluable. Liz Wood, I would like to especially thank you. The notes you took and the depths you went helped me tremendously. Keep on writing. I would also like to thank my boss from Frito Lay, Nick Krul. You always had an open ear to listen to me complain about the work load writing brought. But you also taught me if I wanted something, I needed to go out there, put the work in and go and get it.

Then there is my family. I would like to thank you last—certainly not least, for the genuine amount of support I have received from you since the beginning. Robert Snyder, Dad, you have done so much with your life that I only hope to come close to experiencing all you have. My sister, Christen Snyder, thank you for checking in on my progress and making sure I'm doing okay. My little sister, Erin Mayor, I appreciate how fiercely you are willing to help with whatever I may need— from going around and hanging flyers to talking to news stations to setting up interviews. Your support is precious to me. My loving wife, Sandra Snyder. Thank you for being my rock. Thank you for just being there. Thank you for putting up with me and my shenanigans. Thank you for your patience. Thank you for staying by my side when others would not. I appreciate you and adore you more than you will ever know. I love you.

Author

Tyler Snyder was born in 1984 in Medford, Oregon. As a child, he was captivated by movies, video games, and *Dungeons and Dragons*, along with the worlds these activities created. The original spark that ignited Tyler's imagination was when he wanted to see a movie similar to *The Legend of Zelda*, but the closest film at the time was *The Dark Crystal*. That itch, to this day, has still not been scratched. This led him to books and stories like the pastimes he adored and gave him exposure to a much grander well of ideas and possibilities. Meeting like-minded friends who shared the same hobbies, Tyler developed a passion for creating new worlds. In *Romancing the Darkness*, Tyler explores his world, Ambion, and the countless decisions confronting his characters. Mr. Snyder currently lives in Wyoming with his wife, Sandra. **Tyler-Snyder.com**

Made in the USA
Middletown, DE
11 January 2022

58397835R00149